ORA'S
GOLD

Praise for Ora's Gold

"Even today, across the globe, mothers are forcibly robbed of their choices and rights in childbirth by bureaucracies asserting claim over "safety". Is this our future? Will we sacrifice our mothers, daughters, aunts and nieces in the name of "safety"? Ora's unshakeable belief in herself is the perfect antidote and a must read for every young person. Her strength on her journey of self-awareness and self-determination is enough to take your breath away."

—Bashi Hazard, Lawyer and Board Director, Human Rights in Childbirth

ORA'S GOLD

CHARLOTTE YOUNG

Budding Iris Publications

First published in Australia 2016
Copyright © 2016 by Charlotte Young
The moral rights of the author have been asserted.
A CIP catalogue record for this book is available from the National
Library of Australia.

ISBN: 978-0-9923286-1-0

For enquiries about this book please visit: www.charlotteyoung.com.au

With thanks to:
Damonza.com for cover design and interior design
Yvette Harbinson for advice with interior design

For Boo

It's the agents of our imagination who really shape who we are.

— *Chris Abani*

1

Goodbye

Lucy is hanging off me the way an ivy vine swirls around a tree. I can barely walk, let alone pull my suitcase. The rest of her family trails behind us patiently. The station's massive glass doors open silently, releasing a wave of people moving too fast, streaming past us. One of the wheels on my case gets snagged on a stroller.

'Rraahh!' The toddler in the stroller stands up and waves his toy beast under my nose.

'Great monster!' My best friend leans over, taking me with her. I pull away and tug at my case. It's stuck.

'Grhhh!' The kid's giving me the creeps.

'Sit down Harry,' his mother says, jerking the stroller back.

Finally, the wheels are free. I want to move quickly but there are too many people, and Lucy has reattached herself.

'Why can't you come with us?' Her voice sounds small in the vast interior.

'Which platform was it again?' I stop under the departure board, focusing on the sea of words and ignoring her question.

'I don't want you to go!' She's really squeezing me now.

I glance at the shiny floor and see our reflection. Me, stiff, upright. Lucy, desperate and clinging. Why is she making this so difficult?

'You're the ones who're leaving.' I say, peeling her arms off me.

'But we want you to come with us!'

'Lucy!' Beth cuts in. 'Not this *again*. We've had this conversation so many times. Ora needs to spend time with Dione.'

Even her mum sounds upset with me.

'It's not De-on, Mother,' Lucy snaps. 'Jeez! How many times do you have to get it wrong? It's Dee-OH-nee. Dee-OH-nee. Auntie Dee-OH-nee.'

I smile and then catch a lump in my throat. I can't believe they're all going. I *will not* miss them. I will *not*.

A SIF officer zips by on his motorbike so close he almost catches Lucy's elbow. I look over to where he's headed and see a man in a black hoodie running through the crowds. The SIF siren starts and everyone stands still. No-one wants to be hit by the bikes that have swarmed, seemingly out of nowhere. The officers are wasp-like in their black uniforms with bright orange stripes on the sleeves—the more senior, the more stripes.

'Watch it!' Lucy shouts after the bike. I freeze. Other travellers step away from us. Lucy can be so stupid sometimes.

'I only met her once, *Daughter*,' Beth says, completely ignoring the SIF action. 'And that was over five years ago at the …' She doesn't finish her sentence.

Beth still can't say 'funeral' in front of me.

'Memory like a sieve,' says Lucy, rolling her eyes at me, and I smile. 'I *wish* you were coming with us.' She won't give up.

Maybe I should be going with them. To the land of the kiwi, as Holly used to say.

'I *can't*, Lucy.' I have to shout over the sirens. 'Dione's the only family I've got, apart from Dad.'

'But New Zealand's a free country! No SIF telling you what to do, you can do anything. And think of the food! *Real* food.'

'You still have to work, Luce—a *lot*. Self-sufficiency doesn't just *happen*. Why do you think they opened their doors in the first place?'

The sirens start to die down.

'We won't be allowed in forever, you know. They'll stop letting people in.' She's trying to scare me. This conversation is so old! I know exactly when the trump card is coming. '*We're* your family now Ora.'

'I *know* you are!' How can I explain that I'm never going to leave Mum and Holly? That I need to stay close to my memories. 'And I love you. Always. But … I want to stay in Australia. And I want to spend time with Dione … get to know her again.'

'There's your train,' Hugo's nodding at Platform 14, where the golden bullet has just pulled in. I'm thankful for the distraction. We start moving again.

'I preferred the silver bullets,' he says. 'They looked friendlier.'

'I preferred planes,' Lucy's dad says nostalgically. 'When I win the lottery I'll treat you all to a flight.'

'It'd have to be a big win,' Beth says, 'but it would be nice.'

'Still so frivolous! Haven't you guys learnt anything?' Lucy is on her high horse. 'If your generation hadn't been so greedy there'd have been a bit more oil left for us!'

Hugo whistles the government's jingle, 'Sunny Sunny Solar', as we come to a stop on the platform.

'Shame the government didn't make the changes years ago.' Lucy looks briefly pained before cracking a big fake smile. 'Shiny happy faces on, then.'

Hugo is still whistling and I want him to shut up. Lucy's mum and dad envelop me in a double hug. I squeeze them back, tears looming.

'Thank you for letting me stay with you for so long!' Over three years. I can't believe I'm saying goodbye.

'Bye, Hugo.' I turn and hug him quickly.

Lucy grabs me. 'You have to speak to me EVERY day!' She wraps me up so tightly I can't pull away. I swallow down another lump, inhaling the sweet perfume she always wears.

'I promise.' I hug her back. 'I have to go.'

Finally she releases me. I grab the handle of my case and head for the carriage door. If I turn around I will fall apart.

'Ora!' Lucy calls after me.

I hear her dad say something, but I keep going. My tears have started. I can't look back.

The carriage is empty. I lift my case over the bars into the luggage rack and choose an aisle seat, three rows back. I force myself not to look at the others, standing on the platform, but as the train pulls away I can't help it. They're waving madly. I put my hand up against the cold glass and hope they can't see my tears.

My chest lurches as I think of Lucy. Leaving. The train is travelling at full speed now and the outside world has become a blur. A SIF officer—one stripe—is striding down the aisle of the next carriage, coming towards me. Where did I put my ID? I can't remember. He opens the carriage door, steps past the luggage and smiles as he goes by. I manage to move my lips into a line. I grab my backpack and search it—too many pockets!

My hand closes around the card. Everything is here, in order, as I packed it.

I'm counting tiny fingerprints on the window when a man sprints by, heading towards the front of the train. It's the guy in the hoodie. He's opening the door to the next carriage when he looks back with crazed eyes. My mouth goes dry. Suddenly he turns and runs straight at me, diving under my seat, squishing my legs against the wall of the train as he jams himself into an impossible space.

I sit immobilised. This is *not* happening. The SIF officer returns, stops just after my seat and steps back so he's looking down on me.

'Have you seen a guy in a black hoodie?' His grey eyes are piercing and his neck is too long, his Adam's apple bulging.

Every fibre in my body is willing me to scream that the guy is under my seat. Seconds drag by then I shake my head, no, quickly. I need to pee. The SIF officer takes off again. A minute later the guy struggles out from underneath me.

'Thanks,' he says and is gone.

I can't believe what I just did. What the hell? I don't even know him! The officer bounds past again. I hope the guy gets away. What if he comes back? I need to think of something else. Quickly! I focus on the window again. The surface. I count the fingerprints. One, two. Moving to Adelaide. Three, four. To see Dione. Five, six.

◈

Rough words and heavy footsteps startle me out of my drowsy state. I lean into the aisle and see the SIF officer in the carriage in front, shoving the guy with the hoodie forwards. He's holding him by the scruff of the neck, half choking him. The officer flings open the door and shoves the guy onto the floor, handcuffing both his wrists to the luggage compartment. Right next to my suitcase.

He marches away and returns a moment later with a triumphant grin, pulling a young woman by her hair. She too gets cuffed to the bars. She says something and the SIF officer lashes out, angrily. The woman falls back awkwardly, onto the cases. Her long coat falls open to reveal a huge pregnant belly.

I gasp, completely stunned. My eyes are glued to the massive mound, bulbous and forbidden. She's just lying there. The hoodie guy is going to wrench his arms off if he struggles any more. The SIF officer walks by, winking at me as he goes.

She lies there for ages. Hoodie guy leans over and tries to help her up. Soon they're huddling together on the floor. He's doing a good job of trying to cradle her, but she's shaking her head from side to side.

'No,' I hear her sob. She starts to make a low, howling sound.

My fingernails are digging into my palms. I do not want to be here, looking at them. A pregnant woman! Out. On a train. What will happen to her? We are slowing to a stop. As I try for a better look at her belly, the guy looks up and catches me gawking. I snap my head in, like a turtle, heat flushing my cheeks.

It's time to get off, but I need my suitcase. Passengers are moving past me. I sit for a few more minutes. Dione will be waiting. From the platform, a swarm of SIF officers mounts the train. There are too many people. I'm glad I can't see. But I can hear them. She is hysterical. He is shouting something, I can't make out the words.

They are taken away.

2

Auntie Dione

Dione is late. A chill wind goes through me, making me shiver. The shock of seeing that pregnant woman isn't helping. How could she be so stupid? I can't believe they thought it was worth the risk—they'll probably never see each other again. I wonder if they'll take her womb out now. Dad said they don't do that, but I've heard different. As for the baby …

People mill around me on the platform, making me feel like I should be moving. Spring in South Australia is like being in an icebox. Give me the central hinterland any day.

'Ora!' Her husky tones transport me back instantly. I turn towards my aunt. Love, knowing and grief flare between us, our hazel eyes mirroring each other's. She looks away.

Dione's face is tougher and tighter than I remember. She's got my jaw shape, I realise with a sting of surprise; slightly angular and determined. But the similarities stop there. Her sandy hair, much lighter than my own, is now streaked with silver. Mine is a wild, dark bomb of curls, always escaping. Hers is tied back neatly in a long braid. Everything about her is in place. Pursed lip lines make me wonder if she still laughs like she used to.

I step forward to give her a hug but it's a quick one. 'Come on, it's getting cold.' She pats my arm and strikes out along the platform.

My feet keep pace just behind her but my mind is struggling to take in this new, crisp version of the aunt I used to know.

'There was a pregnant woman on the train.'

Her steps falter for a second but she doesn't turn around.

'Oh?'

'The SIF caught her. And the guy.'

Dione strides on. Maybe she doesn't care about this stuff anymore. I run a few paces to fall into step beside her.

'I can't believe anyone could be so dumb.' The words have barely left my lips before Dione gives me the coldest look, like I'm the dumb one. We've reached the tailgate of a white and battered ute. It's the same car from years ago, but I'm too stunned by the change in my aunt to be comforted by the familiarity. As she throws my case into the tray she slaps out a request.

'You won't call me Auntie Dione, will you?'

She's already in the driver's seat, turning on the engine. My hand touches the cold metal of the passenger door and I'm overwhelmed with a dark longing. I think about saying I need to go back—there's still time—but my body is working against me. I flop down onto the seat. The cabin smells of diesel.

As the road slips by, the silence stretches further, and I start to wonder why the hell I came. This is not the aunt Holly and I played tiggy with, or the woman I clung to at the funeral just a month after my thirteenth birthday.

She makes an effort a couple of times, pointing out a few things as the landscape opens up; a flock of black cockatoos against the blue sky, a massive outcrop of boulders, but I can tell she's uncomfortable. The journey takes forever.

The land is completely parched. No lush greens here, just lots of greys and muted greens. If I held a leaf at home, tightly, it'd slowly uncurl as I opened my hand. Here, the leaf would forget its shape instantly, crumbling into pieces.

We finally turn off the main road and wind our way up Dione's track. It's as long and dusty as I remember. She expertly zigzags around the potholes, holding the steering wheel with ease—she could probably do it with her eyes closed if she wanted to.

Dione mutters something about petrol rations and the length of the journey, but I don't respond. I feel like I'm falling backwards into myself, into a familiar place I haven't visited for years. Maybe I'm just tired.

As we pull into the bottom of the driveway, I look up and see the sign that Holly and I painted: 'Buzzy Bee's Bed and Breakfast'. The paint is peeling and the bee is barely visible—Holly drew it and I added the colour. I remember Holly's bubbly excitement over the name—so *not* Dione, but she could never say no to Holly.

I don't think the B&B ever got off the ground.

Dione parks in front of her old weatherboard home. The white paint is greyer and the house smaller—it's almost shaking with too-loud memories. I'm not quick to get out of the car, but somehow I find myself walking up the path. As my feet sound on the wooden steps of the veranda I flash back to the hopscotch Holly and I used to play here, with the bright pink numbers. She loved that chunky chalk.

We started coming to Dione's when I was six and my big sister, Holly was eight. Dad had these annual doctors' conferences in South Australia, so Mum, Holly and I would visit Dione while he stayed in the city. Fuel was cheap back then. It'd take ages, driving from the New South Wales hinterland, but we had fun in the car; singing, arguing, sleeping and watching the changing scenery from inside our little bubble.

Whenever Mum spent time with Dione, they'd drink

endless pots of tea and talk for hours about the world's diminishing resources and how the corporate food industries and the pharmaceutical companies were destroying the planet for profit. And power. Only a small handful of island countries like New Zealand and Japan dared to fight against the agricultural changes and the scientifically modified 'everything'.

Dione was still a hospital midwife then and she'd bang on about how it all started with birth, which had become an industrialised factory line. If Dione was the birth queen, Mum was the earth queen. Mum's rants were about the horrors of factory farming, genetically engineered food and human greed. Round and round they'd go, firing each other up, bemoaning people's 'little' lives made even smaller by fear. All in the name of safety.

We were visiting the day the SIF were officially appointed. For weeks, we'd heard nothing but news of their imminent arrival. It was even worse than the Sunny Solar campaign: 'The new resource force for Australia, here to protect and preserve!'

Dione went ballistic. 'Special Instigation Force my arse,' she said. 'Sick and Intense Fuckers, more like.'

Holly and I giggled, even if she did make the SIF sound scary. Maybe she knew they'd morph into power-mongering monsters. Later, Mum made her apologise to us for swearing.

It wasn't just Australia. Other countries had their own versions of the SIF. Here, they were initially brought in as 'special' water monitors to investigate water theft and water harvesting. When I was eight, the drought got so bad that the government diverted the water supply and stopped it flowing through the pipes and taps. Mum and Dad were very solemn that day. The first few weekly rations with the black, stumpy containers were new and exciting for Holly and me, but we were young. Reality soon kicked in. One hundred litres per person, per week. Plastic-tasting water became a precious, drop-by-drop part of our existence.

SIF teams sprang out of nowhere and soon their jurisdiction

extended far beyond water, wielding power by numbers, surveillance and arrests. Anyone they suspected of breaking a law—and there were new laws every week—was brought in for questioning. Their method is still the same: break people down and make them confess, even if they're innocent. A 'confession' and an arrest mean points for the team. The more points, the higher the pay. The government loves the SIF. Mum despised them. Dad said he didn't like them, but that they were necessary, even after the Health Minister gave them dominion over women's health.

The only thorn in the SIF's side—and the government's—is the free media, who, like the moon, shine light into the shadows. The internet is their playground and they flash publish reports sporadically; a constant game of cat and mouse where journos risk everything for a good story, all in the name of 'letting the citizens know'. But they're not heroes by any means. They can play just as dirty as the SIF.

Ballistic doesn't come close to describing Dione's reaction when the new pregnancy and birth laws were introduced. It was seven years ago, after all the E. coli deaths. Thousands of people had died. It happened so quickly; the bacteria spawned super bacteria in the rivers and soil, which infected the crops and cattle. And then it jumped to the people. Mum blamed the farming methods, and the lack of rain followed by the freak floods. Antibiotics stopped working and a national crisis was declared.

Babies were being born with severe defects. When the new health minister was appointed he passed a law forcing all pregnant women into state protection centres. The 'Safety for the Future Programs' were implemented overnight across Australia. To ensure the wellbeing of every unborn baby, women had to self-enrol as soon as they found out they were pregnant, and were not allowed to leave the centres until after their babies had been delivered surgically, by C-Section. They were confined to highly regulated environments—bacteria-free zones—which meant no outside visitors.

The law still stands, even though E. coli is under control. If women don't go into a Safety for the Future Program, they risk losing their babies to the state and their wombs to research. Non-compliance is a serious crime.

❧

Dione has opened the front door and is watching me, my suitcase in her hand.

'I've cleared out the junk room for you,' she says gently, and I hear a glimmer of her old self.

I smile for the first time and follow her in.

The floorboards look shinier than I remember but creak a whole lot more, and the passageway is narrower and shorter than it used to be. My bedroom is second on the left, after her study. I wonder where she's put all that junk. Dione's bedroom is opposite, spartan except for her frame drum on the wall and the crocheted bedspread.

Mum made that. I remember her sitting cross-legged on the sofa at home, concentrating for hours on the intricate work.

I want to lie down on it. Smell it.

'Ora.' Dione's gruff voice calls me back and I follow her into my room. A cream cast-iron bed is under the window, with bedding to match. It looks kind of dated, especially on the stripped floorboards, but the mattress feels soft as I sit down and look out at the tree Holly and I used to climb.

I have no control now. The memories are hitting hard, but I don't make a sound as the tears roll down my cheeks.

'Take your time,' Dione says, backing out. 'Dinner's ready when you are.'

She closes the door and goes into the kitchen. The radio volume goes up. I curl into the soft mattress and feel it holding me as I give voice to the sobs in my throat.

3

Fresh Veggies

Dione is folding washing when I go into the kitchen. There's a huge pile of towels, and I wonder if she has some kind of compulsive bathing thing going on. Although it'd have to be dry bathing. She lifts the towels onto the chair by the back door, where night is pressing in at the window.

'You must be hungry,' she says, taking a bowl of salad out of the fridge.

We avoid each other's gaze. I know my eyes are puffy. I open the cutlery drawer—it's still in the same place—and begin to set the table. My mouth is watering; her cooking is the best. Even through my sniffly nose, it smells delicious.

'Where did you get all the veggies?' I ask five minutes later, incredulous and in heaven with my mouth full of her veggie lasagne.

'I still have a veggie garden.' There's a rebellious twinkle in her eye. 'It's just a little more surreptitious than it used to be.'

'You what?'

She nods towards the back door and I get up to take a look. I can't see anything except a sorry-looking lawn, but Dione picks up a torch to spotlight areas in the garden beds: spinach and egg-plants, potatoes, a tomato vine growing over the garden bench, salad and herbs. It's all there, hidden amongst scraggy bushes. There's no way you'd see it via satellite. Even the SIF drones would miss it.

As I sit back down, the danger of Dione's veggie patch hits me. 'Dione, you're mad!'

'Your stomach's not objecting.' She smiles at me stuffing my face.

'I have to hide the evidence,' I smile back, glad to be connect-ing but still feeling a niggling disquiet. 'If the SIF find out, they'll lock you up for months.' She is out of her mind.

'They never come up here, Ora, they're too busy in the city.' She's following the rim of her water glass with her finger. 'And anyway, half of them wouldn't even know what a real vegetable looks like.'

'But where do you get the water from? It's so dry up here.'

She smiles.

'Don't tell me your water tanks are hooked up?'

She gives a small shrug. 'Only the underground ones. The SIF don't know about them.'

'Dione!' I don't know whether to laugh or scream at her.

'I detest that muck they call food. Full of chemicals, no nutri-tional value whatsoever. I swear it's turned everyone into zombies. No-one thinks for themselves anymore.'

'But what if you get *caught*?' A bit of lasagne flies out of my mouth and drops between us. I stuff it back in my mouth. I can't stop eating—this food is making me remember.

'Fear of getting caught is not going to dictate what I put in my garden or in my body. I've been self-sufficient for years, Ora. I'm not going to stop now.'

I know I should back off but she's being so reckless. 'You can't have thought this through! If you wind up in one of those SIF centres, food will be the last thing on your mind.'

She shrugs. 'I still go and collect my water rations like everybody else. The chooks are legal, I just don't feed them that rubbish they call grain. I reckon my hens show more spirit and intelligence than your average SIF officer. Stop looking so worried Ora! They never come up here, and if they did, they wouldn't find anything. This house is one big secret. I used to think Frank was on another planet, but now I think he knew exactly what was coming.' She smiles at the memory of the crazy guy who lived here before her—he'd been paranoid about a mystery enemy invading Australia and built his whole house around the delusion. 'It's like this house was made for me.'

'But—'

'I only water at night and I hide the hoses every time I use them. I've covered every scenario and it's not going to happen. People stopped thinking for themselves when they had to start queuing for water. How crazy is it that the government claims to own every drop of it? There's no way I'm paying for something that falls from the sky! And vegetables that weren't even grown in proper soil? It's ridiculous.'

I carry on eating in silence.

'If you don't like it you don't have to eat it.' She seems annoyed now.

I'm about to tell her again how stupid she's being but there's a sharp knock at the back door. Dione looks at me and then at the door. I sit frozen, my gaze moving over the dishes. How many veggies are in evidence? Dione opens the door just a crack. Two people, a man and a woman, say something in hushed tones then withdraw into the darkness. Dione closes the door and starts to clear the table.

'There's just enough water for washing up, if you're careful,' she says, nodding at the black container. 'Wiping dishes with chemicals isn't my style.'

And with that, she picks up the towels and her torch and is gone. I watch from the kitchen window and see her following the couple up the track that snakes behind her house. The woman stops and bends over, bracing her hands on her knees. Dione catches up with them and gives the man the towels and the torch. She squats down so her face is close to the woman's. He's shining the torch on them. When they stand up my blood goes cold.

It can't be!

Two pregnant women in one day? I watch until they're out of sight and realise they're going up to the cottage, the torch dotting their progress.

Now my brain won't work. It refuses to believe what my eyes have seen. Before I even register what I'm doing, I'm following, trying to tread noiselessly on the gravel. It's dark out here with just a sliver of moon but I know the track well—Holly and I used to play here all the time.

A million questions are making my synapses fire. What the hell is going on? How many times has Dione used those towels? How much time would she get for this? Forget illegal veggies, how about a life sentence! And what about me? Would I get done too? Please let this be a one-off. Surely the woman is just an old and stupid friend. Babies are not meant to be born in the middle of nowhere.

As I near the cottage, the outside light helps me see more clearly. Buzzy Bee's Bed and Breakfast still looks as cute as ever, like a child's drawing in this soft light. There are windows either side of the pale blue front door and two windows above them, on the second floor, the bricks all covered in ivy.

I feel like a criminal as I peep inside. There are no lights on, just a dim, flickering candle. Dione and the couple are nowhere to be seen. The furniture looks a bit faded and the armchair's in an odd position, but it's all just as it used to be—saggy floral sofas and a hotchpotch of furniture.

Where the hell are they? My heart is thudding in my chest and my breath is shallow … I can't go in. They must be upstairs. I wait like this for hours, listening, my senses highly tuned, but the house is dead, and the candle is getting smaller.

Eventually I give up. Tiredness overwhelms me and my feet are too heavy as I stumble down the hill, my body jarring with each footfall. I can only think of sleep.

I head to the bathroom, past the remains of dinner. I remember Mum's bed cover and go into Dione's room. It doesn't smell of Mum anymore, but every fibre of this wool has been through her fingers, and now it's wrapped around me.

I drag my iron feet to my room, still wrapped in the blanket, and sleep.

⌾

In the night I wake and think about calling Dad. He might have forgotten that there's a beating heart in his chest when it comes to me, but he'll know what to do. I grab my mobile and search for his number. Then I stop. What if he dobs Dione in? The doctor in him would be outraged.

For the hundredth time I wonder what she thinks she's doing. She's been on her own way too long.

I get under the covers, still wrapped in Mum's blanket, and try Lucy's number. She doesn't pick up. I let the mobile slip to the floor and wish for sleep to return.

⌾

In the morning, the kitchen is spotless. And quiet. I help myself to home-made bread and honey and once again, my tastebuds delight in bliss. I'm on my third slice and wondering if Dione has her own beehive and where she gets her wheat when she walks in the back door.

'Morning,' she says, walking past me into what used to be the laundry room. I don't bother replying.

'I thought I'd show you around later,' she shouts over the sound of sloshing water. What is she doing in there? 'So you know where to catch the bus into town and where the best beaches are, and how to find the MBD Centre. I have to donate today anyway.' I still don't answer. She carries on regardless. 'The bus stop's miles away but the buses run regularly.' She appears, carrying a basket containing sopping wet towels. I look at them pointedly and can feel her eyes boring into me.

Then she moves to the back door and pauses, asks me if I'm okay, like there's something wrong with *me*.

I'm so stunned that I can't speak. Finally I manage, 'What the hell—'

The door swings shut. I spring to my feet. How dare she? The back of my chair thwacks the floorboards and stops me short. What's the use? She'll just deny it and I don't want to know anyway. I don't want anything to do with her rebellion. The thought of the SIF makes my knees buckle.

I pick up the chair and decide to mind my own business. I need to keep my distance. My chest contracts. Who was I kidding? Lucy and her family have been my only family for years now. Dione didn't bother after the funeral, so why should she now? It was such a dumb move coming here.

I force myself to think about Lucy and her mum, trying to remember how it sometimes pained me to see them together. But I only feel the pain of missing them. They did want me to go with them, even though I convinced myself otherwise.

I look out the window and concentrate on the deep blue of the sky—not a cloud in sight. Could I catch it in acrylic? With French ultramarine and Indian red maybe? I sigh and begin to think seriously about leaving Australia.

Stuff Dione and our connection.

'Right, then.' Speak of the devil. 'I'll just have a coffee then we'll get going.'

I go and sit in the car.

'This is my last year and I cannot wait!' she says twenty minutes later, placing her black pot carefully in the cup holder of the ute. 'Have you got your papers so you can register?'

I nod curtly and turn my head to look out of the window. She gets the message.

I flash back to Mum and how mad she was when the MBD Scheme became compulsory. She and Dad had the biggest row. For him it was a no-brainer—more women and more blood were required, and the scheme was saving lives.

Stem cells were urgently needed to cure all the E. coli survivors who had developed H. coli—a secondary disease that ate away at the tissue of the heart. Some scientist had discovered that menstrual blood contained cells similar to stem cells, won a major award and the newest harvesting program was born: the Menstrual Blood Donation Scheme.

It started off as a voluntary scheme, but not enough women were donating so when the government expanded the SIF's powers to 'Sovereignty over Women's Health'—or as Mum took to saying through gritted teeth, 'control over Blood, Birth and Babies'—the SIF made MBD compulsory. The *great stem cell cure* suddenly turned into the SIF's great tracking device. MBD was the perfect way to have every woman in the country monitored and hooked into a system that would immediately signal new pregnancies *and* ensure direct pathways into the Safety for the Future Program.

Mum refused to go at first. But after she missed two visits, she was summoned for a pregnancy test and given a severe warning. Then she tried conscientiously objecting through a lawyer and an online petition but the SIF hauled her in and kept her overnight. I don't know what they did to her 'cos Dad made us go to our rooms when she got home. But she cried for a long time and never missed a donation again.

It *is* a pain having to deliver blood every month, but the menstrual cups are easy to use once you get the hang of them and there are MBD centres in every town. You don't have to start until you're sixteen and you finish at forty-five. As Dad said, it's helping save lives. Plus, there's one huge bonus although I know Mum despised this part the most—she said it was payment for the blood—but for me, there's nothing like a real shower with two whole minutes of hot water, shampoo that froths and lathering soap.

We pull up in front of the centre.

'I'll be in in a sec,' I say to Dione. No point in spending any more time with her than I have to. Besides, I don't want the SIF to see me with her.

The centre is very similar to the one near Lucy's house. When the scheme was introduced, swimming pools that'd been empty for years were filled in and quickly transformed into donation centres—a perfect use for the dormant spaces. Now a sedate queue of women lines the walls, each one holding a black pot, all hanging out for their monthly cleanse.

Dione is almost at the front. I ignore her as I walk past to the desk. The SIF officer in charge is a cardboard cut-out of the one at the other centre. The slate grey contact lenses they all wear are the worst, hiding any hint of what kind of a person she might be. She's definitely not going to smile.

'Name?' she commands, looking at her screen.

'Ora James.' I hand my papers to her and she taps quickly on the key board, updating my details.

'Pot,' she finally looks at me through her cold contacts. Why do these people always make me feel like I've done something wrong?

I dig around in my bag which is suddenly way too big. I know it's in here somewhere. She sighs loudly with impatience. 'Here it is,' I feel flustered. She snatches the pot, sticks the updated label on it and whacks it back on the counter.

'Is your menstrual cup still in good condition?' She's tapping on her keyboard again.

I nod and walk away, not bothering to say thank you. No point.

'Hey!' She barks after me, stopping me in my tracks. 'Did you hear me?'

'Yes,' I say meekly, turning back towards her. She's standing up now, leaning menacingly over the counter.

'Yes, you heard me or yes, your menstrual cup's still in good condition? And look at me when I'm talking to you!'

'Both,' I say quietly, forcing myself to look at her. Everyone's staring.

'Well next time, answer!' She goes back to her screen, dismissing me.

What a bitch! I'm glad Dione is in the shower room.

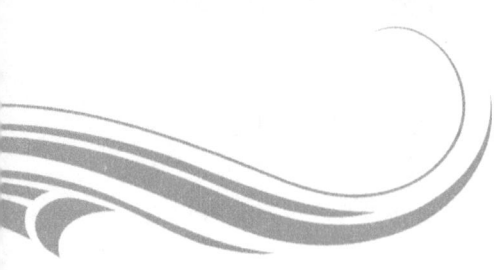

4

Seaboy

Lucy's cheery face fills my tiny phone screen. She's just given me a quick scan of her room, which made my belly flip. It's so bare—stripped of all her posters and stuff. Even the packing boxes that sat open for weeks have now been taped up, ready to go. They're leaving in the morning.

'So how's life in *Adelaide*?' She sounds jokey jealous.

'It's okay.' I string out the 'kay'. 'There's not much to do except draw and go to the beach ... I miss you!'

'Well you should have stayed with us then.' She sounds a bit sour.

'I wish I had.'

Lucy tries to smile but it doesn't work.

'I'm really going to miss you at Christmas,' I say. I've been dreading the thought of just me and Dione. Lucy looks away for a sec.

'Hey, I've got a holiday job at the supermarket,' I sound a touch too bright.

'Woo hoo!' Lucy quips. 'So now you can start saving for the boat fare to New Zealand.'

'I've already started.'

Lucy nods. She thinks I'm joking. 'Will you see your dad for Christmas?'

'Course not, he'll be working like always. It'll just be me and Dione.'

'You sound a bit down.'

'I feel a bit down.'

'How is *Auntie Dione*?'

I shrug. 'She's insane. She's … a frickin' ice queen. I hate it here!'

'Ouch!' Lucy says and looks concerned. Then she starts laughing again. 'Does she torture small and fluffy animals?'

'If only.' It feels good to hear her laugh.

'What then?'

'I can't tell you on the phone.' *I really want to, Luce, I'm just too scared.* 'It's complicated.'

'Ora! You can't leave me hanging. TELL me!'

'I will next time, I promise. Let's talk about something else.'

She sighs. 'Alright.' I'm glad she doesn't push. 'Have you applied for any courses yet?'

'Uh-uh. Still looking.'

'What about the guys there?' She brightens. 'Anyone interesting?'

'Nope. *Very* boring.'

'Oh.'

'Wait, I *did* see this guy at the beach the other day.'

'Oooh. Now you're talking. Nice looking?'

'Very! Except for the seal look.'

'What?'

'He was wearing this full-body wetsuit.' She pulls a face and I laugh. 'It's colder here in spring, remember? Anyway this guy swam the whole length of the beach and back.'

'Did you talk to him?' Lucy asks.

'No, but I smiled when I walked past him.'

'Did he smile back?'

'Kind of.'

'Well, I guess that's something.' I can tell she's a bit disappointed so I throw in some more. 'I've given him a name, wanna hear it?'

''Course.'

'Seaboy.'

'Seaboy?' Lucy chuckles. ''Cos he looks like a seal? Or 'cos he's nuts about the ocean too?'

'Both, I guess.'

Lucy laughs.

'I even like his teeth,' I laugh with Lucy. She wants every detail, like usual. It feels so good to be saying more than two sentences and to have her happy face looking back at me, listening intently.

I don't want the conversation to end. We talk for an hour and twenty-two minutes. Eventually Beth appears at the corner of the screen, flustered, saying they're late for some leaving party. The screen goes blank and I'm left sitting on the bed, surrounded by silence.

❧

The sea pulls me in every time, even in the winter. I go in quickly, ignoring my blood turning to ice. Once the water's up to my thighs I dive. The cold shock penetrates my bones and I come up fast. Since Mum and Holly died I've gone to the beach whenever I can. I used to walk for miles, but since the swimming bans have been lifted, now that the water quality has been declared safe, I prefer to swim.

I was in the shallows when I first saw him, digging my hands into the sandy floor, floating like seaweed. He was looking the other way so I didn't see his face. It was his legs that I noticed.

Defined and strong, just like his arms. I felt smug as he pulled on his wetsuit—not hardy like me, in just my bathers—but I didn't stop looking. He had no idea I was there as I quietly drifted in and out with the waves.

Just as he started swimming, I stood up, feeling in danger of hyperthermia. His speed and grace surprised me. I stared until he was just a vague blob in the distance, then went and moved my towel a little closer to his.

His footsteps crunching in the sand woke me. I'd drifted into a slumber on my belly as the sun dried my salty skin and warmed my bones. I lifted an eyelid and spied him peeling off his wetsuit. After sitting on his towel, he shook his head, spraying drops of sea-water from his dark hair, took out a book and then looked straight at me. I shut my eye quickly and pretended to be asleep, realising too late I was still making circles in the sand with my toes. He must have noticed. I moved my head to the other side and felt a giggle rise up between me and the sand.

He was still there when it was time to catch my bus, so I braved a smile as I walked past. He had a gorgeous smile.

I'm going to the beach tomorrow.

≪

Dione has had her dinner and left mine under a tea towel. She's watching something onscreen. I could go and sit next to her but I eat at the kitchen table instead.

On my way to bed, I stop at Dione's room and look at the frame drum.

'Why do you have a drum on your wall?' Holly's eleven-year-old voice rings out across the years.

In my mind's eye, I see Dione lying across the end of her bed with me and my sister snuggled up under the covers.

'I use it with the women at work,' she said, looking up at the round frame drum with the kookaburra feathers dangling from it.

'So they can give birth the way they want to.' She paused, choosing her words. 'A woman needs quiet and darkness when she's labouring, just like animals, but you don't get that in a hospital so I help them find a special place inside.'

'With the drum?' Holly asked.

Dione nodded, 'Along with their power animal.'

'What's a power animal?' I asked, sitting up.

'You're just trying to stay up!' Dione said.

'No I'm not!'

Holly giggled, 'Yes you are.'

'I am not! I just want to know about power animals.' I loved anything to do with animals. 'And I know you used that drum on Mum the other day. I heard you.'

'Relax, Ora, settle down.' Dione was looking at me intently. 'If you want, I'll do a drum journey with you before you go home tomorrow, okay? It'd be good for you to know your power animal.'

I gave a thankful nod and pushed back into the pillows.

'I never want to have a baby.' Holly said when Dione had gone. 'It sounds horrible.' She had listened in on lots of Mum and Dione's chats.

'Yeah, but the drum journey sounds fun,' I said as I closed my eyes for sleep.

'I wonder what our power animals will be,' Holly said with a yawn.

The next morning when we went to Dione's study, Holly and I were hit by the scent of something herbal burning. When Dione opened her door she was holding a wing—not a feather, but a whole raven's wing!—sleek black night in feathered form. I wanted to touch it so badly. In her other hand she held a smoking stub of leaves, bound tightly with red thread.

'This is sage,' she said quietly, using the wing to direct the smoke over our bodies. I loved the smell of burning green. A lit candle sat on an altar next to a gold bowl of water and a small sculpture of a woman lying down with a big belly and huge breasts. There was also an image of a leopard.

'Right,' Dione said. 'Lie under the blankets on the rug.'

There wasn't a lot of room but we lay side by side with our feet under her desk. She stood against the door holding her drum.

'When you're ready, put the scarves over your eyes. Just rest and listen to your breath. I'm going to drum like this.' And she banged her beater quickly, on the animal skin.

When we covered our eyes I felt the pulse reverberate through the front of my body, and repeated to myself, as Dione had instructed, 'I'm journeying to meet my power animal. I'm journeying to meet my power animal.'

Dione's voice guided us. 'Imagine yourself going into a cave and then down, under the earth or the ocean, or maybe through the trunk and roots of a tree—wherever your imagination takes you. Along the way, you'll meet some animals, or maybe just one. If something doesn't feel right, ask, "Are you here for my highest good?" If it isn't, it will disappear. When it's time to come back, I'll beat the drum like this.' She banged her beater slowly, three times.

A picture opened in my mind. I was walking along a beach, with caves set back into the cliffs. I went inside one, my senses adjusting to the dark. There were some stone steps leading down into deeper darkness. It was so black. I had to put my hand on the damp rock wall to feel my way down. Finally, some light appeared below and soon I found myself stepping out into a forest. A rainforest.

I looked up to see a massive lion standing in front of me, rich amber eyes glowing. I swallowed and said, 'Hello'.

'Welcome to the animal realm, Ora,' he said. The voice was in my head, but it definitely belonged to the lion. 'Follow me.'

He turned and padded along the forest path, tail in the air, twitching occasionally. I followed him, feeling the soft ground under my feet and catching the musty sweet forest scent.

Suddenly, a large snake appeared before me, its eyes huge.

'Ora, I've been waiting for you.'

'Hello,' I replied. 'Ar ... Are you here for my highest good?'

'Yes, Ora. We are always here for you. You're not alone. Remember that. Sometimes you will feel that you are but you're very strong. You have all that you need inside you. The ocean will help you—go there often. And the earth gives you strength. Think of the earth as your mother Ora ...'

The drumbeat changed, but I still had some questions.

'It's time to leave now, Ora,' the lion said.

Reluctantly I turned and there he was, ready to escort me back.

'Start to retrace your steps.' I heard Dione's deep voice.

I walked beside the lion, my hand on his back. He came up the steps with me and stopped just outside the entrance of the cave. I put my arms around his huge neck. I didn't want to let go.

Dione's voice was coming through gently, 'Wiggle your fingers; wiggle your toes.'

I came back into my body and stretched my arms up behind me, warm from the memory of the lion.

But ... a snake? I thought with a little shudder.

Dione sat down on the floor and we told her about our journeys. Holly had met an eagle. Dione said it sounded like I had two power animals: Lion and Snake. I was happy about the lion, but less sure about the snake.

When Dione told Holly that her eagle symbolised power and spirit, I was so jealous. But that was then. Now, I like to think of her flying free with her eagle.

5

First Birth

Dione is out a lot. She never tells me where she goes, just 'out'. A couple of times she's stayed away the whole night. I don't ask her where she's been. I don't want to know.

I'm happiest when she's in the garden.

Now and then we talk a bit, although I feel numb most of the time—apart from when I'm eating her food. It's like I created all this space for her inside me, but she's too busy to notice me, so the space just fills up with pebbles instead. And I'm getting heavier. Full of pebbles and full of food.

Maybe it's more about Mum and Holly. Maybe they were the ones who made the hole, and I was hoping Dione would fill it. Either way, it doesn't matter—she's too busy to care. Sometimes I want to shake her. Her 'screw the SIF' attitude is pathetic in a grown woman. She doesn't realise what she's risking. The SIF are like ants: unseen most of the time, but when there's something sweet they're all over it, hundreds of them. Sometimes I wonder if Dione is just trying to fill all the holes inside *her*—with action.

The beach is where I want to be, swimming and watching Seaboy. We're on 'hello' terms now but I can't bring myself to chat to him. A few days ago I got there before him and sat in his place, but then I moved because it felt far too obvious. I'm thinking of ways to start up a conversation … My favourite scenario so far is the one where I stumble in the sand and fall on top of him.

But I wouldn't know where to go from there.

I don't talk much to anyone at the moment, apart from Lucy, when I can catch her. She's busy settling in.

I've been drawing in my sketchpad—getting lost in the wildlife and the trees. There's this beautiful gum at the back of the property, I've drawn it a hundred times—and used up all my charcoal trying to capture its shape. I should be choosing a course but I still don't know what to do. No direction, that's me.

✍

I'm home alone one evening when a car pulls into the driveway. A wave of nausea rushes through me. The SIF? Dione's had a few 'guests' recently. I open the door a crack and peek out, knowing how suspicious I must look. A woman is walking towards the back of the house. I head through the kitchen and open the back door just as she's raising her hand to knock. She's as pregnant as a hot-air balloon.

'What do you want?' I know I sound unfriendly, but she shouldn't be here. Dad would have a fit.

'Is … is Dione here?' Her eyes flit behind me into the kitchen, all mad and starey, like a fox in a trap.

'She's out.' Stupid woman, putting herself and her baby in danger. *And me.* 'You'll have to come back another day.' I begin to close the door.

'Please,' the woman puts her hand on the doorframe. 'The baby's coming.'

She puts her other hand up and leans forward, breathes out

through her mouth, all slow and forced control. Now I'm really scared. Is she going to drop her baby here on the back step? I want to slam the door but her fingers are in the way. I back into the kitchen and suddenly I'm shouting.

'WHAT ARE YOU DOING?'

She just stares at me, confused, still gripping the doorframe and doing her heavy breathing.

'You're breaking the law!' This time my voice comes out low and even.

She says nothing, but those eyes bore into me. I step forward. 'You should be in the Safety for the Future Program!'

She starts to moan—probably to protest, but I stop her immediately.

'See, that's what I mean. Do you know how dangerous this is? What about your baby?' I'm alive with purpose. Someone has to talk sense into her!

Now the woman's hands have slipped down to her side. She looks sort of glazed, like she's going to cry.

'What if the SIF catch you? They'll take your baby. Why can't you just be normal and go to the centre like everyone else? Why'd you have to come here?' My voice has become strangely high-pitched. I feel I might burst. 'People like you—'

'Ora!' Dione's voice booms down the passage. She strides force-fully into the kitchen and pushes past me, car keys still in hand.

'I'm so sorry,' she's saying gently to the woman.

The woman lets out a choking sob. Dione's stroking the hair around her face and then she starts guiding her down the back steps.

'She doesn't know what she's saying.' Dione says to her, glanc-ing back like she hates me—it's a punch in the guts. 'She's just a teenager.'

What the hell? I'm eighteen! Dione barks a command at me over her shoulder.

'Get Lyndal's bag out of her car and bring it up to the cottage.'

Me. Is she talking to me?

'You're kidding me!' I shout the words.

'Just get it!'

The woman has to stop and hold onto Dione.

I storm into the passage, slamming the kitchen door behind me. I trip on the porch steps but manage to save myself before falling over. Then I'm running down the driveway, desperate to burn off this fire inside me. Only when I'm gasping for breath do I stop, crashing into the post of the Buzzy Bee sign, which starts swinging, grating metal against metal. I spring up, full stretch, to bring it down, screaming, shouting, roaring out my fury. It's too high. I grab the post and shake it, kick it. Stub my toes. Shouts turning to sobs, I put my head against the post and slump against it, finding my way to the ground.

Car tyres on gravel rouse me and I sink lower in the overgrown bushes. My tears and snot are all over my face. I wait for the car to go by, but instead it turns in, clipping the verge as it revs up to the house. The driver doesn't notice that he's nearly flattened me with his frenzied steering. The father, I guess.

I flash back to the woman's face at the door, her bewilderment and fear all mixed up with my words. I close my eyes and see my lion's face over my own. Breathing deeply, I imagine my arms around his neck.

Troubling thoughts start to plague me. I was screaming in that woman's face. What if I made her cry so much that I stopped her baby from coming out? Can a baby stop when it's on its way out? I try to stop torturing myself as I make my way back up the drive. *She's* the one who's put us all in danger—I'm just the fool in the middle. But shame is squirming in my gut. My self-righteous anger has deserted me.

By the time I get to her car, I don't even flicker with hesitation. It's like there's a magnet pulling me to open the door. I lean in and smell lavender—a small bunch sits on the dash. Her bag is faded brown and the leather is soft. I shut the door quietly and walk around the house, up the path, steadily towards the cottage. For the briefest of moments, I imagine my lion is beside me.

'You're Dione's little helper.' Mum's words from years ago echo in my head, making my anger flare up again. This isn't for Dione! It's for the woman. I need to make sure she and her baby are okay.

The cottage is empty when I step inside. I lean against the rough wood of the door, momentarily dazed. It's too quiet.

Where are they?

'Uuhh.' A deep powerful moan thumps the silence, making me start and bang my head on the low beam. It sounds like there's a beast downstairs—but this cottage doesn't have a downstairs. 'Uuhh.' I don't want to move but my body is already heading towards the sound.

The floral armchair, sitting at an awkward angle in the middle of the room, has been pushed aside to reveal a trapdoor lying open. I hear another groan, deep and primal. My heart feels like it's going to punch a hole in my chest. I hoist the bag onto my shoulder and turn around to grasp the metal rails either side of the stairwell. The ply board steps are steep and they creak and whine as I make my way closer to Dione's freak show. How did the woman get down here? My instinct is to run, but a mystery pilot is in charge and taking me down.

I pause on the bottom step, looking back up at the trapdoor. Maybe I should just dump the bag and flee. I start to slip the handles off my shoulder.

'Ora.' Dione's voice is gentle.

I turn and see the woman sitting back in a deep round tub of water, just big enough for her. Dione is leaning over her, tenderly wiping the woman's face. The man is the other side, supporting her head. Her bare breasts are full and arching up towards the ceiling, shiny from the water. She looks like she's sleeping. But then her head snaps forward and she looks straight at me, making me jump.

'Get her out,' she says loudly, a she-wolf baring her teeth.

Dione gestures with her head for me to go back up the steps, dismissing me.

But I don't go. I'm a mess of fear and rage and longing. I want to stay in this little cave of warmth where the air is gentle and expectant and full of all the nurturing that Dione used to shower upon me. So this is who she's saving it for! I'm locked to the spot by a swirl of emotions, clutching the woman's bag and looking at her breasts. Her baby is coming. Dione is coming towards me when another wave takes the woman.

I finally find my words, 'You shouldn't be—'

'Uugh!' The woman's cry overpowers my voice.

I drop the bag and run.

6

Not Swimming

I spend the whole night thinking about running away. To New Zealand, or back to Dad's. Maybe I should just move to Sydney or Melbourne and lose myself there? I go back to thinking about Dad, but I can't live with him again. At least Dione can look me in the eye *sometimes*. I was so stupid to think we would have a connection. She's totally lost it with her crackpot birthing unit. I have to get away. I want to tell Lucy but I can't. Not on the phone.

By the time the first bird starts calling my head is fuzzy and full of white noise. The beach. I have to get to the beach and into the water. Then I'll be able to think straight.

I creep out into the sepia dawn and see the sun's first glow offering some colour. The morning chill hits my bones. I forgot my hoodie. The bus won't be running for ages, so I start walking. I need to get away.

I walk until my feet are sore. Eventually I get on a bus. At the beach I head straight for the water. I get to the buoy in no time and just keep going. All the thoughts and memories and hurt that have been torturing me surge out of my arms and legs as I push through the water. The rhythm soothes me, but the hurt explodes inside my chest.

When I saw Dione with that woman I knew the truth. She only cares about pregnant women. She doesn't want me anywhere near her—she won't even hug me.

It's hard to cry when you're swimming.

Why can't she love *me*?

It's even harder to swim when you're crying.

My dad can't stand the sight of me. I know he wishes I'd died instead of …

I have no one.

I'm over halfway across the bay when I have to stop, I'm crying so hard.

Why did they have to die?

I am back inside the raw, grisly grief of losing them. The hole that they left is too big. I can't stand it anymore.

My sobs roll over the water into nothingness. Lion and Snake flash briefly through my mind but I push them away.

I hear the sound of a motor, then an orange boat swishes in beside me. Before I know what's happening, I'm being scooped up by a bronzed, round-faced lifesaver. She flashes her straight white teeth as she heaves me over the side.

What is she so bloody happy about?

'You looked like you were in a bit of trouble there.' She looks me over closely, deciding whether I need medical attention.

'I'm fine,' I sob, embarrassed and angry. And cold. I start to shake uncontrollably. She puts a towel over me and settles herself into position.

'Don't worry, love,' she says. 'I'll have you back in no time.'

'I was fine!'

'It's no bother. Better safe than sorry.'

How dare she pluck me out like a rag doll? I want to scream at her but all the air goes out of me, making me slide to the bottom of the boat. I rest my head against the hard rubber side and shut my eyes, concentrating on the whir of the motor.

I am jolted into the present by the crunch of sand underneath the boat. She has expertly surfed us in on a wave. I get ready to disappear as soon as my feet touch land. All I want to do is slink back to my towel and burrow into it, hiding my shame. I look along the beach to my pile of things and there he is, sitting just outside the flags not far from my towel, looking straight at me.

No!

'You'll have to rest for a while, love,' says the lifesaver, smiling again. I want to hit her. 'Just so we can keep an eye on you. Have you got someone we can call?'

I sigh and shake my head.

'Well, let's get you out of the boat and you can sit here for a bit. I'm sure you'll think of someone soon.' She's smiling brightly, and doesn't move away until I'm sitting on the sand.

I hug my knees hard and look straight ahead. People are looking at me, curious about the girl who needed saving.

'Drowned rat' is taking on a whole new meaning—my hair has started to frizz into a wild afro and I feel wretched. I pretend to zone out into the horizon as I feel my self-esteem belly flopping into the ocean.

Out of the corner of my eye, I see Seaboy get up and start walking towards me. I stop breathing and look down. *Please walk past. Please.*

'Hey,' he says, sitting a little way from me. I can't speak. He picks up some sand and moves it between his fingers. 'You know, I'm the only one around here who can manage to swim across the bay?'

I look at him and he's wearing this grandiose grin and just for a second I forget myself.

'Well excuse me, Mr Weedy Pants Wetsuit!'

He opens his mouth—I've surprised him—then laughs. 'I have to wear it, it gets way too cold out there for that long.' I smile and try not to think about how crap my eyes must look after all that crying.

'I'm Jake, by the way.'

'Ora,' I say, shaking his outstretched hand. The gesture is more matey than formal. His skin is soft under the grains of sand.

'So what was happening out there?'

I drop his hand and look back at the horizon.

'Ora!?' Dione's voice travels up the beach.

'Oh no,' I say. 'My aunt.'

Seaboy raises an eyebrow and we watch her marching towards us on the uneven sand.

He starts to stand and so do I, feeling wobbly.

'Ora!' Dione comes to a halting stop and there's an awkward silence.

'Hi.' He holds out his hand for a second time. 'I'm Jake.'

'Dione,' she says, shaking it briefly. She looks at me. 'I'm glad I guessed the right beach.'

My insides feel tight when I look at her.

'We need to talk,' she says.

Great. I finally get to chat to Seaboy and she ruins it! Just like she's ruining the rest of my life.

'I'll see you another time.' Jake turns and walks back to his towel before I can respond.

'Let's go home,' she says.

'No!' There's no way I'm going back to that house. Not with her. I start walking towards my stuff.

'Iced chocolate?' she calls after me. 'The Star of Greece?'

The years fall away when I hear the name. Every visit, we always had to go there—Me, Holly, Mum and Dione—the high-up café overlooking the sea.

I walk stiffly to my things. I can't look at Seaboy ... Jake ... whatever. I want the ground to swallow me up.

The lifesaver says something to Dione.

I walk away from the sea and away from Dione, towards the bus stop. I have to get away.

But where to?

7

Justification?

I slump onto the bus-stop bench and dump my bag beside me. Dione has followed me.

'Aren't you wasting your precious petrol, coming here?'

She doesn't sit next to me, thankfully. 'I needed to check you were okay. I just had a feeling that—

'—you were a mental bitch?'

'Ora, I know you don't—'

'Don't want to live with you anymore? Too right.'

'Ora ...'

'I can't handle all your preg—'

'Shhh.' Now she's looking around, worried.

'You've treated me like shit ever since I got here, Dione. Why didn't you just tell me not to come?'

'I tried! I wanted you to go to New Zealand, remember? But you *insisted* on coming ...' She looks at a man approaching the bus stop and speaks quietly. 'I knew how hurt you were over your dad ...'

The man stops beside us. He could be an undercover SIF officer. The thought's enough to make me move.

Dione's ute is hot and airless but the car's speed and open windows soon have my hair dancing. We drive in silence except for the radio music. I don't care where we're going. I'm too busy squirming over the past twenty-four hours: Seaboy—Jake—seeing me get picked up by the lifesaver. The woman in the tub and her snarling face. Dione dismissing me.

We pull into the car park overlooking the sea. There's only one other car here. The café hasn't changed, solid and white against the blue sea and sky, neat rows of sash windows with pink and orange flowers tumbling from their sills.

I feel so old.

Dione turns off the engine and I have to swallow hard to keep my tears in.

'I didn't mean for any of this to happen, Ora.' She turns and reaches for my hand. I don't let her touch me. Why is she being so nice all of a sudden? It's ... too much.

The last time I was here was with Mum and Holly.

I feel sick.

'God, Ora,' she says, shaking her head. 'I'm so, so sorry ...'

I want to spew my guts over her. Fury. Nausea. Pain. I want her to know everything. To feel it as deeply as I do, this searing emptiness that won't go away.

I force the tips of my teeth together.

'You're ridiculous, Dione. All your *stupid* birth stuff. You're possessed by it ... That woman last night ... you were ... so soft ... and you shouted at me like I was ...' I shake my head, trying to delete the memory.

'When I was swimming, all this sadness ... I started feeling so ...' The tears are rolling down my cheeks now, but I'm not sobbing. 'I miss them.'

She shakes her head and squeezes my shoulder, looking stricken. Her eyes are soft now. She reminds me of Mum.

'I've been so stupid, Ora.'

'Yeah, well, that's stating the obvious.' I push her hand off me.

'But I needed to keep you out, to shield you.' She's still shaking her head.

I stare at her. Nothing makes sense. We sit for ages, looking through the windscreen to the sea.

'Ora, I've *always* wanted you here ... I just couldn't see how to make it work with the birth stuff.'

I need to get out of the car.

'Will you let me explain? Please?'

I look at her, knowing it's not a good idea, but I need to find out how deep she's in.

We're halfway to the entrance of the café when she stops in front me.

'The only reason I didn't have you here from the very beginning is because I couldn't offer you the stability you needed.' She looks very earnest, her face scrunched up against the sunshine. I can feel some heat seeping back into my heart.

She puts her arm around my waist and hugs me from side-on. I want to snuggle in, but I pull away. We walk over to the railing at the top of the cliff.

'When I heard you might be going to New Zealand I was distraught, but I knew it was for the best. I knew you were happy with Lucy and her family, and New Zealand's got so much more going for it. But you wouldn't listen ...'

'If only I had.'

The bell above the door announces our arrival. Perfect glimpses of the ocean greet us as we step inside, each window framing a moving palette of blues. There's a new deck at one end that offers the privacy we need. Dione orders peppermint tea and iced chocolate and we sit, staring out to sea, until the drinks arrive. I look at the milk. It'll be genetically engineered, but I don't care.

'D'you know I was at your birth?' Dione asks, pouring her tea.

'I think so.' I know so, but I want to hear about Mum.

'I only just made it,' she says, smiling. 'I booked my ticket two weeks before your due date but you decided to come early. When there was no one at the airport to meet me I guessed something was up and jumped in a taxi. You were coming out just as I stepped through the door.'

I shrug.

'That was the last year homebirth was still legal.'

'I can't believe Dad let Mum have me at home.'

'He didn't have a say.' Dione smiles again.

I shrug again and inhale a waft of seaweed.

'I didn't plan any of this, Ora.' She's got her activist voice on now. 'It just happened. When the government changed the rules, it flicked some kind of switch in me. I was outraged. Safety, safety, safety,' she spits. 'It's just one big excuse to control us.'

I use my finger to scoop some iced chocolate into my mouth.

'Then after your mum and Holly died ... I stopped working altogether. I just shut down ... until an old client turned up on my doorstep. She was very pregnant and on the run from the SIF, so I hid her in the cottage.'

'Dione, the Good Samaritan,' I say.

She continues, ignoring my scorn. 'Her partner was a plumber, and he fixed up the shelter with the birthing tub and did some building work to make it right for her. I told myself I was only going to help her, but then her friend wanted help soon after. Every time I tried to stop, another woman would contact me. Maybe I was easily persuaded, I don't know, but before I knew it, I was running an underground birthing centre.'

There's a long silence.

'How do the women not get caught once they've had the baby?' I wonder aloud. 'And how do they get around MBD?'

'They get friends to share their blood. The donor centres don't identify or measure the blood—it's too expensive. As long as you show up with a donation, that's enough. As for the birth records, there are a few master hackers out there who can get into the system, make it look like the babies were born into the Safety Programs. I don't know how they do it, but it works. There are also some skilled forgers who create fake papers.'

'So there's a whole racket going on! A kind of underground revolution? I bet that couple on the train were part of it.'

'I don't know about the couple on the train but all of them are just people who want sovereignty over their own bodies, that's all. There'll never be a revolution. All the Programs and centres are way too big now. It just comes down to what each individual believes is right.'

'What's right? These *individuals* don't care one bit about the safety of their babies. I can't believe you're doing this!' I'm finding it hard to speak quietly.

'What makes you so sure the babies are better off in the centres, Ora? Have you been so brainwashed?'

'It's been proven. What *you're* doing is dangerous. And negligent.'

'Do you know what happens in those centres? They're like prisons. Women are sedated as soon as they step inside. You have no idea. The centres are overcrowded—twenty women to a dorm— and there's nothing to do for the entire pregnancy! No wonder they come out half deranged. The births are all scheduled and the babies are whisked off to incubators as soon as they're delivered. The mothers don't even get to hold their newborns. What chance have they got of bonding? We're creating a zombie nation, all in the name of safety!'

'What if something goes wrong? Do you have a back-up plan? You're too far from a hospital to get help.'

'Listen to how fearful you sound, Ora. Everyone is a seething mass of fear. We've turned into sheep, running to do whatever the government asks. And the centres haven't been *proven* to be safer. They've just managed to convince everyone that it's a big scary world. All that E. coli and H. coli propaganda. It was nonsense.'

'Thousands of deaths does not equal nonsense, Dione.'

'It was never thousands. It's all about control. They've found another way of controlling women. That's the bottom line, Ora. If you control the way women give birth, throw enough fear in there, you've got the whole of society sewn up.' She's fidgeting in her seat now. 'Do you know when it all started?'

I sigh loudly and sit back for the lecture.

'Way back in the sixteen hundreds when women started lying on their backs to give birth—and guess who for? The king! Louis the Fourteenth got a kick out of watching his mistresses give birth, so he ordered the doctor to make them lie down so he could see better. After that, the doctor realised it made things so much easier—for him! Soon it was all the rage. The doctors loved it because they didn't have to kneel anymore, and the women just followed the fashion, like they always do.'

'But this isn't about lying down, Dione.'

'Women never got up off their backs!'

'How would you feel if a baby died? Or a woman? I can't believe you're being so blind. The hospitals and government wouldn't have made the rules if it wasn't in our best interests.'

'How can you be so naive?' She looks shocked.

'*How* would you *feel* if a baby died?' I'm starting to raise my voice.

'I didn't realise how much of your dad you had in you.'

'Leave him out of this.' I'm shouting now. I pull in my breath sharply. 'Will you just answer my question?'

'There are two reasons I do this; for the women who dare to birth the way they want to, and for the babies, who deserve to come into this world without being pumped full of drugs to "save them".'

I stab at the ice in my glass.

Dione's eyes are shining and her cheeks are flushed. 'It all starts with birth, Ora. New babies need to be with their mothers, skin-to-skin, heart-to-heart, to give them the best chance of connecting deeply for the rest of their lives.'

'You still haven't answered my question,' I say in a sing-song voice.

'Do you realise we've buggered everything up? We've never been sicker, as a race.' Her words are grating on my nerves. 'The reason there are so many autoimmune diseases, where the body's own cells turn against themselves, is because we've buggered up our ecosystems—with antibiotics, with chemicals, with electro-magnetics. Just like we've buggered up the earth's ecosystems.'

'You're insane, Dione.'

'And just like we cut the earth up to extract all the resources, now we're cutting open—'

'—I'm not listening anymore.' I stand up. The waitress appears and I ask for the bill.

Dione is simmering down. 'I'm sorry. I just want you to understand.'

'You still haven't answered my question,' I say for the hundredth time.

A group of people come and sit at the table beside us. Dione follows me out. When we're in the car she asks me if I want to go back to the beach. A wall of exhaustion hits me.

'I just need to sleep,' I say, overwhelmed. I can't decide anything right now. All I want is to get into bed.

As we come to a stop outside the house, she says slowly, 'Every birth I attend, I weigh up the odds of the baby dying or the mother dying, or both. I'm not so blind as to think it won't happen. If you're talking about birth you have to talk about death too—they're two sides of the same coin. Not even the doctors can prevent death sometimes.' She's talking gently now, not lecturing. 'If it happens, I'll have to live with my conscience for the rest of my life, but ... maybe it won't ... or maybe I'll get caught first.' She smiles thinly and I see a massive crack zigzagging through all her fighting words.

As we climb the veranda steps I say, 'I still don't agree with any of it. None of this is about freedom of choice. Not really.'

She looks at me, puzzled, still lost in her activist world. I carry on talking.

'It's about your own shadows, Dione. What you're running from. Do you remember when you called to persuade me to go to New Zealand?'

She nods and pushes against the door, stumbling into the passage, then stopping to look at me.

'I was complaining about Lucy leaving Australia and you reeled off this long list of things to weigh up in my decision making: health, friendships, money, the SIF. You said it was part of the human condition to suffer but the most important thing was to know your priorities and stay busy.' She nods.

'You never mentioned family in your list, or loss.' I pause, watching her closely. 'Do you know, today was the first time you've mentioned losing Mum and Holly?' I see her face hardening, but I push on.

'You haven't come close to facing your grief. You are *so* in denial. It's rubbish, all that stuff about keeping busy! Look at Dad with his job, and you! All this birth stuff, it's just to distract you.'

I look at her accusingly. She stares back at me, a mixture of disbelief and truth.

She speaks very quietly. 'It's not rubbish. It is better to stay busy. If I stopped … Where would all the mothers be? They need me Ora.'

Her eyes fill with tears. The tougher Dione feels safer, but this one is more real. I reach out to squeeze her fingers before she turns and goes into her bedroom, shutting the door.

I go into my room and get under the covers. My ring catches on Mum's crocheted blanket.

Dione's blanket. I think it's time to give it back.

8

Mum & Holly

'Where are you? I can hardly see you.' Lucy's squinting face peers out from my phone.

'I'm under the covers.'

'It's the middle of the day Ora!'

'It's after four o'clock here. I'm just exhausted, that's all.'

'You look it. Can you put the light on? I want to see how bad you look.'

'No.' I feel terrible. I needed to talk to her but now I wish I hadn't called.

'Just tell me what's up?'

'Nothing.'

'*Nothing* is the problem, Ora. You're not doing *anything* up there. It's not good for you, all that wilderness. You need some friends. And you need to decide on a uni course. All the places will have gone by the time you get your act together.'

I don't say anything.

'And Dione clearly isn't the wonder aunt you thought she was.'

'Too right!'

'So start TALKING!'

'She … she interrupted my first ever conversation with Seaboy.'

'What?'

I can tell her some of it.

'I'd just got brought in by the lifesaver and Seaboy saw everything but came over to say hi anyway, and then Dione stormed up and scared him off.'

'What? You're breaking up. Will you sit up so I can see you?'

I come out of my cocoon slowly, taking a weird pleasure in her frustration.

'Did you nearly drown Ora?' She looks so serious, I crack up.

'No! The stupid lifesaver was on a power trip. I was fine. But it was really embarrassing.'

She still looks serious. 'Get me Dione. I want to talk to her.'

'What?'

'Get her, Ora. She's not looking after you. I can see. I'm going to tell her.'

'Lucy, I'm fine, really. The move has just been harder than I expected.' She looks at me. 'That's all.' I sigh. 'I'll find a friend before I next talk to you, I promise.'

'DIONE! DIONEEEEE!' Lucy starts shouting her lungs out.

I turn the volume down and watch her face getting redder and wilder as she shouts. I laugh, and a couple of tears escape. It's too much. I turn the camera off so she can't see me.

'I have to go,' I whisper when she finally stops. I don't want her to hear the waver in my voice. 'I love you.'

⁊

My heart hurts and my mind won't shut up. I miss Lucy. She was right about me needing friends. Echoes of Dione's words keep swirling round and round in my head. Images of the woman in the tub are disturbing me—she was so peaceful, until she noticed me. The memory of Dione's tenderness makes me fidget. And the warmth. And the normality. I see myself crying in the sea, and the lifesaver ... and Seaboy. Jake.

I should get up, go for a walk. I need to still my mind.

A drum journey ...? I haven't done one for years. Not since we moved into the flat.

I hated that flat. After Mum and Holly died, we stayed at Lucy's for a bit. Each night, I'd cling to Dad, sandwiched between him and the wall, never letting go. But her house was small, with paper thin walls that couldn't contain our grief.

The new flat was all hard, with furniture fit for an office. I yearned for Mum's handmade cushions. She'd got some bright pink and orange fabric from an Indian woman at the market and made about ten cushions to hide the sofa. They screamed at you whenever you walked in the room, even she'd laughed at them, but eventually we stopped noticing them.

I've wondered about those cushions, whether the flames took on their colour before they were burned to ashes.

Holly died instantly, Mum two days later.

Dad was on shift. Mum managed to drag me out of the house in my sleepy, smoke-filled state, then she went back in for Holly. Holly's room was at the back, where the fire had started, so I don't think she would have felt pain. Just drifted off into another world, carried on the smoke.

To the stars, Mum would have said.

A neighbour got Mum out, but the damage was done.

The hospital let us wash her after she'd gone. We couldn't do the same for Holly. There was no chance to say goodbye. But I'd had two days to think about this goodbye, and I convinced Dad we should do it.

It was weird and beautiful and a nightmare. Her body went from warm to cold. She was there but not there, her skin no longer alive to the touch. I wanted to shout at her to stop mucking about, to wake up. Dad and I didn't talk. We didn't even look at each other. Lost in the confusion of Mum's dead body under our hands, our love for her, stronger than ever, breaking our hearts.

It felt like days before Dad and I spoke again, but we were connected anyway. Forever, I thought.

The hospital wouldn't let us take Mum's body home. Dad didn't want to anyway, and besides, we didn't have a home to go back to.

Faulty electrics, apparently, in the home I used to love. And dead batteries in the smoke alarm.

The worst thing about my new bedroom was that it didn't have Dad in it. He told me I had to learn to sleep through the night without him. The sheets were new and scratchy–a perfect match for the cold and empty room. I took to clinging to Dad on the sofa, and he'd have to peel me off at bedtime, pulling and gently nudging me into my room. Shouting at me when I pushed him too far.

I had to find something to help me sleep, and that's when I remembered the drum journey download Dione had given me years before. Soon I was listening to it every night, eager for the monotonous beat to take over and lull my anxious mind into a beautiful nothingness.

Later, when sleep became elusive again, I decided to take myself on a proper drum journey, and called to Lion, who appeared immediately. We went into a forest where thick, green leaves the size of dinner plates hung off willowy branches above our heads.

A structure lay ahead, like a giant, golden walnut shell. The entrance was a soft arch and the shiny walls curved back into a smooth, candlelit cave. Peace. Except for Snake, who was coiled up inside. But she looked like she was smiling. Beside her sat a large, round cushion, just for me. I sat down and Snake welcomed me.

After that visit, I went every night. Lion and Snake were

always there. We talked a lot. Me mostly, telling them about my days, my grief.

One night, the round cushion was gone and in its place was our old sofa, with the colourful cushions … and Mum and Holly.

I flung myself on top of them, intent on holding them forever. There were tears, but joyful ones. We stayed there for a long time, holding hands and looking out at the forest, as I filled up the cracks and the holes that had been crumbling me away.

I went often over the next few months. Sometimes they were there, sometimes not. I didn't get it. I'd figured out I was the one controlling it all, so why couldn't I summon them whenever I wanted? Lion and Snake were always there, but Mum and Holly seemed to have their own visiting hours.

I would go to sleep curled up with hope in my heart, which was ironic, seeing as they were dead. But it was the closest I got to having them back. A new family, including a big cat and a snake, was forming in my little forest temple. Sometimes I wondered at the weirdness of it but mostly it felt right; they were all a part of me.

Lying on my bed in the late afternoon sun, I listen to the drumbeat. Lion and Snake arrive instantly, but Snake starts talking all sorts of rubbish and gives me some crazy advice about trusting Dione. I finish it early and go for a walk. When I come back Dione is out—she must be up at the cottage checking on the woman and the baby. I make us some sandwiches and eat mine in my room, not ready to see her yet.

I wonder if she'll ever stop.

9

The MBD Centre

guess she's my age. I remember her from last month. I like her hippy chic look—except for her boots, which are more farm than French. Her hair is in a Japanese-style bun on the top of her head and I'm just wondering how long it is when she turns and smiles.

'These lines kill me!' We're queuing for our showers, donation pots in hand. 'This whole thing kills me. Donation, my arse! They make it sound like we're giving out of the goodness of our hearts.'

'The goodness of our *wombs*, you mean,' I say, and she laughs.

'Why do they still call it donation? There's nothing *voluntary* about it.' She looks around and sniffs. 'I used to swim here when I was a kid. Funny how it still smells like a pool, isn't it?' I nod, imagining the centre as it once was, full of splashes and shouts. 'If you were given the choice, would you still give your blood?' She seems like a bit of a radical but I like her. Kind of earthy, in spite of her tailored clothes.

'I don't know,' I say honestly. 'I love my shower. And the blood helps a lot of people.'

'You reckon? You really think they use it for the H. coli victims?'

'For sure. My dad explained it to me. He's a doctor.'

I got my period for the first time when I was thirteen, not long after Mum died. Dad made a big deal about it and bought me flowers, saying how important it was and how in a few years I'd be able to donate and save lives. By the time I had to make my first donation I was living with Lucy, and I was glad to have her there to show me how to use the menstrual cup.

'So he works in diseases?'

'Emergency,' I say, and she scrunches her nose.

'Doesn't count. He wouldn't know what they do with the blood.'

'How do you know?'

She shrugs, 'Just a hunch.' She turns away.

I've blown it. I'm not sure if it's because of Dad's job or what I said about loving the shower. I don't want to stop talking to her.

'How about you?' I ask the back of her head.

She leans against the wall and looks at me again. 'Nope. Not in a million years.'

'Really?'

'The showers are just the carrot to get us here. Brainwashing. Bodywashing. Same thing. Just a ploy to make you believe the government owns your blood as well as the water that falls from the sky. Oh look, right on cue.'

A long parade of SIF officers marches past, looking straight at us. Their cold eyes make me feel dead inside.

'There they go,' she says to their backs. 'Flexing their muscles. Every two hours, like clockwork. Have you ever wondered where they're going?'

I shake my head. I have no idea, but it was the same at the other centre.

'Every centre, every two hours—a little march up and down.

A little show, just for you and me, to remind us who's in charge. Works a treat. So if we have children we can tell them what a scary-wary bunch the SIF are and how important it is to be vewy-vewy good.'

I'm shocked. She is mega-radical. Surely the SIF have a base here too, like they did at the other centre? Maybe I should stop talking to her. She doesn't care who hears. What if we get reported? But then she leans in close and whispers, 'I only give them half.' She smiles, holding up her pot. 'The other half goes back to the earth.'

I don't know what to say. But I've worked it out. I knew she reminded me of someone.

Mum.

'I reckon the plastic company has made a killing.' She's talking loudly again. The woman in front turns to give us a dirty look, like we're a couple of termites.

'Millions of menstrual pots and trillions of water containers. The government's probably got shares in them. In fact, they probably own the company.' It's like she wants everyone to hear.

'I'm Melissa, by the way.'

'Ora.' I can't help liking her, even if she is a radical. Once she's had her rant, she tells me about her passion for fabric and making clothes. I tell her about my sketches, although there's not that much to say. But she gets quite excited—she's looking for someone to work with on fabric design.

By the time we come out of the centre we've exchanged numbers. Who cares what Dad thinks? Maybe he doesn't know everything after all.

10

Christmas

When I find the courage to go back to the beach I sit as far away from the happy bronze lifesaver as possible. I wait all day, but Jake doesn't come. It's the same the next day, and the one after. I've a sinking feeling that I've missed my chance.

I sketch him in my pad, even though it makes me feel like a stalker. Finally, after dozens of attempts, I capture him. The image bears a striking resemblance. I pin it up on the back of my door—I don't want Dione seeing it.

Dione and I have been getting on better since the day at the beach. Neither of us has mentioned the birth stuff—it seems to work if we stay well away from the subject. We've started eating dinner together and have gone on a couple of bush walks, chatting about different courses I could choose. She seems okay with me not knowing what I want to do. I think she understands that I need some time. She's even talked about Mum and Holly, twice, remembering different things about them.

It feels good.

I've been to see a movie with Melissa, and last week she came to the beach. She's invited us for Christmas day—there's only her and her brother and nephew at the moment, so she said it makes sense to celebrate together and Dione seemed okay about the idea of spending the day with people she didn't know. She didn't pull a face when she heard how far away Melissa lives, either. I think she's really trying.

For Christmas, Dione gives me two pre-paid driving lessons—they're mega expensive and it seems kind of redundant to be learning, but she says she's saving for an electric car. Dione loves my present—a silk scarf I coloured with natural bush dyes.

It takes me a while to decide what to wear. I've never been good at dressing up, but Melissa always looks so nice. In the end I choose the funky patterned top that Lucy gave me on our last day together and a pair of nice shorts. It's going to be hot.

When we're almost there, Dione asks if we're going to a horse property. I nod, and explain that Melissa is looking after her sister-in-law's horses.

'I've been here before.' Dione is smiling broadly as we turn into the driveway. 'I know the couple who live here.'

I get a sour taste in my mouth. Surely not in that way?

Melissa comes out to meet us. She doesn't recognise Dione, so that's a relief. Melissa's brother is called Tom. He has a toddler—Little Tom—who looks like he lives in the crook of his dad's arm.

'Dione!' Tom booms, giving her a massive hug. The writing's on the wall, especially when she starts cooing over Little Tom, saying how big he's got. I'm seething inside but I don't want to ruin the atmosphere, so I smile at Tom when Melissa introduces us. He must be at least ten years older than Mel.

'Where's Sarah?' Dione asks, looking around—for the mother, I assume.

Tom shakes his head and looks forlorn. 'She's in the Program.'

'What?' It's Dione's turn to be shocked.

He nods. 'She'd had this eye infection for weeks so went in for some tests. Why they tested for pregnancy too, I have no idea, but they found out before we did. There was no getting around it, Dione. I tried to get into the system, but it's a lot harder taking people off the records than putting them on. Before we knew it, she was gone.'

Dione has her hand over her mouth, like Sarah has just died.

What is it with her and birth, and why can't she get away from it? I feel like spitting nails at the pair of them. It's like she's this magnet for birth-related bullshit.

'I'm so sorry, Tom.' Dione is shaking her head. They start talking about how terrible the Program is.

'Do you want to look around?' Melissa suggests. I'm out the door before she can finish her sentence.

'Are you okay?' Melissa asks, catching up with me.

There's no point in complaining to her, she probably agrees with them.

'Sure. Come on, show me around.' I force another smile.

We walk through dry horse paddocks—there are acres of them, stretching to the bottom of a mountain range. Towering gums dot the landscape, majestic and ancient, standing with their giant limbs spread open, saying, 'This is my land'.

Melissa moved up here when Sarah left, to help out with the horses and Little Tom. She wants to show me the new foal. The horses are Sarah's—Tom runs an IT business. *I suppose he's into hacking, too,* I think snidely, but I hold my tongue.

'They're paying me really well—Tom earns heaps—so I'm saving for a new sewing machine. One of the shops in the city is going to start selling my clothes, can you believe it? Hey, did you bring your sketchpads?'

'I just want to work on them a bit more before I show you.'

'I'm sure they're great. You *have* to show me next time, okay?'

I nod my agreement. I wish *I* was sure.

The foal is extra cute. His spindly legs look like they're about to shoot out from under him. He makes me laugh as he runs around playfully, and I forget my anger. I can't change what's in the past, and there haven't been any women around recently— maybe Dione is trying to change.

⤳

'Thanks for not saying anything,' Dione says after a while, on the way home. The sun's just gone down and there's an orange pink tinge to everything. 'I know it was a bit of a shock.'

'Too right!' There's an uncomfortable silence that drags on for a bit, then I break it, 'It's like we can never get away from it. How many births have you actually been to?'

She doesn't answer immediately. 'Probably over a thousand, all up, including the hospital.'

'A thousand?!' Why did I ask? But I don't have the energy to fight with her. And besides, she sounds kind of apologetic.

I'm just starting to doze off when she pipes up. 'Hey, guess what I found out?'

'What?' It better not be birth related.

'One of Tom's cousins helps out on the property and guess what his name is?

'What?'

'Jake!' I look at her and sit up straighter in my seat.

'And apparently he's this amazing swimmer!'

'No way!'

She nods, keeping her eyes on the road. I told Dione about Jake a few days ago. I couldn't get hold of Lucy and I had to talk to someone. I was feeling so down about not seeing him.

'That would mean Melissa is his cousin too!'

She's nodding, 'Tom said he's in Queensland at the moment training to be a lifeguard.'

'Queensland?'

'His mum lives there, apparently. He went up for Christmas. But how small is Adelaide, hey? Can you believe it?'

11

Second Birth

The day I get my driver's license is the day everything turns to shit.

It starts well. I pass without a hitch thanks to the top-up driving lessons and all the hours I'd clocked up with Lucy's parents. They were so good to me, letting me drive them everywhere, even after the petrol rations came in. When I get home, Dione has made a celebratory lunch. She says she knew I'd pass. She pulls out a bottle of French champagne that one of her clients gave her years ago. The bubbles go up my nose and we both get giggly. It's the best time I've had with her yet.

In the afternoon, she has to go and collect her water—they don't deliver this far up.

The sun is shining but it's not baking hot, so I offer to put the compost around the veggies. I'm feeling pretty pleased with myself. And excited—Melissa told me Jake is coming back in a couple of weeks.

I've got the radio on and my head's under a bush when a man's voice makes me start.

'Quick! Help!'

I stand up too quickly and lose some hair in the foliage. I'm cross that he's startled me out of my gardening haze. A woman is sitting on the tomato vine bench, leaning forward, holding her belly. I didn't even hear them arrive. They must have parked out the front. He shoves her bag against my chest and turns to go.

'I can't do this,' he says to her, and takes off, back around the house.

I'm gobsmacked.

'He's scared of getting caught,' the woman says, rocking backwards and forwards. Then she roars like a wild woman.

I drop the bag. A bead of sweat trickles down my spine. Think. Get her up to the cottage. Call Dione. Towels. What?

I can't move. This isn't happening. Tell her to go. Now.

She's left it too late. Her noises assault my ears and I know she's left it too late. The sound reverberates deep in her throat, in and around her body. She's trying to squat and take off her undies at the same time.

Here in Dione's veggie garden.

'I can feel its head,' she says urgently, her hand between her legs.

My hands reach out towards her and I snatch them back.

Why isn't Dione here?

I'm moving towards her before I can stop myself, taking off the gardening gloves.

She's lowered herself into a kneeling position and shifts forwards, onto her hands. She crawls a little way forward and then another wave takes her. She's on all fours and roaring, bearing her baby down. I could let the panic take me—it's rising fast—but there isn't time. I move in beside her.

She kicks off her undies and shifts back into a squat, grabbing my arm and the bench, squeezing me like she's trying to squish my bones.

I dare to kneel down and look between her legs.

It takes all of my self-control not to grimace.

'Breathe,' I say, more for me than her.

She goes back onto all fours. The head is coming! An orb with black hair, coated in creamy stuff. The woman's skin is stretching and arcing around the head and being pulled taut, like a rubber band. She pushes again and the head comes out a bit more, then goes back again. This happens a few times, and I see more of the baby each time. Then suddenly, with one deep, guttural chant, the head is there, just between her legs.

It looks dead, face pointing to the sky. It isn't moving. The baby's skin is purple and it isn't moving.

The mother reaches between her legs, feeling the baby's head. Then she puts her hand on the grass again and makes another powerful, low tone, and in one slimy glide it's coming out. I don't know what I'm doing but there are my hands, reaching, guiding, touching the slippery body. My jelly-like grip tightens as the baby half falls into my hands and lap. The cord is around its neck and I fumble, my breath getting stuck in my throat. The warm, wet body, streaked with blood and oily cream, almost slips away from me. I'm trying to unravel it. Instinct is moving me.

The mother is breathing heavily, waiting for me to pass her baby between her legs so she can hold it. Finally it's free and I breathe out.

I lean forward with her treasure and see that it's a boy. I let out all my breath when a tiny yowl sounds from his mouth.

He is alive!

She holds him close, wondrously, her eyes drinking him in. He gazes back with a heavenly newborn stare; two souls meeting in the flesh. Sacred.

I am lost in their moment, where only the two of them exist, inside a mystical sheath. She has opened her shirt and put him against her breast and he's nuzzling, searching for her nipple.

When she looks at me, her eyes are so clear.

I smile then look at the baby again.

We can't stop looking at him.

In the distance a car horn sounds and I'm flung back into reality. I've got to hide them. Gently but urgently I coax her up to a kneeling position. As she starts to stand, legs shaking, a fierce contraction courses through her. I've seen enough nature docos to know that the placenta's coming out.

I squat down and make a better job of receiving it. It's like this mega chunk of liver, warm and wet with the grey, rubbery cord stretching from it to the baby. It's disgusting, but I don't have time. I'm pure action, placing it carefully on the bench beside her. I register the colour of blood against the wooden slats. Her legs are still shaking. Into the laundry I run, reaching for the picnic rug and a couple of towels.

When I see my blood-soaked hands a drop of fear slides through me, then more adrenaline kicks in. All I'm seeing is the need to get this woman up to the cottage.

Dione's ute arrives in the backyard as I'm coming out the door. I point at the woman in the garden with her baby and Dione drives over the plants to park beside her. She wraps the baby and placenta in a towel and I put the rug around the woman. Dione opens the passenger door and bundles them in.

'I'm bleeding,' the woman says, looking between her legs. Dione is in the driver's seat already. I jump up onto the tray at the back, landing awkwardly on the water container. We tear up to the cottage and Dione rushes inside, reappearing in seconds with a syringe, which she injects into the mother's thigh. She instructs me to go and get more blankets from upstairs, and bends to examine the amount of blood coming out of the mother.

'We'll get you warm,' I hear her tell the mother. 'You're going into shock.'

It's all a blur and I'm holding my breath again. Dione is speaking to the mother in a soothing voice. She's still holding the baby feeding at her breast. Some colour is returning to her cheeks. Dione nods at me reassuringly. She's going to be alright.

It's only when they're tucked up in the room downstairs that it hits me. I start shaking uncontrollably. Dione tells me to go upstairs and have a hot bath—there's enough water. She gives me a towel and a big hug, rubbing my back hard and telling me what a great job I did. I feel completely numb as I stand there, shivering. I can't move. She has to guide me up the stairs and into the bathroom. She turns on the taps then puts her wet hands on either side of my face.

'You're going to be fine, Ora.' Her face is so close to mine. 'You did great. The mother's safe, the baby's safe and you're safe.' She gives me a little shake. 'Come on, into the bath with you.'

⊰

I'm a hotchpotch of flashbacks—good and bad—and flash-forwards, where fear, with a red-hot branding iron, stamps 'SIF' all over my body. One minute I'm seeing the joy and the wonder of new life, the mother's eyes, her tiny baby, and the next I'm getting my limbs ripped off by the SIF.

The bad flashbacks keep running in my head like an old projector reel, spinning uncontrollably—the man's bulgy, fear-filled eyes; the woman's vagina stretched around the baby's head; the baby's slippery body; the cord around his neck; his purple face. What if he had died? What if the mother had died? Dione spends hours with me, debriefing. For the first couple of days, she keeps urging me to go up to the cottage to visit, but I refuse.

My anger returns full throttle. I shout at my aunt, a *lot*. WHY is she running this place? Is she insane? Putting us *both* in danger.

And what about the mothers and babies? Someone is going to end up dead. Why can't she stop? What if she hadn't had that syringe? How could she have stolen so many supplies when she worked at the hospital? What happens when they run out? The conversations go around and around until I'm tired of them. It's like I've used up all my energy on asking too many questions, trying to make her see that she has to stop.

She tries to make me see it's the world that's wrong, not her.

When I realise I'm totally over it and not getting anywhere, I just stop talking to her. I've had enough.

I want to go back to how we were, celebrating my driving test.

My blood-chilling fear of the SIF slowly subsides and my insomnia is gradually replaced by a low-grade anxiety. I start to feel a lot calmer once I discover something new—I begin to imagine Lion asleep, beside my bed, ready to pounce.

12

Phone Call

My biggest saving grace is the beach. Next is my sketchpad, which I'm starting to take with me to the beach. I'm almost ready to show Melissa. And third is the daily game of Scrabble. I think Dione was as worried as I was about the rift between us—we'd only just found each other again—so when she suggested a game I agreed straightaway. And now we're hooked, losing track of time, focusing our minds on letters and words, each intent on winning. Here is a place where there is no blame or excuses, just delight in our own genius and the memory of Mum, who loved this game.

'How was the beach?' Dione asks as I open the back door, sticky and hot.

'It was *really* good,' I reply with a smile, brushing sand off the tops of my feet. 'Jake is back!' I can't wait to tell Lucy.

'Jake?' Dione looks vague.

'You know, Jake! Tom's cousin?'

'Oh yes. Good,' she says absently, then brightens, grabbing the Scrabble board. 'We've got time for a game before dinner.'

I want to tell her how I went and said hello, how we chatted about the surf and the shark that was sighted last week. And how gorgeous his eyes are, but she's not making the right noises—she's too busy picking her letters.

I will definitely ring Lucy later.

'Ok,' I say, sighing loudly and sitting down at the table, across from her.

We're halfway through when her mobile rings, making us tut and scowl, but she answers anyway. She always does.

I can't work out who she's talking to. It's someone she knows, but there's an edge to her voice, and she's taking care with her words.

'Hang on a minute. I'll get her,' she says.

I feel a small flip in my stomach—it must be Dad.

'Hello?' I say softly into the phone.

'Ora, how are you?' His voice sounds strange.

'Dad! Hi … Yeah … I'm good thanks.'

There's a silence.

'I tried your mobile,' he says.

'I need to charge it.' I really should do that, so I can ring Lucy. Another silence.

'How about you? Are you still at work?' I imagine him sitting at the nurse's station, looking tired.

'No, love. I clocked off early tonight. What've you been up to?' Is there a tinge of accusation in there?

'Oh, not much,' I say vaguely. 'Going to the beach a lot. Why?' I ask, biting back an accusation about him suddenly remembering he still has a daughter.

'I just thought it was time to check in.'

'My sketchpad's nearly full and I'm looking into fabric design courses, although I might have missed this round of intakes. And I'm swimming nearly every day. It's such a lovely beach, Dad. I think even you'd spend some time there.'

'Yeah?' he laughs a bit.

'Yeah.' It's good to hear his chuckle in my ear.

And my heart.

He says quietly, 'I miss you, Floss.'

'D'you know Dad, I've been here for nearly four months?'

'God, is it that long?'

'*And* you haven't been to visit me once!'

'I'm busy here. You know that.' He's closed up again. I shouldn't have criticised him. 'I've had a call. I've just told your aunt and now I'm telling you. I don't know what you two are up to but I know it's serious if the SIF are ringing me in the middle of the night.'

'What?' My world slows and my legs become hollow.

'That's right. They rang last night.' There's a long pause. 'What's it about Ora?'

'What? Why would they ring you?' I am trying to sound innocent, and failing.

'I don't like it, Ora. You know what they're like. Once they get a sniff of something, they strike like wildfire. They wanted to know where you've been living in Adelaide.'

'But they would know that from my MBD registration.'

'Well, I don't know why they called me but they did.'

There's a silence, which I know I'm meant to fill. He's waiting for me to tell him. But not a word comes out. I clutch the phone tightly … maybe they are listening in, this could be a trap!

Finally, he says, 'Alright. Well. I'm going now, but stay away from trouble. D'you hear?'

'Yes, Dad.'

'And you can tell me if Dione's up to no good.'

Another silence.

'I'll try and get down there after Easter,' he says gruffly.

'Bye, Dad,' I say meekly.

Dione gets up and takes the phone out of my hand.

'I'll make some tea,' she says with a sigh.

I stand for ages. My brain won't work.

'The SIF,' I say. My eyes feel too big. This isn't supposed to happen. Not when I'm just beginning to feel good again. 'What are we going to do?'

'We'll work it out,' she says, bringing the tea to the table. 'I thought something was up yesterday. The cottage had a funny feel to it. Like someone had been in there.'

'What?' I say, fear writhing in my gut. 'They were here yesterday? How could you keep that from me?' My skin prickles with indignation.

'I wasn't a hundred percent certain, Ora. And I didn't want to worry you,' she says, stalling the anger that's about to explode. 'You've been upset enough already.'

I take a deep breath. My heart is thumping.

'I'm really scared, Dione.'

We sit in silence. I can almost hear her mind turning over.

'Well, the good news is they don't have any solid evidence, otherwise they'd have cleaned us out already.'

Momentary relief.

'I'm guessing it was an anonymous tip-off.'

'None of your women would snitch on you.'

'I know, but that father from the other day …'

I nod slowly. Of course.

'He wasn't happy when he came to pick her up.' She looks at me regretfully. 'We have to think of a plan. The SIF are bound to pay us a visit any day now, and I don't want you here when they do. You're not up to talking to them.'

'I don't want to go to Dad's.'

She nods. 'The less he knows the better. We need to hide you for a few days, just until they've come officially. I'm sure they won't find anything, but we can't risk you being here. Not with that birth being so recent.' She pauses. 'Shit!' She gets up and starts pacing.

'That stupid couple. I only took them on last month. I didn't want to. I wanted to stop.'

She bangs the bench with her fist and stares out the window.

'I've got it!' she turns to me suddenly, looking pleased. 'We'll hide you up the mountain. I can tell them you've gone to stay with friends and be all vague. How do you fancy going bush for a few days?' she says with a broad grin, as if we haven't a care in the world.

Before I can form a reply, she rushes on.

'You can take my camping gear. I've got enough food that will travel light, and the forecast is great for the next few days. I'll come and get you once the SIF have been.'

'Couldn't I go to Melissa's?'

'Too risky. They might start investigating Tom and Sarah.'

'I don't know, Dione, this is all feeling too rushed.' But I don't have any other ideas, except going to Dad's. The SIF will come looking for me wherever I am, if they decide they want me. I force a load of air into my lungs. I can't breathe properly.

Dione packs food and water for me and talks me through pitching her tent. She wants me to go beyond where we've walked, right into the bush.

It's well into the night by the time we're ready. We head out together, thankful for the moon, and walk for an hour in silence.

'Right,' Dione says, coming to a stop, all matter of fact. 'I'll be up in a few days. If I'm not, just come back down again, okay? I'll cover everything up as best I can. And remember, you know nothing.'

'But this doesn't feel right! How will you find me? Can't you come with me?'

'You know I can't, I've got to make the birth suite look like a spa as soon as I get back, in case they discover it's down there.' She gives me a quick hug and points up the mountain. 'It'll take you most of the day to get to the top of that ridge. Camp somewhere along it, but just below and make sure you hide the tent as much as you can. Go easy on the water.' She gives my shoulder a squeeze. 'Don't worry, you'll hear me coming.'

I nod slowly.

'And one more thing. If ever it comes down to it, which it won't but just in case … it was me at that birth. You never even met them, okay?' She squeezes my shoulder hard this time.

I could turn into a zombie right now. Tune out. Sink down right here. But I start walking as fast as I can under the heavy pack. The water weighs so much.

I need to move faster than my fears are building. Already they're bombarding my being, a steady stream of fighter jets.

13

Who's there?

It's dark by the time I've pitched the stupid tent. I'm too tired to eat. The sleeping bag is musty and there's a big rock or root running all the way underneath me, so whichever side I move to, I can still feel it. I don't sleep all night. There are too many sounds penetrating the canvas, assaulting my senses. The shrill cry of an animal before it gets devoured. That will be me next. A persistent scratching just beyond my head. The wind tearing through the branches above. I hate it up here. I remember the story about the camper who was crushed by a falling tree limb when he got up to pee in the middle of the night. Death by tree. The branches above me are creaking. I try to imagine a good story where the camper gets up and his tent is flattened instead of him … Damn! I need to pee.

The first day drags on forever. I can't decide whether I'm safer in the tent or outside it. I spend the whole time jumping sky-high and bracing myself for the inevitable team of SIF officers, swarming up the mountain, here to arrest me.

By the third night I am so sleep-deprived, I start hallucinating. Lion and Snake attack a sniper who is waiting for me behind a bush. They rip him apart. Silently. Then, I don't know what to do with his body parts. Or his gun. The SIF will definitely kill me now. I will keep the gun.

But in the morning it's gone and so have his remains. A cooling glug of water brings me back to earth.

I wish Dione would come. Maybe they've got her? What if I never see her again? What if she's told them? Should I confess?

Sleep. I just want to sleep. On the fourth night I stop hating the tent and cannot believe it when I wake up after the sun has risen. I eat the last of my nuts, I venture over the ridge. The land is beautiful.

I see a snake. It's real.

I go to sleep with the sun.

Day six … or is it day seven?

Still waiting up here.

The sky is big. Pinpricks dance inside the blue. The ocean is up there too. And the smell—maybe the taste?—of the mountain air is sweet and dry.

Up here, in the middle of nowhere, I think about Mum and Holly.

And Dad.

And the SIF.

A circle of rocks is around my fire. The circle is perfect. The flames are beautiful.

Where is Dione?

There are no people sounds up here. No drills, no engines. I'm just sitting, lying, on the earth. On my mother. Snake said that. The earth is my mother. Lion is my father.

I'm lulled by the trees, the breeze. Birdsong.

There is no fear. No SIF. No women birthing underground.

Sometimes I'm angry with Dione, sometimes I miss her. She

was going to stop. For me. Why did she say yes to that couple? That spineless man. That stupid woman.

It's so hot today. I'm moving slowly—there's nothing to do.

Dark clouds fill the afternoon sky. It's hot and clammy. A thunderstorm in February?

Snap!

I'm up, alert, cells out on stalks.

Panic rises in the back of my throat. I half squat, half kneel towards the sound, pick up one of the rocks from my campfire. A big one.

Crack!

It's definitely someone. There's a footfall, and another snap.

It's not Dione. She'd call my name.

My once-camouflaged tent now looks like a neon beacon. I oscillate; stay low, still on the ground, or run as quickly as I can? I crouch down like an animal, close to the earth.

'Ora?' A loud whisper. A man's voice through the trees. And again, urgently, 'Ora!'

'Friend or foe? Friend or foe?' I want to shout, and feel ridiculous and hysterical and wild, remembering the game I used to play with Holly in the forest.

'Ora, it's me, Jake … from the beach … Where are you?'

Jake! I almost stand up. What is *he* doing here?

He's heading straight for my tent.

Is he with the SIF?

I drop my rock and start pelting down the mountain, pounding my feet on the earth, hell-bent on getting away. But his legs are swifter and longer.

'Stop!' he shouts.

There's no way I'm giving up.

He tackles me. The ground crashes up to meet me and we lie panting. He's still holding me.

'Sorry.' His voice is deep. 'But you wouldn't stop. Your aunt asked me to come …'

I'm breathing heavily, my nose just a few centimetres from the ground. He lets go and eases himself into a sitting position, leaning over me, ready to catch me if I take off. I roll onto my back. We stare at each other for a long time, eyes blazing, energy firing. I'm suddenly distracted by what he's wearing. I've only ever seen him in his beach gear. I like his black T-shirt … Wait, really? I'm having a fashion moment *now*?

'Ora—' He looks like he's coaxing a kitten out from under a car. His lips move, but at first I don't hear what he's saying. Then I tune in.

'—to bring you some food and stuff. Dione's under surveillance, that's why she can't come. She's worried they're going to send a search party up here. She says you need to leave and get as far away as you can. They might bring dogs.'

'It's not Dee-on,' I correct him, willing him to feel stupid. He's just tackled me like a sack of potatoes.

'What?'

'It's not Dee-on, it's Dee-OH-nee.'

He shrugs. 'She hid a note in my towel on the beach yesterday, when I was swimming.'

I look around, bracing myself for SIF officers to jump out of the bushes. I've spent hours near this guy, imagining all sorts of things. But not this.

'Look.' He pulls out a tatty note from his back pocket. The paper with the spiral motif, from Dione's notepad. I recognise her writing,

Dear Jake, we met once at the beach. Please help!
I've just been released by the SIF after days of
questioning and am under surveillance. Because Ora

lives with me, she is now wanted for questioning too. She's hiding out on Mount Best (see map below) and needs to move on from the ridge ASAP. If she follows the creek bed as far as she can go and then takes the track into the town she'll be safer there. I've enclosed money for her to stay at the Best Inn and will contact her soon. Thank you in advance, if you do help. I'm sure you know it's risky. Yours hopefully, Dione. PS She will have run out of food by now. PPS Please destroy this note.

She must be desperate! If the SIF had got hold of this note we'd be toast. I tear it into tiny pieces and bury it in the soil. What if the SIF had seen her plant the note? Dione can't be thinking straight.

I sigh and sit up, getting ready to talk. Jake is not one of them. He's taken a huge risk coming up here for two people he doesn't even know. He's talking again, and looking at me earnestly.

'…I hate them' is all I hear—I keep getting distracted by his eyes. I sit up straighter and focus on his words. 'And when Melissa told me she knew you … and last year my friend got taken in …'

I'm finding it hard to keep up—I haven't had a conversation in nearly a week and I've got no idea what he's saying.

'I remember all those protests and rallies, I thought it was just a load of hype, but the SIF are out of control now and like I said, he didn't do anything, just a bit of street art.'

As he unravels the details of his friend's trauma—graffiti is a very big sin in the eyes of the SIF—I understand why he's sitting here with me on the forest floor, and a small frond of trust begins to unfurl towards him. His friend was bullied and shamed by the SIF, and hasn't been the same since.

I'm enjoying the sound of his voice when my stomach

interrupts us with an embarrassing gurgle and he breaks off, noticing me looking at his backpack.

He grins. 'Hungry?'

After a couple of days without food, I need something fresh and light.

'Don't suppose you brought any fruit? Or an avocado?' He pulls out a paper bag and there, unbelievably, is a small avocado. I don't care how mutated it is.

'Thank you!' I say. He smiles, and for the second time I feel my energy lurching towards him.

He's got his knife out and has already cut the avocado in two. I am *so* hungry. He gives me one half, then removes the stone and holds out the other. I gesture for him to have it but he shakes his head and presses it firmly in my hand.

The skin peels away easily and I bite into the soft, firm texture. My tastebuds are going wild, sending fireworks into my brain. They don't care the food's been messed with or normally tastes like cardboard. I have to force myself to take small bites, to savour it—I just want to stuff the whole thing into my mouth. After a few more mouthfuls, I realise he's watching me.

'Thank you,' I manage, looking up. My pleasure in the taste makes me sound all sensuous, and I pick up a banana, feeling the colour flame my cheeks. I can feel him smiling but can't look up. Our bodies are so close. This is far too intimate. Maybe he senses this, because he shifts back. I want him to move in towards me again, but carry on with my banana meditation as another kind of yearning dances in my belly. I finish chewing and force myself to look at him. He's clearly comfortable with the silence.

'You did well finding me,' I say, needing to take control.

'You reckon? I've been up here for hours! I was just about to head back when I saw your tent.'

'Dodgy positioning.' I smile at him again.

A drop of rain hits my face. I look up and realise there's only about an hour of light left. 'You won't have time to get back down,' I say, thinking aloud.

'That's okay, I can find my way in the dark.'

'The clouds will cover the moon. Have you got a torch?'

He doesn't.

'You'd better stay.' Did I say that too quickly?

He clears his throat. 'I'll go in the morning then. Looks like a storm is going to break anyway, so the SIF won't do anything tonight.'

'They'll be too busy monitoring the water.'

Another pause.

'Okay then,' he nods.

And just like that, it's decided.

He's moving in.

We get up stiffly and start walking back to the tent. I feel like a hermit who's lived a thousand years in solitude and lost her voice … I have no idea what to say. Thankfully, the rain takes over and we break into a run. By the time we get to the tent it's pouring, and we dash and fumble into my cocoon. His backpack snags on the entrance and once he's pulled it in, I surprise myself by zipping us in.

I turn back towards him slowly.

The light is fading fast, and it makes his smile seem huge. He leans back on his elbow and looks around the tent.

'This is pretty comfortable.' He definitely looks comfortable.

'Yeah,' I manage, deciding to take off my boots. He sits up and does the same, maybe out of politeness, maybe because he doesn't like mud in the tent either.

The downpour has passed but thunder is rumbling in the distance. I open the zip, needing more space, and the wet-dry scent of rain on parched earth hits me. I can't believe it, it's been so long since it's rained!

'That smells so good,' I say, to drown out the annoying voice singing in my head, Jake is here! Jake is here. In my tent! With me!

'So,' he says. 'Are you still swimming like a mad woman?'

My jaw drops at his cheek and I quickly make it drop further so I look dramatic on purpose.

'I could ask you the same question,' I say, sitting with my arms wrapped around my knees, determined to keep some distance between us. I need to work him out.

'Every day,' he says. 'I swim in a squad at another beach, but that one's the best.'

'Do you compete?' I ask.

'Yeah. I used to all the time—I got entered in the nationals but then the ocean bans came in, and I moved overseas anyway. Killed my chances of getting anywhere.'

He looks a bit wistful but doesn't say more, which unnerves me—most people like to go on talking about themselves, especially when asked the right questions.

'And you're a lifesaver, right?'

He nods. 'I just finished my training up north, although I've done a lot of helping out already. What about you? Why do *you* swim so much?'

'Oh, I just like the sea.'

'Without a wetsuit?' he pushes, but I just smile.

More silence. He's waiting for more.

'Do you live near the beach?' I ask, feeling myself wanting to tell him more. To tell him why I started going to the ocean as much as I could.

'Yeah,' he says. 'I grew up just around the corner from that beach. I still swim there because there usually aren't any rips. And there are some interesting people who hang out there, too.' He smiles at me broadly.

'Do you work?' I ask. It must sound like I've ignored his flirty remark, but I'm only just registering it.

'Yeah, part-time job at the surf shop,' he says. 'Need something to get me through uni.'

'What are you studying?' I wonder how old he is.

'Marine Biology. Second year this year. How about you, Mystery Molly?'

He must be a few years older than me. This guy is tricky. It's maddening. He's asking as many questions as me.

'I'm kind of in the middle of deciding. I used to live in New South Wales, and I finished high school last year. I didn't get great results.' I'm sounding like a drop-out.

'What about the stuff with your aunt?' he asks. He's clever.

I pause, deciding whether to plunge in. He knows some of it already from the note, and I find myself wanting to tell him. All this time alone up here has shown me that I do like talking after all. I've also realised how much I miss Lucy, and how I've abandoned her recently. I've been so busy missing Mum and Holly and trying to get to grips with all the birthing drama.

But four months of enduring Dione's secret women's business without telling a soul has been long enough.

'It's hard to know where to start,' I say.

The impact of all that's happened rises up, hot and lava-like inside me. My lower lip starts to wobble. I can't believe I'm about to cry. I widen my eyes, struggling to dispel the tears that are forming.

'You know when you do something really challenging, like a long day's hike or a marathon maybe,' I say, 'and you don't realise how hard it is until you stop?'

He nods slowly.

'Well, there's maybe a moment or two when you have a bit of a freak out, but you just keep going. But at the end when you finally stop, your whole body aches and you know you couldn't walk another step even if a bushfire was tearing up behind you?'

'I sometimes feel like that after swimming.'

'That's how I feel right now. Just really, really tired.' And then this huge sob wells up from my very depths and before I know it, I'm crying. He moves close, wrapping his arms gently around me. My first impulse is to push him away. It's been years since I've cried in anyone's arms. I could struggle out of his grip but I don't. He holds me a little tighter and I lean into his chest, briefly registering his musky scent. I'm making his T-shirt wet with tears and snot, but I'm past caring. His warmth and strength are comforting.

He sits quietly, holding me. I can't stop wailing. It sounds so bad, demented, like a strangled cat.

After a long while, I'm cried out and completely self-conscious. My hair and body are covered in six days' worth of camping and I feel completely exposed.

He gently lets go of me and, still without saying anything, urges me into my sleeping bag. I curl up into myself, burying my face. I feel his hand briefly on my shoulder and he says something about making a fire.

Once he's zipped the tent back up I stretch out on my back and let out a heavy sigh. Did I just drop my bundle or what? I squirm and move myself into a ball again, full of embarrassment. I don't even want to think about what just happened. I'm staying here all night. And maybe he'll stay out there by the fire. That'd be best.

14

Middle of the night

Before I wake, just for a moment, there's this lightness. I'm home, Holly's in her room and Mum and Dad are in theirs, all still asleep.

I sit up with a start and then the dragging feeling is back in my chest. I hear movement outside and listen intently. It must be Jake.

Jake.

The gentle cracking and popping of a fire makes me want to go out there. I sit up. Lie down again. I want to go out. No I don't. Yes. No.

Before I delay myself with any more thoughts, I'm unzipping the tent and moving out towards the warm flames. When I see him I think about retreating, but he beckons me forward.

'The ground's wet but my jacket's big enough for two.' He sounds cheerful. I grab my jacket as well.

The sky has cleared and there's a fresh chill in the air. The stars are out in all their glory. I feel like I could sit really close to him and he wouldn't mind, but I put my jacket down next to his instead, my frantic urge for control re-emerging.

'How're you doing?' he asks.

'Okay,' I say, looking into the flames. 'Thanks ... for before.'

He keeps looking at the fire and nods. 'No worries.'

The silence extends. I want to start talking but I don't know where to begin. There's so much swishing around in me, some of it has to come out. I look at him, then back to the fire.

'Do you remember before you went away, at the beach ...?' I struggle to find the right words.

'When you got saved by the lifesaver?'

I wince. 'She overreacted. I was fine.'

We look at each other briefly, then turn back to the flames.

'Well, the night before that ... I'd just witnessed my first birth with Dione.'

It's his turn to pick his jaw up off the floor. I nod and take a deep breath. 'She's an undercover midwife, fighting this secret, *stupid* war that she should've let go of years ago.' He lets out a long whistle as he absorbs my words. I want to tell him about the birthing centre too. It's not a good idea, for his safety or mine, but the floodgates are open now, and I can't stop.

'Maybe I was thrashing around a bit in the water, but I was really upset.' I need him to understand. 'Dione didn't want me around—she was so taken up by "her work"—and my dad is a lost cause. And my mum and my sister are—'

'Hang on,' he touches my wrist briefly. 'Does your dad live here too?'

'No! My dad lives in the middle of nowhere in Victoria and has forgotten I exist, which is kind of ironic because he's already—'

'Ora,' he interrupts me again. 'Could you please slow down? And ... start at the beginning?' He raises an eyebrow and I look away.

'That would mean starting way back when the world went crazy and people lost their rights and forgot how to grow food.

And water became a political commodity and the earth got depleted because the corporations were taking over …'

His shoulders are shaking and when I look at him he's laughing. I can't believe it! I start to get up.

'Stop,' he grabs my arm.

'You're laughing at me.' I pull my arm free.

'No, please. I'm not.' He's looking at me, waiting for me to look back, but I stare hard at the fire. I will not cry again.

'It's just that …' he pauses. 'You either don't say anything or you talk so fast I can't keep up.'

I still can't look at him.

'I'm sorry, Ora. Can I … Would it help if—'

I blow out of my mouth slowly. This is not going to be easy.

'Just don't patronise me, okay?'

He's quiet, then nods briefly.

I swallow and take a breath in. 'My mum and my sister died when I was thirteen. Me and my dad moved to Victoria a few months later—from the rainforest hills—for his job. He's a doctor. A new start, and all that.' I look at him briefly.

'We went to this crappy country town where the land was flat, the sky grey and no ocean for miles. The kids hated me. They called me 'Feral' because of my hair, and because I didn't have the right clothes. They thought I was weird because I loved animals instead of boys.'

I pause, expecting an interruption, but he nods, so I go on.

'There weren't any birds in that place, which says it all … Well, maybe a crow or two, and an owl at night, once.'

He's still not interrupting, so I keep going.

'Dad started working at the hospital whenever he could— which was most of the time. I watched him morph from this big, solid giant with a heart to match, to a shrunken shell that I didn't recognise, like he'd been taken over by an alien that sucked out all of his greatness.'

Jake smiles, but it's a sad smile.

'Even the shape of his face changed; it got tighter, and his lips got stuck in this permanent line. Maybe I'm exaggerating, but "heart the size of a pea" sums him up pretty well.'

'He seemed to just forget I was there.' I lean forward and put some wood on the fire. When I sit down, we're shoulder to shoulder, and his arm feels warm against mine. I look down and see that I'm sitting on his coat ... I must have moved closer.

'I tried cooking his favourite dinners, keeping the house tidy, that kind of stuff, but it didn't work. Then I tried the "Look at me, I'm depressed" routine, but he didn't notice any of it. The lights were on but no one was home. So I gave up.

'I was there almost a year and a half ... months and months of drawing, I must have filled a hundred sketchbooks. Trees, mostly. I had to copy animals out of books. Escaping into novels helped, too. Mostly, though, I felt as bleak as the landscape. When kids from my old school got in touch, I never replied, except to my best friend Lucy—I didn't have anything to say. In the end I stopped drawing and just vegged out and watched movies.

'Then, Lucy's mum rang out of the blue and before I knew it, I had a holiday planned at their place.' I fall silent. I'm thirsty after talking so much. 'I ended up staying with them for over three years. When they moved to New Zealand a few months ago, I moved in with Dione.'

He leans closer and says, very quietly, 'Shit', which feels like the appropriate response.

We sit silently for a while.

'Do you miss your dad?'

'Sometimes,' I say. 'But he changed so much ... we just stopped being a team, you know? Like somewhere along the way he dropped the ball. Maybe I kept reminding him of Holly and Mum. Maybe I kept him soft when all he wanted was to be hard.'

Jake reaches out, putting his arm around my lower back, and squeezes me gently.

I like the feel of his arm.

'How about you?' I ask. 'What's your family like?'

'Two sisters.' He takes his arm back. 'Kate's still at home with Mum in Queensland. They moved there two years ago. And my big sister, Jenny, lives with her partner in the city.' He pauses. 'So what exactly has Dione been doing then? What did you mean, "Birth war"?'

'It's safer if you don't know.' I wanted to tell him so badly before, but the less he knows the better.

'Was she involved with Little Tom's birth? They've never told me what happened.'

I need to change the subject. 'How old are you?'

'How old do you think?'

'Forty-five?' I smile.

'Ha!' He bumps against me, making me lose my balance. 'I'll be twenty-three next week, thank you very much.'

'And do you live near the beach?'

He nods. 'I'm renting with a mate. I moved back in after I got back from America.' He pauses. 'My Dad's a lost cause too.' His lips purse, only slightly, as he gets lost in the flames for a moment. Then he sits up straighter and does my changing-the-subject trick. 'So what's it like living with Dione? I can see why you spend all your time at the beach. She must be a bit of a fruitcake.'

The expression makes me laugh.

'It's one of Mum's,' he smiles. 'So …?'

'She's a mixture of grace and grit. When I first moved in, she was all grit—except unlike Dad, she was only pretending, which is bloody good 'cos I was ready to give up on my family completely. She's got a big heart and we get along fine, so long as we avoid the birth stuff.' I know he'll think it's dumb, but I say it anyway. 'We play a lot of Scrabble.'

'Scrabble?' He chuckles and looks at me in a puzzled kind of way. 'You've got to get out more Ora, you really do.'

'Are you saying I'm a fruitcake?'

'Possibly,' he grins.

I yawn, then shiver. The fire has died down and we've used all the wood.

'It's going to be an early start,' I say, yawning again.

'You're right,' he says, standing, and pulling me up.

I turn, avoiding his eyes, and stomp off into the bushes, saying over my shoulder, 'Bush wee.'

When I get back into the tent he's lying under his jacket. I climb into my sleeping bag and he beckons me closer.

'Could you come here a minute and warm me up?' He shudders. 'Grrhh. You might have organised some better guest accommodation.'

I jab him in the ribs. 'Don't be rude about my tent!' I say, and before I know it, I'm lying next to him.

'It's freezing up here.' He shudders, pulling me closer.

'You should have brought your wetsuit,' I say, unable to believe I'm nestling into him in response.

But this feels right, even if it is kind of quick. I don't care about anything outside of this tent right now. I listen to his heart beating below my ear and enjoy the feel of his swimmer's chest under my hand. He smells clean and musky and herbal all at once. I smile in the darkness.

I think back to this afternoon and see his eyes and his lips. His lips ... I want to kiss him. I savour the urge, enjoying the desire. I take some deep breaths and relax my whole body against his. He's warm, and comforting.

'Thank you for trekking up here and risking the SIF,' I say, still not quite believing my luck.

'Wouldn't have missed it for the world,' he says with another squeeze of my shoulder and a yawn.

It takes me ages to fall asleep.

15

Flight

A raven's caw wakes me. The sun is high. Jake is sound asleep, lying on his back. I still can't believe he's here. But there's this gnawing tension beyond the zip of the tent adding an urgency to the atmosphere. I study his features, taking in his nose with its straight and determined line and his long, dark lashes. His mouth is full and relaxed in sleep, tempting me to lean up and over him. I pause for a few seconds, then lower my lips onto his.

I watch as he stirs into wakefulness. He smiles and kisses me back. Our eyes meet briefly before I close mine and sink into the feel of his lips. Our tongues meet tentatively, just the tips, but soon they're probing softly and moving together. I slide over, still in my sleeping bag, until I'm lying on top of him. I have never been so daring.

A new kind of hunger is pushing at me, dancing between my hips, making me want to push into him. He's just lifting his arm to my sleeping bag when a distant sound brings us out of our bodies, wide-eyed, back into daylight.

A dog. Or a few dogs? Far away, barks rolling up the mountain, breaking the quiet.

'Shit,' he says.

I scramble out of my sleeping bag, my body moving ahead of my thoughts. Every cell is in flight mode—I need to get away. My boots are on before I know it. I fling on my jacket. Jake is rushing too. I unzip the tent and grab my backpack, moving into the annex. We lock eyes for a split second.

'I'll head for the creek bed,' I say, making it clear I'm going alone. The authority in my voice surprises me. Jake is right behind me. No time for goodbyes, just a look—panic, desire, sorrow, rolled into one.

I'm off up the track behind the tent, tripping through the thick undergrowth. I can still feel his lips on mine. The track is almost non-existent. I race over the ridge and down the other side. Dione's instruction is all that drives me. The creek bed, the track, the town. My lungs heave for air, my gasps tearing my throat. The ground thumps through me as I barrel down the hill.

The dogs sound further away once I'm at the bottom of the ridge. I send up a silent prayer that I'll get away—Jake, too. I can't go fast along the creek bed—the rocks and pebbles make me stumble. I trip, and almost fall.

Crazed dogs! They sounds too close—at the top of the ridge.

Not a chance. The thought forms in my head and I run faster. I hear men shouting. Their excitement hits me between the shoulders, and adrenaline pumps through me, thumping in my ears.

The dogs are closer now, though the men sound further away. Perhaps the dogs are off their leads? I surge forward, picking up the pace. Frenzied barks, too close, hunting me. Everything goes into slow motion as I spin around. Two Rottweilers charge me, paws slapping stones. Snarling. Teeth. Wild eyes.

The dogs separate, working together, one behind me, the other in front. I lock eyes with the dog in front. It's rabid. A long, low growl tells me it's about to attack.

'Freeze!' The shout from a few metres upstream jolts through us both. The dog whines momentarily, then snarls again. I tear my eyes from it and look up. Two SIF men rush towards me, and white fear surges through my body.

'Gotcha!' One grabs my arm roughly, like he's won a prize. The other is rewarding the dogs, which have morphed into family pets, wagging their tails. He looks up with a mean twist to his mouth.

'Ora James,' he says, shaking his head slowly.

I am trembling violently. My breathing has slowed and I cross my arms over my chest, protecting myself. I need to stop the shaking. I want Dad. I'm alone in this wilderness out here—me, the dogs, and two clowns from a nightmare. They are power happy, coming down from the high of the chase. I am something to play with.

The dogs are on leads now. One of the men shoves me forward. Everything slows. I brace myself.

'Start walking.'

Hope touches me briefly; they are not going to hurt me. He shoves me again.

'Get moving!'

I begin to retrace my steps. For the moment, I am safe—they've had their fun. The ridiculousness of my situation overwhelms me. I have no words.

This was never my battle!

How did it come to this? Will they hurt me? Torture me? Tears blind my eyes, and I brush them away furiously.

We tread a steady path back up the ridge, down past the tent. Jake and I were here only moments ago. The officer in front gives the corner a kick, ripping the canvas near the tent peg. He might as well have kicked me.

Sobs of fear and fury escape my throat, and the dog behind me growls.

'Move it!' The handler shoves me hard. No sympathy for the wicked. I am made of sterner stuff than this. Aren't I? My legs feel so weak, like they're going to crumple underneath me. I want to bury myself in the leaves and soil, feel the earth meeting me in a welcoming embrace. My mother.

The shove this time is violent. My head snaps back. I need to pull myself together. I can't collapse. I look down, focus on my boots, putting one foot in front of the other. The leather. The rhythm. My breath.

My boots, my steps, my breath.

Hours later we hit an unmade road, and I finally look up. We are at the bottom of the mountain. A van is parked up ahead. Will Jake be in it? I desperately want him to be. I desperately want him not to be.

What if I'm put in with the dogs? A new fear uncurls itself. When we get closer I see a dog van parked beside the first car, and another SIF van as well. I feel a momentary relief when I'm bundled into the back of the car and handcuffed to the door. I am so thirsty.

There's a third guy now, talking to them. Finally, they shake hands, laughing. The dog handler is putting the dogs into his vehicle as we drive off. I breathe in and make a wish for Jake's safety. He's risked so much coming out here, tracking down a girl he barely knows.

Tears threaten again and I close my eyes. I can't watch the familiar countryside slipping away.

The drive is interminable. I keep my eyes shut, trying to stop the thoughts and fears shooting through me in waves.

How did this happen? There's one golden rule with the SIF: don't break the law. It's simple. My fury at Dione boils in my blood. She should have kept me out of this. We should have remained strangers.

I open my eyes, then close them again. Memories crash into my thoughts.

Reggae rhythms. Mum and Dad in their bathers, dancing in the kitchen. Stinking hot day. Me and Holly, little, drawing at the table, giggling. Mum doing outrageous moves. Dad not knowing what to do with her ...

My heart feels too big in my chest when I think of Dad. He'll help me, I know he will. They'll have to let me phone him. He tried to warn me. I need water.

16

The SIF

I am being watched. The room is bare, except for a table and chairs and bright, fluorescent lights which hurt my eyes. It feels like a flock of vultures are observing me behind the darkened viewing window. I'm not naked in this puke-green, hospital robe, but I might as well be. They even took my underwear.

I can't stop shivering. My hands and feet are blue and my heart is a chunk of ice.

The walls and floor are metal. I sit at the table and tuck my legs under me. The edges of the chair are sharp and dig in, but I stay like this. The more of me I can feel, the better. The temperature must be below zero.

When we got here, they dragged me into a decontamination unit. I was dunked and blasted with chemicals that have made my skin peel and itch. I tried to make myself disappear through the corner walls, crouching small and covering my head with my hands. Shock kept the pain away at first. Now my whole body aches. The chemicals must be inside me now.

The door opens and two guards come in wearing thick puffa jackets. They look warm and rosy, like they've been drinking hot tea. But there's nothing rosy about them. Steely grey eyes, tight lips, squat bodies with dull, thinning hair. She looks tough, he looks mean.

They have come to break me.

I breathe in and close my eyes, calling for help. Lion and Snake arrive immediately. Lion jumps on the table to block the guards, ferocious and cool. Snake is beside the female guard, lower body coiled, upper body rippling from side to side at her elbow.

'Open your eyes, now.' The male guard's voice is too loud.

I keep looking at Snake in my mind's eye. 'Draw a circle of light around yourself,' she says. 'Bring it up into a pyramid point above your head. It will protect you.' I see myself inside a case of light and a glimmer of warmth starts to move in my belly.

The guard bangs on the table and shouts at me to open my eyes.

I do.

The ends of their noses are red with cold and they have shrunk. He is a rat with a twitching mouth. She is a slug. Snake is elegant and graceful beside her.

The slug leans in over the table. I'm glad my hands are tucked under my legs, I think she'd snatch at them. Lion roars and I only catch the last word of what she says, and then Lion is gone, and Snake too.

'—Jake?'

She smiles. She's snagged me on her line. Now she is going to reel me in, savouring her words as she casts them.

'In the hospital.' She smiles. 'Coma.' Pause. 'Stupid boy.' Another smile. 'Running down a mountain! Doesn't he know about rock faces?' She sniggers. 'What a hero.'

Movement returns to my icy fingers and my feet make contact with the ground. I will throttle her.

'Your circle, Ora!' Snake is loud in my ear. 'Keep it around you. And the pyramid. It's your only chance.'

I slump back, scrabbling to re-draw a shield of light as images of Jake lying at the bottom of a cliff torpedo into my heart.

'He won't be swimming again,' says the rat to the slug, shaking his head and raising his eyebrows in feigned compassion. 'With both legs broken …' he trails off, turning to me with a hateful smile. The image of Jake becomes more defined, his legs at right angles to his crumpled body.

'And then there's Dione,' she says, sounding almost bored.

I close my eyes tightly, a mantra forming. *Circle, white light, pyramid. Circle, white light, pyramid.*

A blow to my ear knocks me to the ground. Stunned, I vaguely register that my head is pounding. I am half deaf.

'Get up, and don't close your eyes again.'

The slug is leering over me. I scramble back onto the chair. Small. I am small. And cold. And not cut out for this. I press my lips together tightly. I will not cry. I will not. I keep my eyes open and take another breath. I feel Lion sitting on my right. Very close.

The guards are looking at me. I want to ask about Dione but I won't give them the pleasure. Snake is with me too, dancing and bobbing on my left. I know what I have to do. I breathe in again, rebuilding my wall of light, then sit up straight, staring at the window behind them. I resist the urge to lift my chin. Disdain won't help.

The rat flings his chair back and comes around the table. I imagine him tripping over Lion's tail. And then, weirdly, he stumbles. Just momentarily.

Warm tingles cascade down my spine as my imaginary world suddenly becomes a lot more real.

When the rat grips my shoulder, threatening to crush my collarbone with his fingers, I don't scream. Or cry. I take another breath and look ahead.

'If you don't tell us where she is, we'll make sure your lover boy doesn't come out of his coma.'

Everything goes still as my emotions collide. Relief floods through me—Dione is still free. And black, coal-like fear. Jake. In a hospital bed, surrounded by guards with drug-filled needles.

'I don't know where she is!' My voice sounds raspy in the dank air. I haven't spoken or eaten for hours. 'The last time I saw her was before I ran away.' I sound desperate. I am desperate. I have to make them understand.

The guards look at each other briefly. They don't give anything away. The rat's grip tightens even more and I let out an involuntary yelp.

'Why did you run?' He is speaking through gritted teeth. Now he is a terrier who will never let go.

'I wanted to get away!' *Circle, white light, pyramid.*

His cold hand moves over to my throat. Is this how it ends?

'Had something to hide, did you?'

'Jake! I wanted to be with Jake!'

He lets go with a shove.

'Dione didn't like him. She … we argued …' I rub at my sore neck and shoulder.

Their eyes are searing into me. Can they tell I'm lying? I look back at them, trying to look convincing.

'Please, is he going to be okay?' Oh God I hope he tells them the same story. If he wakes up.

Just like that, they leave. The door slams. I take a breath in and my defence crumbles. I turn away from the window and clutch the back of the chair. The last time I cried this hard was two nights ago in Jake's arms. Rage and distress, fear for his life. I am crying so hard I don't feel the cold.

✍

They spray me daily with toxic chemicals that sear my skin. By day three I'm a mass of open sores which seep and burn every time they blast me again.

The only time I am with people is when I'm being interrogated. Mostly, by Slug and Rat. They have jagged, gashing tongues that slice me with their words. It was my fault Mum and Holly died. Dad wishes I had died. I am a waste of space, wanted by no-one. On and on. I am lost. They know everything about me.

They try so many ways to get me to talk about the births and dob Dione in. They start being all friendly which is totally creepy. I don't touch their food offerings—probably full of drugs. Lion and Snake see me through and keep me sane—which is mad, I know but as soon as I'm on the edge of breaking, one of them does something to distract me; Lion jumps on the table, Snake starts dancing. Something. Always something.

I come closest to talking on the third day when they send in a new officer. A man. Monster really. His neck is like a giant tree stump and he has a deep scar that runs across his cheek. He bangs and thumps the wall incessantly. And pounds me with his questions. I go into a deeper catatonic state than before. He carries on for hours. When he punches a hole in the wall and starts towards me, I jump up and fling myself into the corner, facing the wall. I'm just about to turn, to talk—the garden birth is on the tip of my tongue—when I lose control of my bladder. There isn't much because I'm so dehydrated, but that warm trickling down my thigh ignites a bone-deep determination to keep quiet. I will not give them what they want. They will not control me.

He keeps saying the spa wasn't really a spa. I feign surprise. I kind of am surprised—could Dione have pulled it off? Slug and Rat return. I tell them I don't know anything about a birthing centre, and I convince myself I *don't*. The B&B *was* operating as a B&B and spa, wasn't it? I believe what I'm telling them. I have to, to survive.

I had nothing to do with the people who stayed. I only ever

saw them in the distance. And the only pregnant woman I've ever seen was the one on the train. They know about her.

I just wanted to be with Jake. Away from Dione. She didn't like him.

I discover I am good at lying.

The SIF hold me for a week. The 'lies' get easier each time they interrogate me. My story sets hard and strong, the longer I am here. But the rest of it—being caged and blasted—takes every ounce of my determination. And as for being up close and personal to people who take pleasure in another's suffering … I don't know if I'll ever trust in true goodness again.

The fear ebbs. The cold doesn't.

The tip-off must have been brief, because all they keep saying is that a woman gave birth at Dione's. I don't know what they're talking about.

I am good at lying.

Dad would not be proud of me.

Dad. They won't let me ring him but every day I wake up and think, *this is the day he's coming. He is going to stop this nightmare and tell them it's got nothing to do with me. That they have no right to keep me here.*

I start to hope that they'll blackmail him into coming. I have to see him. But he doesn't come.

I ask if I can ring him, but the guards just laugh at me.

After three days, white-hot anger settles in my stomach. What a piss-weak shell of a man. The longer I wait, the more clearly I see how he's disappeared up his own arse since Mum and Holly died. Mum was the one who held Dad up and blew all the life into him. Now she's gone, he's just a shell.

Where is he? What is he doing while I'm locked up in here like a murderer? And where has he been all these years? He hasn't visited Dione's once, and he only came to Lucy's three times.

I stop wanting him to come. I begin fantasising that he was the one who died in the fire.

I know Mum loved every cell in my body. Sure, she could shout and rave sometimes, but she loved me and Holly completely. I think Dad just loved us because she did.

I hope he will be disappointed in me. Desperately disappointed. Stuff his stupid reputation.

The SIF's power-hungry zeal starts to dull—they have no fear to feed on. Their questioning becomes robotic, indifferent. They're going through the motions now, just like me. I begin to wonder what I was so afraid of.

By the time they let me out I have a hacking cough—who knows, maybe that's what motivates them to release me. That, and my threat about going to the free media when I get out. It was worth the slap from Slug. I struck a nerve—she knows they've kept me too long. As for my skin, who knows whether it will ever be the same again?

They give me my clothes back which are damp, and stink of mildew, but I don't care.

The sunshine feels sublime. I savour the rays seeping into my bones as I sit at the bus stop, grateful for freedom and the five-dollar note that's always in my backpack, thanks to Dione, tucked into the little inner pocket, just in case.

17

Invitation

There's no sign of Dione anywhere. Her house looks like a graveyard that's been dug up and turned inside out. The cottage, too. And it feels like there are eyes in every corner.

The only good thing is the chickens, who have somehow survived. They carry on like wild things when I go to them, took-tooking at me madly. I don't know where they've been getting water or food but they look well.

It's like Dione has slipped into another dimension. No clues, nothing. I keep walking around the house expecting her to appear. I don't dare ask around—I know the SIF are watching me. Maybe that's another reason they let me go—to lead them to her.

SIF cars come up the driveway daily. They sit out the front, engines running. At first I'm terrified. But after a few visits, fury sets in, and I plant nails all over the driveway.

Lion doesn't leave my side.

My body feels older. The cough takes a while to shift—sometimes it's so bad my lungs ache for ages afterwards. In the mornings I sit out in the sun, imagining that the rays are making me stronger.

I try to find Jake. I call Melissa but she hasn't seen him. Neither has Tom. I can tell Melissa's annoyed at me for not calling. How do I tell her I've been in a nightmare for days? That the SIF are probably listening in on our conversation, that her cousin might be dead because of me?

I ring every hospital in Adelaide but they won't give me any information. I sound completely stupid—I don't even know his surname. But there can't be that many guys with two broken legs. Nobody at the surf shop knows where he is. I refuse to believe he's gone too. Hope makes me daydream long and hard about meeting him again.

I go to the beach every day and wait for him, hoping. Every night I come home empty. As the days stretch into weeks, my hope fades and a dark ghoul takes its place, filling my mind with nightmare scenarios of him being tortured at the hands of the SIF.

After a few days, I force myself to blank him out. I have to hold onto some sort of sanity.

But I can't control my dreams.

I've spoken to Lucy twice. The first time she told me what a bitch I was for not returning her calls. I tried to laugh her out of it but she was so furious she hung up. I was devastated. The second time I called, she hardly said a word and I struggled to feel anything, except stiff and hard, like old leather toughened by the sun.

I've been here alone for three weeks.

I stop going to the beach. Dione will come back soon, she has to. I know she will. My phone is by my side constantly, always charged, and I go to town weekly to collect the water and check her mail box.

The general store is old-fashioned, with a wooden veranda and ornate iron lacework. The mail boxes are outside. I sit down on a nearby bench to sift through Dione's letters, hoping there's some sign of her. Unopened, they're like an oracle holding the answers to my fate, but opened and read, they become scraps of useless paper that I want to hurl as far as I can.

The pile on the hall table just grows steadily.

One envelope catches my attention with its rough and earthy paper. It's addressed to the two of us, from Tom. He mustn't know Dione's missing. I don't understand why the SIF haven't paid them a visit. It makes me think Jake must be dead. But then, surely they'd know? Unless the SIF have covered it up.

It's an invitation to a 'bush doof under the stars', in three weeks. Little Tom is almost two, Tom is turning thirty and Sarah and the baby will be home soon. Tom wants to celebrate with some dancing.

I wonder how Melissa will feel about me being invited.

I put the card on the mantelpiece, thinking fondly of them all. But I won't go. Melissa hasn't returned my calls. Besides, a party is the last thing I feel like.

Time drags by. I have nothing to do. The house is sparkling, the garden thriving. Dione was right about the veggies—the SIF didn't find them. They would have ripped them up if they had.

I am running out of money. I've been going through my savings with care but the money is dwindling fast. I'll have to start thinking about another job—maybe the supermarket will have me back? But I'm not ready to try. If I did get a job it'd be like accepting that Dione's gone, and not coming back.

Saturday night, I'm moping from room to room, treading a familiar path. I pass the mantelpiece and the invitation jumps out at me. I read it again and realise the party is tonight. I look at the time. Nine o'clock. It'd take me an hour to get there. Would the SIF suspect anything? Their visits have slowed to a trickle, they may not even be watching me anymore, especially not on a Saturday night.

Without giving it another thought, I decide I'm going. Maybe I'll tell Melissa what's been going on. I pull out the old green suitcase from under my bed. Dione gave it to me soon after our visit to the Star of Greece. It has some of Mum's clothes inside, and a book—one of her favourites, by Lao Tzu. These are the only things I have of hers, other than my memories and the box of journals from the garage. I click the brass catches and open the lid. Out wafts a faint scent of clary sage.

I pick up the book and open it at random:

'Being deeply loved by someone gives you strength, while loving someone deeply gives you courage.'

— Lao Tzu

That's all I need! A reminder of how few people I have in my life to love or be loved by. Tears prick my eyes as I riffle through the musty clothes and do a bitter tally. Mother and sister—dead. Father—who cares? Aunt—missing. Jake—probably dead. Lucy— not speaking to me. Melissa—no idea.

My hand closes on something cool and slithery. Astonished, and suddenly a whole lot lighter, I feel a slow smile come to my lips. Do I dare? Nah … Leggings with silver sequins? Way too disco. How come *these* have ended up with Dione?

A memory flashes: Mum's 'Oooh!' as she pulled the leggings from the rack. Holly and I roaring with delight at her crazy moves as she strutted around the shop. We were going to have a party in honour of the sequins.

But she never wore them again.

Right here and now, feeling more alone than ever, the memory of Mum's wild side ignites something in me and I decide these leggings are going on an outing. I won't know anyone other than Melissa and Tom, but I don't care. I'm going crazy on my own. Besides, a bush doof is much more outrageous than sequinned leggings.

I pull on my knee-high black boots over the shimmering pants and dig out my favourite black top. The fabric is soft and gently swings and slinks as I walk; good for dancing, I think, with a bubble of excitement.

≫

There are tea lights in jam jars lining the long driveway as I make my way up to the house. I've been on edge the whole way; my wild need for release is battling anxious thoughts about what'll happen if a SIF van sees Dione's car. What if I'm putting Tom and his family in danger by coming here?

The beat of the bass enters my body as soon as I get out of the car. A moment of doubt washes through me as I look down at my shiny legs, striding towards the music. But I don't stop.

An open-sided marquee stands at the back of the house, filled with tables, chairs and food. People are dancing already, while others stand and sit, talking merrily. I'm taking it all in when I find myself scooped up in a big beery hug.

'Well, if it isn't Dione's niece, Ora! How are ya darl?' Tom asks with a lopsided smile and a bit of a slur. He looks behind me for Dione.

'She's not here. She's been gone for weeks,' I blurt, forgetting about the usual pleasantries. Everything goes still as he looks at me, taking this in.

'I read something about a crackdown but I just thought it was free-media bullshit.'

'Have the SIF been here?' I ask, holding my breath.

'God no! Little Tom is in the system like he was born into it. We made sure of that. They have no idea we employed Dione.'

I don't know whether to be relieved or worried that he doesn't say anything about Jake. I can't ask, not yet.

We stand awkwardly, not knowing what else to say. Tom looks straight at me. 'She'll be all right, Ora. She's a clever one, that Dione. Come on,' he says, grabbing my hand. 'Let's get you a beer. It's a winner, even if I say so myself.'

Melissa appears and gives me a hug.

'Hello, stranger.' Maybe she isn't mad at me?

As Tom passes me a beer, she says, 'I reckon Ora would prefer the punch over your home-brew.'

Tom raises his eyebrows, puts the beer down and pours us each a long glass of something that looks more like pink toilet cleaner than anything drinkable.

'But watch out,' Melissa grabs my hands like we're still friends, which makes me smile. 'It's got a kick in it too. Why haven't you called me back?'

'What? You're the one who hasn't called *me* back.'

'Rubbish! I rang and texted loads, which was pretty nice considering you never bothered to reply.'

I'm about to bark back something similar when I realise the SIF must have been meddling with my phone. Haven't they got anything better to do? I look around, trying to decide if it's safe to tell Melissa what's been happening. I've already lost Lucy. I can't lose another friend. There are too many people at this party, it's overwhelming. I can't think straight. But I'm going to pop if I don't say something. So I start talking, unpacking the past few weeks—but only the bare minimum. My voice is strange and kind of removed. I know I'll start blubbing if I'm not careful. I don't mention Jake.

I can't.

Shock, compassion and anger roll over Melissa's face. Her eyes widen and her forehead crumples. She keeps saying she can't believe it. I feel like I'm about to cry. Seeing it through her eyes makes things worse.

I have to change the subject.

'Hey I came here to have fun! Not talk about this stuff. How's Little Tom?'

'Oh, he's great.' I can see she's worried, but she goes along with the subject change. 'He's talking more and more. Mum's looking after him tonight, but you'll see him in the morning.'

I don't tell her I'm not staying. I ask her about her clothing label. She's been experimenting with transferring my designs onto fabric!

'That's great!' Finally, something to be happy about.

'That's why I was trying to get hold of you. I needed your help'

'I'm sorry, Melissa. Let's get together next week. We won't let those SIF bastards get between us!' I'm about to ask her about Jake when some of her friends come over. She keeps trying to pull me into the conversation, but the small talk is doing my head in.

I drift away and sit down near the speakers. Soon my whole chest is pumping with the music. The first sip of fruit punch makes me recoil—it's way too strong—but the alcohol warms my veins and I can just taste the fruit flavours. After a few mouthfuls, I push the drink away.

The dance floor is under the stars, as promised, just beyond the marquee. It's in the shape of a huge square, flanked by giant gum trees towering above us on one side and a paddock fence on the other. The DJ has set up her console on the far side, opposite the marquee, enclosing the dancers comfortably. Behind the DJ, rolling paddocks stretch to the horizon. People are dancing freely, immersed in the music. There's one couple locked in an embrace, and occasionally people connect, but mostly the dancers are following their bodies, eyes closed, arms undulating, legs moving.

I stand up too quickly—I'm dizzy. If I watch any longer I know I won't dance, so I step onto the dusty ground, feeling the beat rise up through the earth, letting my feet slide and turn, circling, spinning me around.

I sense someone watching me from the middle of the marquee,

but instead of looking, I sink into the glorious feel of my body loosening up. I have been watched for too many days. Besides, whoever it is, they're looking at the leggings, not me.

I hang forward from my hips, upside down, the top of my head just above the ground. My feet and legs gently step on the spot and my upper body sways. Holly showed me this trick years ago, to let the music in and 'your thoughts fall out'. It's true, there's no room for thinking, and when I stand up the dance is in me, my mind a distant whisper.

The sequinned leggings strut their stuff and I'm away, letting the movements take me. I don't care if people think I'm dancing too hard or wildly. My body has taken over, shaking out the last few weeks of my life.

It feels like the DJ's playing songs just for me. Some of them I know, but a lot are new. She's playing them in waves; starting with slow and flowing beats, blending each tune seamlessly. Building in crescendo, moving into rock with a jagged beat that makes me find my edges. Then she moves us into a frenzy, bringing out the wild side in every dancer on the floor. Just when it feels like I don't have any energy left, she plays a few lyrical tracks that reach high above us, making my steps light and my arms stretch up to the stars. Then she rolls in the last part of the wave with music that has a stillness at its core, driving me to move from the centre of my breath.

And we're off again, on another wave. I can't remember how many songs I've danced to but suddenly I get a stomach cramp. The pain makes me double over, but I can't stop dancing; something makes me keep moving through it. I know if I stop, my thoughts will crash in. I put my hands on my thighs and lean forward slightly, rocking from side to side like a sumo wrestler, breathing into the heart of the pain in my belly, and feeling the excruciating wrench as something rips at my insides.

Flashbacks come thick and fast: the interrogation centre, Jake in his wetsuit, Dione's face, swimming and crying, dogs chasing me, birthing mothers, the SIF, the mountain, Dad, Holly, Mum, Dione again. I breathe harder and the pain shifts.

I start to move and open up the front of my body as much as I can, opening my shoulders, leaning my head back so my throat arches up to the night sky. It feels like something is coming out of my stomach, just above my navel. I have the crazy thought that I am giving birth, here, on the dance floor. It feels so real. The pain is real and the breathing is real. The image of a dragon coming out of my belly soars into my mind. Suddenly I *am* the dragon, wings and claws finding their way out of my belly. I am moving as the dragon—breaking out and free.

Once I'm out, the pain vanishes and I become the wildest whirling dervish. Turning and jumping at the same time, my great black wings lifting me high off the floor mid-turn. The power is phenomenal as I leap and stretch, twirl and shimmy. I am breathing fire from my throat and flying all around, weaving in and out of the other dancers.

The chaotic music shifts into lyrical, bringing me out of my frenzy and into a glide. I am soaring now. My consciousness expands across the paddocks and up into the air. No SIF bastards can get me now!

Gradually, gently we move into stillness. A Tibetan singing bowl chimes deeply over the speakers and a throat singer pulls me back into the world of the living. I stand in one spot, rocking and swaying, ever so slightly, feeling my heart pumping inside my chest and my ribs lifting, gasping for air.

I don't want to open my eyes. My mind is crashing in and I'm starting to freak out. What *was* that? What just happened? I am going mad. The music is already on another wave, flowing into the darkness of the night. I can't move—my body feels so tired. I sense someone standing opposite me and open my eyes slowly.

Jake?

Here?

'Hello, Ocean Woman,' he smiles, taking my hand gently. I've barely caught my breath and here is in front of me? Back from the dead. Am I imagining him?

He starts leading me to a table. I follow, dumbfounded, trying not to notice the curious stares drawn by my crazy performance. But I feel them anyway, eyes roving over me. Jake moves a chair out for me and guides me into it.

'I'll get you a drink,' he says, and moves towards the bar.

'Water ... please,' I croak, tasting the dry and bitter remnants of the fruit punch. What did they put in that drink?

As Jake returns I see he's limping. Gone is his easy grace. He still stands out, a head above the crowd, moving confidently, but there's a definite falter. My stomach drops to my toes. Does he blame me? He sits in the chair beside me and plonks a bottle of water under my nose. It's been in an icebox and is covered in condensation. I take great gulps, freezing my throat. When I put it back on the table I watch the trickles of water running down the outside of the bottle. I've wished for this moment so often, but now I don't know what to say.

We sit, trapped in an awkward pause that lasts for weeks. I still can't look at him. Something about Jake makes me want to cry.

'Shall we go somewhere else?' he asks quietly.

Yes. That's what I need. I love you ...

Where the hell did that come from? Terror instantly replaces the thought. But one look down at Mum's wild leggings makes me take his hand and start walking out to the paddocks beyond. I see a gum tree beckoning in the distance and gesture towards it. As we walk, I think I sense the dragon above us, flying silently.

I feel a newfound strength; my feet and legs are sure and steady as we make our way to the tree. We slide our backs down the trunk and sit against it, shoulder to shoulder. I visualise the giant roots below, reaching out as far as the branches above. The night-filled countryside is the perfect backdrop for the thousands upon thousands of stars blazing in the sky.

Eventually, I break the silence. 'I'm so sorry.'

'Huh?'

'About your legs.'

'Legs? I only broke one.' I take this in slowly. 'The physio reckons it'll be back to normal in a couple of months. If I keep swimming hard, the limp will be gone altogether.'

Relief seeps and settles into furrows worn deep by worry.

'Were you in the coma for long?' I ask.

He looks puzzled again. 'I was never in a coma.'

I stare at him, rage building. I speak very slowly. 'They told me you were in a coma.'

'*They* are bastards,' he says, equally slowly. 'They told me you'd done a runner to New South Wales.' We fall silent, seething at their lies and our own gullibility.

'Fuck!' I shout, jumping up. My voice carries far into the paddocks. 'Shit! Bastards!' I don't want to swallow this. I want to scream it out. All the nights of heartache and guilt, imagining Jake in a hospital bed, crippled or dead. When I finally sit down again he smiles. 'They didn't break us though, did they?'

I snort and search the horizon, then look back at him.

'But why haven't you been at the beach?' I can feel the anger wanting to hone in on him now.

'I've only just got out of rehab.'

'Oh.'

'I couldn't get about for weeks. I had to use the hydro pool every day. I didn't contact Tom or Melissa for ages, I was too worried it might lead to trouble. I went to the beach once, but it didn't feel right, just sitting there. Anyway, I thought you'd gone. I had no way of finding you.'

'I tried to find you!' I take a breath and imagine the fury

sliding off my back. I won't let the SIF interfere in my life anymore. I will never be that stupid again.

He smiles widely and leans back against the tree. 'But here we are again, away from it all, surrounded by nature.' His voice is deep and comical. 'A tree above us, instead of a tent ...'

I see the humour but can still feel echoes of fury ricocheting inside me, despite my efforts.

'So did they interrogate you?' I ask.

'They tried. But I just kept telling them that we'd gone camping together. I acted all indignant that they were even talking to me.'

'That was clever.'

'I'm a clever kind of guy,' he jokes.

I sit back against the tree, feeling easier. His arm comes around me and I lean into him, instantly remembering his warmth from so many weeks ago.

What was that quote about strength and love and courage? His muscles and his breath feel good as I let him hold me. I smile into the darkness, giving him a squeeze, noticing his presence in my heart.

'I'm thinking about my bed at home,' I say, remembering how sweet it was to spend the whole night next to him.

'Mmm?' he answers.

'And, erm ... it might be more comfortable than a tent with baying hounds outside ...' I trail off, stunned at myself. Am I really propositioning this guy, who I hardly know? But I feel like I do know him.

'Mmm?' he says again, eyes shining, possibly enjoying my discomfort; clearly liking the invitation.

I stand up brusquely, embarrassed. And then he's up too, holding my shoulders and staring at me, into me. His hand moves to the back of my neck and we lean into each other. My hands go around him and our lips meet. He feels tender. Tongues touching, knees softening, searching each other out. My hands move over his back. I can feel the frenzy from the dance floor return. I want to inhale him, consume him.

'Whoa,' he says, coming up for air, and I burst out laughing, delighted and horrified by my passion. He laughs too, thankfully. We stand hugging, giggling, swaying ...

'I think we should head home,' I say thickly, finding some self-control. And before he can answer I take his hand and find my stride.

18

Alone

We can't find Melissa to say goodbye but we let Tom know we're off. We walk down the driveway still holding hands, neither of us talking.

Jake climbs into Dione's passenger seat like he's done it a thousand times before. I'm totally self-conscious about my driving. Here I am cruising through the dark with this beautiful guy sitting next to me, making me feel a hundred things at once.

I'm glad I have the steering wheel to hold onto. He looks all nonchalant sitting there, like he's out for a Sunday drive with his granny.

Just as I'm thinking this and snatching a quick look, Jake breaks into his big wide grin.

'What?'

'I'm just remembering your dance,' he says with a laugh. 'You were pretty wild there for a minute.'

'So?'

'Hey, you were great. You've got some moves!' He laughs again.

'It was the other dancers, they didn't know what'd hit them.' He's chuckling now. 'They just stopped and looked at you with their mouths open, like you were some kind of tornado!'

I start laughing too, realising how funny it must have looked, a lunatic going off on the dance floor. Even if the lunatic was me. Right now I don't care.

'Were you channelling some kind of spirit or something?' he asks. The laughter is still in his voice, but he's staring at me hard.

I keep my eyes on the road, glad of the distraction. Holly's voice rings in my ears. 'Just tell it how it is!' she'd say when she saw me struggling for words.

I take a breath in. 'I *was* channelling something, I think.' There's a long silence, then I add, 'But it wasn't bad or anything.'

He's definitely going to know I'm mad now.

'So what was it?' This guy doesn't give up.

'A dragon,' I say quickly, and wonder where the dragon is now.

He's looking at me strangely, possibly like I'm some kind of psycho driving him home to kill him.

'Can we not talk about this?' I say.

'Sure.'

A full five seconds pass before I can't bear it any longer.

'It's never happened before and I know it sounds really weird but it doesn't mean that *I'm* weird. Just that weird things happen to me.' I'm digging myself into a hole.

He's gone very quiet, like he's slipping into some internal landscape. Minutes drag by. I need to think of something else to talk about, to shine the spotlight on him.

'When I was in the cell at the SIF,' I say, breaking the film of ice between us, 'I thought about you. When I wasn't worrying about your legs or your head, that is.'

He smiles.

'And I tried to guess things about you, like I was colouring in a picture. Because I had the outline and the feeling of you but none of the details or the facts.'

I feel totally vulnerable telling him how much he's been in my head. Living with Dione must have rubbed off on me; she's not one for many words but when she does speak, it's never small talk.

'You want me to talk about myself?' He is actually squirming. I can feel it.

I nod, wanting to stare at him but keeping my eyes straight ahead.

'Well, I'm not a big talker,' he says, shifting slightly in his seat, looking uncomfortable.

A happy little surge of realisation rushes through me…He is human after all!

'I'll have a go though,' he says, sighing. 'You already know about my sisters … Erm … I was born in Adelaide.' He stops abruptly.

'Did you have a happy childhood?' I turn my head briefly and he's looking at me like I'm asking too many questions.

'I love knowing this stuff,' I say, looking back at the road.

He sighs again. 'Mum did a good job of bringing us up on her own.'

The silence is awkward, but I hold my tongue.

'I was ten when Dad left. He was a bastard with a drinking problem. That was around the time I got serious about swimming.' His words come out in a rush.

I wish I could see his eyes properly. I can't read what he's feeling, but I can hear the emotion under the flatness of his voice. I'm about to ask another question, but he cuts me short.

'That's it.' He shrugs.

'What about girlfriends?' I ask.

'What d'you mean?' He sounds really guarded now.

'Well, how many have you had?' I ask, surprising myself.

'What kind of a question's that?'

'A blunt one?' We look at each other briefly. He has a hunted look in his eyes. 'Sorry, I'm just curious, that's all.' I smile, wanting to make light of it. 'I'm trying to figure you out.'

'You're meant to ask me about music, films.' He's lightening up now. 'Not about how many girls I've been with!'

'Come on, you can tell me …'

A flirty kind of silence falls between us. It's true—I do want to know about the girls he's been with. Why is that so wrong? Indignation starts brewing in my belly and I blurt out, 'I'm bringing you back to my house. I've invited you into my bed, which I'm still in shock about, by the way, and you think it's rude that I want to know more about you? You're the first boy I've ever wanted to do this with and I'm meant to feel bad about asking personal questions?'

'Hey,' he says, as I pause to take a breath. 'I'm not trying to make you feel bad, but I've never been grilled about my private life by someone I hardly know.'

'And I've never shared my body with someone *I* hardly know!' I say in a rush, raising my voice, calling my fear to the surface.

There's a horrible silence. The city lights shine into the car, making us both too visible. I drive faster, longing to get out the other side, into more darkness. But that means we're getting closer to Dione's. What have I done, inviting this stranger back to my house?

'Would you like me to get out?' Jake asks in his uncanny way, echoing my thoughts. 'There's a bus stop not far from here.' He sounds far away, and maybe a little sad.

'I don't know, I …' I open my mouth and close it again, pulling over to the kerb. I need to see his eyes. He puts his hand on the door, ready to get out. This is all wrong.

'I'm sorry,' I say, touching his arm. 'I just don't know how to do this. I …' The thought of going home on my own makes my insides feel dense. How can emptiness be so heavy?

Jake leans over and kisses me lightly, fleetingly, on the lips.

He draws back and looks at me. 'You're a swimmer, Ora. And a dancer. You know how to listen to your body. Sometimes thoughts just get in the way. So do words.'

He opens the door and I feel my energy being sucked out with him.

'Wait.' I want to get our closeness back. How have I pushed him away? The glow and excitement from earlier have vanished. I can't let him go. His foot is on the pavement.

'Can we exchange numbers?' I try to sound cooler than I feel. I know I should let him go but there's this huge tidal wave of hollowness threatening to wash over me. The longer we stay talking, the longer I can keep it at bay.

A smile brightens his face. 'You know where to find me.'

Both his feet are on the pavement now. I can hear the roar of the wave crashing towards me, rendering me mute.

He leans in. 'Come swimming soon.' He closes the door gently.

Everything is still and soundless. My eyes are dry. I see my hands gripping the steering wheel tightly but I don't feel them. Something inside me has clicked off. Not thinking, not feeling, not seeing. I've fallen asleep, sitting up, with my eyes open.

19

Another invitation

My senses return along with the early morning light. I straighten up and stretch, feeling stiff. On the way home, thoughts of the SIF briefly stop me from thinking about Jake. How dumb could I be—sitting there all night like a mad woman!

I go back to thinking about Jake. I can't get him out of my head.

What if I've chased him away with my questions? Maybe he's decided I'm not worth the hassle. What if he isn't interested at all? This thought visits often, but I push it away.

I replay our kisses and time in the tent and then start having these wild fantasies about him doing all sorts of things with me, to me, under me, over me ... This guy has really gotten under my skin, literally.

His advice was to trust my body, but it's my mind that keeps concocting wild scenarios. And because I've been 'listening' to my body, I find myself swimming in full-on desire, filled with lust. But every now and then, sensible thoughts find their way in. I hardly know anything about him.

Mostly though, my fantasies win.

Never before have I pleasured myself with a particular person in mind. Usually I have some vague scenario going on, but always with someone unknown and faceless. Now, Jake is with me; in my touch, in my mind. As I caress my own body, his energy comes through. I wonder if I'll be disappointed if we ever get it together in real life, and not just in my messed-up imaginings.

I need to swim.

How can he be so sure I'll come and find him? What if I don't? If I was a complete flake and stayed at home, would he get my number from Melissa, or my address from Tom? I don't think I can wait to find out. I call Melissa but she doesn't pick up.

Part of me is furious that he's so laid back. He's acting like he knows I'll come running. How can he be so sure? Maybe he's got heaps of girlfriends and hasn't given me a second thought. Maybe he's just really full of himself.

I have to find out, one way or the other.

I spend the longest time getting ready for the beach. Thankfully, I only have two sets of bathers to choose between. It's what to wear over them that's the problem.

The sky is grey and there's a slight wind bringing an early autumn chill to the morning. In the end I decide on my favourite cotton pants, kind of combat style. They're green and if you look closely are patterned like a spring meadow. My faded pink T-shirt, grey hoodie and sneakers finish the look. Strong and relaxed. When I see my reflection, I imagine Mum nodding her approval. I don't want to look like I'm trying, even though I am.

When I'm finally ready, I pack a basic lunch and my sketchbook. I've only done two sketches since the party, both of the dragon. One shows her flying, wings outstretched, gliding. The other is of her face. Her eyes are dark round wells that I lose myself in. They hold so much love and wisdom. I know dragons are mythological and are meant to be fierce and wild, but all I see is compassion.

The bus is almost empty. There are a couple of kids at the back, wagging school, laughing and gossiping, and a man at the front, reading his paper. It's just before lunchtime and my stomach rumbles. Maybe it's nerves.

The ocean glistens in the sunlight. Patches of blue sky are winning out over the clouds. I inhale the fresh sea air and am tingling with excitement at being back at my beach, where I might finally spend time with Jake.

He's not here! Neither is his towel. I plonk my stuff in my usual spot and strip off to my bathers. I don't care. I won't. The ocean is enough, even if he doesn't come all day. Why did I stay away so long?

It feels glorious to be in the water again. My body delights in stretching out as I dive into the gentle waves over and again. Down to the sandy floor, then arching up and out towards the blue sky. I am lost in the meditation of movement when I hear a familiar deep voice.

'So now you're channelling a dolphin, right?'

Jake is standing in the waves next to me, hands on hips, barechested with faded bathers. Clearly he's gone for the relaxed look too.

For a moment I'm tongue-tied. I want to say something funny about a cross between a dolphin and a dragon but the words won't come. I smile and dive again to hide my red face. When I come up he's gone. I turn a circle in the water but I can't see him. Suddenly, he's right in front of me, coming in on a wave.

He lands a salty kiss on my lips and draws back before I have time to respond, smiling broadly.

'Fancy seeing you here, Ora Dragon. You took your time.'

'Well, Seaboy Jake,' I smile, 'it seems I couldn't keep away.'

He sits beside me in the shallows so we're both looking out to sea. I am suddenly aware of my nipples, pert under my bikini top, as the cold water laps around our legs. I lean back on my elbows, hoping to conceal them under the water, but it's a bad move. The water is going back out—now they're on display even more! I'm totally out of my comfort zone, wishing for another wave to hurry up and come in.

Suddenly the horizon is completely fascinating.

Jake's glance takes me in. He lies back beside me, then flips quickly onto his belly. I wonder if he has anything pert to cover up, too, and feel a smile twitch at my lips. I turn over, enjoying the feel of my upper arm sliding against his with the water between us as we both look back up the beach.

'Ouch,' he says, laying a finger gently over one of the scars on my shoulder.

'The SIF,' I say with a shrug, moving slightly. My skin has healed really well but there are still a few marks across my shoulders and back that will be there for longer. I don't want to be reminded.

'Are you going to swim across the bay today?' I ask.

'I was about to, but now I'm not so sure.' I love the way he makes me feel welcome. 'Hey,' his whole face has lit up. 'Can you horse ride?'

'Yeah, but it's been a long time. My best friend had a horse when we were growing up. I've got a funny habit of making them bolt.'

He looks at me with a question in his eyes.

'I don't mean to. They just sense something in me.' I smile, wanting to make light of my insecurities. 'Probably my madness!'

'Probably your dragon,' he says, looking cheeky.

'Shut up about my dragon.'

'Just sayin'.'

'It's kind of new, so I'm feeling a bit sensitive about it.'

'What, you mean there're others?' he jokes again.

'There could be, just a couple.'

'Seriously? Like what? Unicorns?'

'No!' I push him over, ducking the question. I won't tell him about Lion and Snake. He pushes me back and we start wrestling.

'What then? Phoenixes? Or … or Trolls?' We're laughing.

'A lion and a snake actually!' I sound kind of proud. So much for not telling him. He has a hold of my wrists but I'm putting up a good fight.

'Are they like animal totems? Do you have indigenous blood in you?'

'Maybe,' I say. 'Half Koori, half Cherokee.'

'Right.' He thinks for a minute. 'That's an interesting combo. But shouldn't you have some African in there too? I've never heard of a half Aussie, half American lion.'

'Ha ha.' He looks surprised at how strong I am as I free myself from his grip. It's my turn to take his wrists and I kneel up to get more height. 'You want to be careful, you might get eaten.'

'So is it here now?' he's looking up and down the beach.

'Not telling.' I start pushing him backwards and before I know it, I've fallen on top of him, across his torso. I kneel in beside him and pin his arms into the seabed, laughing at my win. Then I realise I'm waving my breasts just above his face, so I let go and move down to kiss him instead, stretching my body alongside his, not quite touching.

Our lips come together boisterously, playfully, but we soon slow down. His fingertips gently touch my cheek. I remember sliding on top of him in the tent but we had my sleeping bag between us then. That'd be way too confronting now.

But I want to.

Cautiously, I lift my leg onto his thigh, loving the feel of his muscles underneath my own.

'I think we should go riding,' he says.

'Here?' I say suggestively, raising my eyebrows. He laughs.

'Horseback riding! There's this beautiful track behind Tom and Sarah's, and they've got a couple of horses we could ride. If the weather stays nice we could take some food and camp out.'

I nod my agreement with a big smile, liking the sound of horses, camping ...

And Seaboy Jake.

20

The Shack

'It's like a French picnic,' he says with a good French accent. I'm impressed by his imagination as I look at the block of yellow, processed cheese and plastic looking bread in our supermarket basket. At the last minute I agree to some red wine. I'm not sure I'll drink it, but it fits in with the French theme.

Jake has an electric moped that just makes it up to Tom's—the tyres bulge underneath our weight, along with the added burden of sleeping bags, pillows and food.

It's clear he's spent a lot of time around horses. I watch his easy grace as he leads them into the yard and starts preparing them for our trek. He's gentle yet firm, a reassuring hand always on one of them, as he checks bridles and girths.

By the time we've chatted to Tom and cooed over Little Tom, it's well after three. I don't know where Melissa is but I'm relieved she's not around—this is all too new to be fielding any looks or questions.

We pack our gear into old leather saddlebags that are soft and well used. Jake puts something extra into one of them, but I don't see what. Excitement floats around inside me. One of the horses shifts and scrapes its hoof on the paving outside the stables. I study them closely, trying to sense which one is least likely to take off on me.

Surprisingly, Jake hands me the reins of the bigger one, a dappled grey about eighteen hands. He is huge! 'Don't worry,' Jake says. 'Duke's a gentleman.'

I heave myself up onto the horse from some steps on wheels. My body's memory kicks in as soon as I'm in the saddle. This feels good!

Jake's mount is a black mare, more delicate and spirited than my gentle giant. She dances about in protest until she's used to his weight. I am relieved to be riding Duke.

Tom and Little Tom wave us off as we go through the gates. We start out along a track that winds around the mountain to the east of their property. It's lined with lilly pillies and I can smell the zing of a lemon-scented gum. The afternoon sunlight filters through the trees and I hear the distant laugh of a kookaburra.

We ride beside each other and Jake and I grin broadly. The wind has dropped and the rhythmic thud of the horses' feet along the grassy path lulls me into dreaminess. It's familiar, yet unbelievable, being here in the bush with him and two beautiful horses.

I keep stealing glances at him, enjoying the way he looks in the saddle. The mare has been a bit skittish but he's remained calm and centred with steady hands, and she's relaxed a bit. He looks like he's been riding all his life. He catches me watching him and I don't hide my appreciation.

'You ride well.'

'Thanks,' he smiles. 'So do you.' After a pause he says, 'I've been thinking about your questions.'

'I'm not sure I want to remember that conversation.'

'I was a bit defensive and ... I'm kind of private but ... I get where you were coming from.'

The bridle clinks as Duke tosses his head. The flies are bothering him.

'Thanks.' I don't know what else to say.

'I haven't had many relationships, a couple of girls at school—one in year ten who dumped me pretty quick. I was heartbroken but then I went out with a girl in the year above. She got way too serious, too fast, so I ended it. After that I just hung out with my mates and got through year twelve.

'That summer I was volunteering as an assistant lifesaver and I fell for someone.' He pauses, looking into the distance, eyes closing slightly against the sunlight. 'An American, ten years older than me, here for a writing sabbatical.'

'What was her name?' I don't really want to know, but I can't help myself.

'Kat. Katherine. We got talking one day and before I knew it, we were together. She made the first move—she always knew what she wanted. We were pretty serious for a while. After she went back to the States, I saved up and followed her a few months later.'

He pauses again and I want to ask him more, but I make myself wait.

'I fell pretty deep. She was strong, you know?'

I nod yes, but I don't know.

'It was good to be in another country, seeing new things. For the first time I felt free.'

'I guess you didn't have to look out for your mum and your sisters,' I say, needing to say something.

'Uh huh,' he agrees. 'The US has got its own version of the SIF, but resources didn't seem so tight. I guess they didn't get all the diseases like we did.'

We sit for a moment.

'I could just be this wild, new man. This anything-I-wanted-to-be man.' He pauses. 'Except it turned out to be anything *she* wanted. I started to jump through hoops for her. I was out of my depth.'

He looks at me and I nod again.

'I didn't know anyone else, except her friends, who were a lot older. In the end I got some cash work, gardening, and saved the money to get away for a while. When I got back she ended it, and that was that.'

'Oh,' I say, surprised at the finality of it.

'Yep.'

There's more silence, but I'm not going to fill it.

'I was gutted,' he says. 'And relieved. I knew it was for the best but I was pretty low for a while. I ended up travelling all over the States.' He's quiet and then says, 'But it's true about time healing. And sometimes,' he smiles and looks across at me, 'there's something amazing around the corner.'

My heart skips a beat.

Now I realise why it took so long—all those weeks on the beach together, not talking. I was too shy, and he was getting over a broken heart.

'What about you?' The cheeky glint is back in his eye. 'You *must* have kissed someone before? What about when you were five or six?'

'Oh, my cat, you mean? Yes, I used to kiss him all the time.' Can he see that I'm way out of my league? His ex is fourteen years older than me! She must have been so experienced; I can't bear to think of them together. I feel like a kindergarten kid lost in the high-school yard.

I kick Duke on to hurry him up and he jumps sideways in surprise, barging into Jake's horse. She tosses her head and looks insulted and suddenly we're off, galloping along the path, neck and neck. I hold on with my thighs, giving Duke all the reins he needs to push ahead. The pathway narrows and he surges forward.

Jake's horse is right behind us and I can sense that they want to be in front, but Duke and I are in the lead and loving it. The pathway narrows even more. Up ahead I can see it curves back on itself, up and around the hill. I lean forward, readying for Duke's change of weight.

'Ora,' Jake shouts, out of breath. 'Slow down! There's a bridge ahead. You have to STOP!'

I start reining Duke in and feel him resist. This is where I often lose it with a horse—I like the feel of them being free.

'Ora!' Jake sounds more authoritative, even though he's further away; he's slowed the black mare down.

I lean right back, pulling hard, and Duke, the well-trained horse that he is, slows to a fast canter and then suddenly stops, nearly tossing me over his head.

Jake trots past me on the high side of the hill. He looks at me angrily but doesn't say anything. His face says it all. It was stupid to gallop off without knowing the way but I'm not going to apologise.

The bridge turns out to be a rickety old wooden thing over a deep ravine. We have to dismount and lead the horses across it. It's been built for walkers, not horses, and I'm alarmed at how dangerous it would have been to clatter over it at a gallop. The horses could have broken their legs. I want to say sorry but I can't. I have withdrawn.

We get back on the horses and walk for a long time, lost in our thoughts and the countryside around us. Perhaps he's thinking about Kat and his time in America. My thoughts are flitting all over the place. Only a short while ago I was feeling so close to Jake, all wrapped up in intimacy, and now he's a million miles away. How can things blow so hot and cold between us? I don't get it.

Memories of Mum and Dad and Holly on a family horse-riding holiday keep popping into my head, mingling with thoughts of Dione.

Apprehension about the night ahead begins to creep in. Is it too late to turn back? Why did I agree to come away with a guy I hardly know?

The forest path ends abruptly and opens onto endless hilltops that roll into the sky in slow waves. The expansiveness lightens my mood. We look at each other and smile.

'That's where we're headed.' Jake points to a shack on the next ridge, a dot in the distance that looks more like it's grown out of the hill than assembled by human hands. 'Tom built it five years ago—"The Escape",' he says. 'So he and Sarah could take holidays—she can't leave the horses for long.'

The hills have turned golden in the sunlight and the silver bark of the gum trees really does look ghostly. Something about all the space and being so close to the sky makes me open up. He asks loads of questions about Holly and Mum. Most people are too afraid to ask. But talking about them makes me feel like I'm holding a smooth pebble, rather than a fistful of sand that's slipping through my fingers. For the first time, I really share what it's been like to lose them. Not in relation to Dad or Dione or Lucy. Just me—a kid who lost her mum and sister.

'When do you feel it most?' he asks, looking curious.

'In the mornings. Across here,' I gesture to my chest. 'It's like this dark shadow that I wake up with, pushing in on me. When I get busy it goes. But it's there when I stop. And sometimes it's like there's this hole. Like my heart has a crack that makes me notice different colours—the murky ones—and hear different music. It's hard to explain.

'Holly was always there. We sparked off each other. Always together; giggling, imagining, arguing, annoying. She always sat beside me, never opposite. I don't know why. I didn't realise until she'd gone how she made me whole.

'And Mum was like this crazy mixture of wild and deep. Not wild in an unsafe way, but she'd have these crazy impulses and we'd get carried along by them. You know those glittery leggings I wore to the party? They were hers.'

Jake smiles.

'When she wasn't being wild she was quiet and soft and always knew what we needed.'

Jake is a great listener. I even tell him about my one and only two-week-old boyfriend who I went out with in Year 11. I explain that I was scared of getting too close to anyone so I ended it soon after it'd started.

'What about your animal guides or totems or whatever they are?' he asks, out of the blue.

'What about them?'

'Well I still don't get that about you. Like, how do they fit in with the Ora who plays Scrabble?'

'Oh, I don't fully understand them, either. But some nights it's really weird, I turn into a lion and go prowling around and then, before dawn, I transform into this giant snake before I slither home to bed.'

'Really?'

I nod. 'But it's very hard on my body, morphing from one to the other and then back to me again. And picking out the Scrabble letters with a Lion's paw, that's really difficult.' He's looking at me with big eyes, and then cracks a huge smile.

'You had me!' I nod and burst out laughing. 'But only for a minute. Come on Ora, you have to tell me!'

'Seriously, Jake. I don't really know how they work. They're kind of like an aspect of myself or my imagination. Different parts of me that have an animal form, maybe?' He nods. Smiles. He's actually really listening and doesn't think I've cracked it. 'Dione taught me these drum journeys years ago where you meet your power animal. I ended up meeting a lion and a snake and at different times—usually when I'm stressed—they pop into my head.'

'So … do you … hear voices?'

'No! Yes! Kind of.'

Now he's looking a bit worried so I start speaking very quickly in case he wants to turn around and go home. 'But it's usually only when I've got a drumbeat that I meet them. Apart from in the SIF, which was totally extreme.'

He's still here, nodding. So far, so good.

'Mostly, I just listen to the drum recording which produces an altered state of consciousness. Ages ago, I read up on it and apparently the beat makes the hemispheres of the brain connect in a way that synchronizes them.' Jake nods again. Maybe he understands. I hope so.

'Perhaps it's a bit like lucid dreaming,' he suggests.

'Maybe. But I've never done that so I'm not sure. Sometimes, Lion appears without the drumbeat, but not often.'

'Except in the SIF?'

I nod. 'Like I said, it was totally extreme in there …'

'Do you want to talk about it?'

'I don't think I'm ready … but I'll tell you when I am.'

'Okay,' he says then smiles. 'But what about the dragon?'

'I don't know …'

'Right!'

'I mean, I haven't worked it out yet.'

'You and me both!' he says with a chuckle and his horse does a little dance-y move at the same time which makes me smile.

'I think the dragon arrived because it was the first time I let my hair down after the SIF—maybe I was just having a good freak out.'

'It was definitely that,' he agrees. We both laugh for a moment. If he was closer, I'd whack him.

We walk on in contented silence. As we get nearer to the shack, I see it's been thrown together with bits of old timber and sheets of corrugated iron. There's a stout brick chimney at one end, making it look homely. Pink panes of glass and an old stable door give it a picture-book feel.

I slide off Duke and hobble like a bow-legged cowboy to look inside the hut. It's tiny, like it was built around the roughly hewn wooden bed. A bright pink blanket covers the comfy-looking mattress. And there are candles everywhere, as well as a whole load of wax.

'No power,' Jake says. 'And Tom and Sarah love candles.'

The sun is low in the sky by the time we take the horses' saddles off and tie them up with feed from one of the saddlebags.

Jake suggests I walk to the top of the hill to watch the sun go down while he makes a fire in the hut. I'm glad for the chance of some space. I'm not used to being so long in the company of anyone—especially a guy I'm about to get naked with.

There's a feeling of inevitability lurking in the background and I can feel the contrary part of me resisting. This is all too contrived. Does he bring lots of girls up here?

I don't know if this is what I want. Is this how it's meant to be? Shouldn't I wait until I know him better? It's feeling too quick, rushed, like he's rushing things. I'm totally out of my depth, stuck up here, unable to run.

What if *he's* the psycho?

I barely see anything of the sunset; I'm trying to recall the route we took, wondering if I can walk it in the dark. Where is the moon? Usually I know whether it's waxing or waning but things have got so out of whack since the SIF caught me. Suddenly I miss Dione's little kitchen. And her frittata.

Jake's footsteps make me tense up. I hunch my shoulders and hug my knees. He sits down beside me, not too close, and hands me a tin cup half filled with red wine. I smile a small thank you and take a sip. It tastes strong, velvety, as the dark liquid slips down my throat, heating my belly. I want to take great glugs of it now. If he wasn't sitting here, I would. I don't even like red wine.

The sun crowns the hilltop before sinking behind it, colouring the sky. A short while later we're enveloped by blues and greys coming to end the day. The beginning of night. I've tried to capture it so many times.

I want to tell him this is my favourite time, but I can't. I feel sick with self-consciousness. He puts his arm around me and I'm not sure if I like it. I go to take another sip of wine but the cup is empty. A horrible slurp sounds out as I try to suck in the last drop. I start giggling inanely.

It's better than crying.

He leans in close and kisses me tenderly on the lips. He calms me and maddens me at the same time. How is he so in control? I don't like it.

And I do.

He stands and pulls me up, placing something cold and metal in my hand. It's a torch.

'Watch your step,' he says, starting off down the small track to the hut. I keep my eyes fixed on the ground the whole way, careful not to trip over and embarrass myself further.

When we're close to the hut I look up and am surprised by its hearty glow. Warm candlelight dances in the pink windows, calling us inside.

He opens the door and a magnetic gold light springs out—there are so many candles, and the fire is roaring. I see the food on the mantelpiece along with the bottle of wine. He's made the bed with a sheet and laid out our pillows and sleeping bags.

'Wow!' I'm stunned by how magical it looks. Completely blown away.

He leads me in and I sit on the bed, holding up my mug as he pours more wine and passes me some bread.

'To soak up the wine,' he smiles, and hands me a small board with the cheese on it. When he was pouring the drinks I noticed his hand shaking, which made me feel better. I can't work him out.

He's so laid back and nonchalant, but he must be pretty organised to get all this happening.

'So where's the orchestra?' I joke, to hide how overwhelmed I am.

'They did a runner when they saw how far they'd have to come,' he replies, not missing a beat. 'But I do have my phone.' He gets up to put on some music. It's a band I vaguely recognise. They sound tinny and distant without speakers, but it's good to have some music to fill the silence.

Jake stokes the fire and helps himself to food. I'm busy stuffing my face and gulping more wine, even though I'm not especially hungry or thirsty.

He comes and sits behind me. I stiffen and stop chewing mid-mouthful, feeling his hand on the back of my neck, gently stroking it, making every cell there tingle. We stay like this for ages, him in no hurry and me frozen to the spot. I manage to swallow the bread in my hand and sip some more wine.

Do I turn around or stand up? I can't look him in the eyes and I don't want to move away so I carry on just sitting, enjoying the movement of his hand. He's running it up and down my spine now. He kneels behind me and places both his hands on my shoulders. My zip-up hoodie has come off one shoulder and he's caressing the bare skin under my T-shirt sleeve. Now both hands are near my neck again, massaging.

He leans around and kisses me on the cheek. My mind is working furiously, trying to keep up with my body's enjoyment. Should I say something? Pull back? Take more control? But instead my head turns and finds his lips.

He reaches to the stretch of my neck that is exposed and runs his hand down over my shoulder, to the bare skin on my arm again. My hoodie is off my other shoulder now, pooling around my wrists. His fingertips are spidery on my arms. My skin becomes sensitive; it's singing under his touch!

The music has stopped and all I can hear is the crackling of the fire and our breathing. It feels like we're in a cocoon … and it's shrinking.

I get up and put my cup on the mantelpiece, pulling my hoodie back on. This is going too fast.

'Are you okay?'

'I … This … It feels a bit quick.' I turn back slowly towards him.

'Do you want to just get into bed?'

'Under the covers sounds good,' I say, looking at our two separate sleeping bags.

That's not going to work …

'Shall we try zipping them together?' he asks, reading my mind. 'So they make a doona?'

'Let's give it a go.'

We cajole the zips into a haphazard kind of union and in the process, end up having another wrestling match.

'You think you're so strong,' he says, trying but failing to pin me down.

'That's because I am!' But then my laughter overtakes me and he breaks my winning streak.

'So you *do* know how to have some fun, Ora James.' I like the sound of my name in his mouth.

We're out of breath from laughing so much and slow our rough and tumbling, ending up in a snuggly heap, facing each other.

'We can just sleep if you want,' he says gently.

'I don't know,' I say. And I honestly don't. I want to tell my mind to shut up and let my body go. This guy who I fell for so many months ago has brought me here to this magical place and I want him, with my heart and my body. And I want to please him too. But it feels forced. Like I *have* to, and something in me is baulking. Maybe I *am* contrary. Mum used to say I was. I just don't want to rush. I know he's the one. There's no question. So why do I need to go slow? Am I just being contrary for the sake of it?

You don't have to go all the way on your first night. My own words echo in my head from ages ago. Lucy was going to a sleepover at her boyfriend's for the first time.

'What are you thinking?' he asks sleepily. His hand is stroking my arm again.

'About going all the way,' I reply.

His eyes open. 'Do you want to?'

'Yes, but not right now,' I say quietly, knowing I risk losing the magic of this moment.

He hugs me close. 'It's okay.'

He lets me go and rolls onto his back. I'm shocked. It's like there are two lights—red or green—but amber's out of the question. I roll away from his arm, wrapping the makeshift doona close to my body.

'Oi!' he says gruffly, 'stop stealing the covers.' He folds his body in behind mine, and pulls me close.

'Maybe we should unzip them?' I say grumpily. 'We'll both be warmer.'

'No chance,' he says to the back of my neck, pretending to snore loudly.

'Are you really going to go to sleep?'

'Yes.'

'Right.'

'You just said you didn't want to *do* anything.'

'I didn't! I said I didn't want to go all the way *tonight*. That doesn't mean I don't want to do *anything*. Do you only have two speeds?'

'Thanks a lot!' He rolls over to his side of the bed, taking the covers with him.

If I could storm out I would.

I knew this was a trap.

He turns around again, sighing loudly, and looks up at the ceiling. 'I'm trying to give you space, okay? This is all new, and I'm no expert.'

'You know a lot more than me!'

'But it's different. You're different. I'm different. This is new. It's not like there's a guidebook.' He's sounding worked up and looks like he's holding a lot in as he grips his arms tightly over his chest.

In a lightbulb moment I suddenly see how this is for him. It isn't a trap! It's a big-hearted attempt to make this special, and it must be so far removed from how he was with his ex. She would have been the driver—experienced and sure of what she wanted. Predatory even. And here I am, the complete opposite, expecting him to know what to do because he's the one with the relationship history.

But that was *their* history.

I have to do something to connect us again.

'We could get naked,' I say, surprising both of us.

'What?'

'We could take our clothes off and jump under the covers.'

'Really?' He's smiling now, hopefully not thinking I'm completely mad. 'But I don't know—'

'Race you,' I say, before I can begin to feel stupid.

I sit up and take off my t-shirt and bikini top. He's a bit quicker, but I had a head start. We lie back in sync and fling off our bottoms at the same time.

'I won!' I declare, hugging the silky sleeping bag fabric close to me.

'You did *not*, I was way ahead!' We're giggling now, and we turn towards each other, lying on our sides but not touching. The electricity under the covers must be sending out some sparks.

'What I was about to say, before I was so *rudely* interrupted, is that I don't know if I can be trusted if you're lying naked here, next to me.' He places his hand on my naked hip.

I look into his laughing eyes. 'I trust you,' I tell him, and feel a surge go through my heart because I really do.

Is this what love feels like?

Maybe it's lust … I want to feel my breasts against his chest and the length of him against me. His arm goes around my back and mine around his as we shuffle closer. Every cell in my body lights up at the feel of his skin pressing against mine, our muscles and bones kissing. My blood is coursing through my body at a million miles an hour and my thoughts are registering all of his body parts against mine—the most obvious one pushing against me, warm and hard. Then there's the pulsing and tingling in my own body, which is going off like a pinball machine.

I dare to put my hand on his bottom and pull him closer to me. We're kissing and he lets out a little sound. I'm feeling wild—it's like a hunger—and now I want all of him.

'Seriously, Ora,' he says breathlessly. 'I'm not sure I can do this.'

'But this feels right,' I say. 'And good,' I add, pushing up against him.

'You have no idea!' He takes my hip again and pushes me away gently, creating some space between us. 'You tell me you don't want to go all the way and then practically jump on me.'

'Oh. I …' I don't know what to say.

'Whatever happens, we're not going all the way tonight because that's what you wanted earlier. But I'm not made of steel—'

I start giggling.

'What?' he asks, as his hand starts tracing the length of my thigh.

'Parts of you are!' I laugh some more. I don't want to shrivel up inside and let embarrassment take me. He smiles, watching me thoughtfully.

'I feel okay about that now,' I say, remembering my yearning from a minute ago. 'I think I was just being contrary before. I actually, really … want you.' I can't believe I'm saying this, but I don't want to feel like the other night, like I'm being left behind.

'And I so want you.' He looks at me very intensely and all my fears of him walking away leave me. 'But I heard you before and I'm going to make sure that your wish is my command.' He's making a jokey attempt at sounding chivalrous.

'Shall we put our clothes back on then?' I ask, with that sinking feeling in my belly.

'No, but I might need to take a breather sometimes.' His hand feels so good on my body. I close my eyes. This is all too intense. My mind wants to gatecrash and sabotage everything, but before my thoughts can distract me, his hand comes around to my belly and gently urges me to lie on my back.

He spends what feels like hours, tracing patterns and circles over my belly and chest—everywhere but my breasts. So much so that every time he gets near them, I find myself pushing them up, yearning for his touch.

The sensation sets off tingles in all directions.

He leans down to my belly and kisses it gently, then blows on it, and strokes it again. I giggle and he smiles. He comes up and kisses my lips, then asks if this is okay. I nod, and he takes one of my breasts in his hand.

This guy is driving me crazy, playing, making me feel my desire so hotly. I push my breast into his hand.

He carries on with his patterns in his slow and gentle manner.

It's glorious, sensual and all too much. I can feel myself yearning for his touch between my legs. He runs his hands over my thighs and I arch towards him.

He brings his hand back to my breasts and surprises me when he finally makes contact with my nipples. He leans down and kisses my breasts. There's so much desire racing around my body, I'm half expecting to see steam. His steady pace is making me wild.

'Is this okay?' he asks again, and I want to shout, '*What does it look like?*' But I manage a quick nod and close my eyes, sinking into the pleasure.

He runs his finger from my collarbone down to the top of my pubic bone and back again. Over and over.

Slowly, slowly he finds his way between my legs. He keeps kissing my nipples as his fingers gently discover me. It feels like he's creating this triangle of intense pleasure between the three most sensitive parts of my body. I move with him, responding ecstatically to his touch. He takes me to the edge and holds me there, suspended. My head is arching back and I feel so open and wild. When my body starts to shake and release I lift my head and look into his eyes. *Wow.* It's amazing, and scary—*big*—letting him see all of me. Letting myself be totally vulnerable.

I snuggle into him for a bit, catching up with myself—feeling the gorgeous intimacy of it all.

When I sit up, my shyness threatens to overwhelm me but instead I let my lust take over and enjoy his gaze upon my nakedness. He sits up too and we start kissing. Soon, we're kneeling together, our bodies pressed against each other. My hands dance across his back.

I push against him and he returns the pressure. I can feel his hardness and want to touch him. I gently explore the length of him, my fingers stopping at his balls, tentatively exploring first one, then the other, then both. The skin is slightly ribbed and they are cushiony—the complete opposite of what they're attached to.

He looks at me and smiles.

It's my turn to discover and play and his turn to breathe a lot deeper. He opens his eyes and we exchange a powerful look; love, lust, tenderness, passion. His lips look swollen and his cheeks are rosy. I hold his gaze for a long time, feeling bold as my hands become familiar with his body.

After a long and loving kiss I make him lie down and slowly, fumbling to find the right position and rhythm, I bring him to similar shudders of ecstasy. He holds me tightly as his body rocks against me. We lie for a long time looking at each other, smiling.

He rolls over and gets me some tissues. Then he takes a gulp of water from the bottle and bends down to kiss me, surprising me as he fills my mouth with cool water.

Stroking, smiling, kissing a little, the reflection of the flames dancing on our bodies. He gently pushes a lock of hair off my face. I close my eyes and smile sleepily.

Through the night we wake and discover each other's bodies again and talk more, then sleep again.

When daylight comes, I thank him for keeping his promise and tell him we're free of it now. He doesn't take much convincing. He's gentle, but it still hurts a little, momentarily. Our lips are grazed from so much kissing and parts of me feel quite sore, but it's a nice kind of sore. I wasn't expecting our bodies to fit so well together. Nature is amazing!

I want to stay here forever in this beautiful hut, high up on the hill. As the morning turns into afternoon, the horses start to stamp their feet and huff and puff in their shaky-lipped way, telling us it's time to go.

Neither of us wants to leave. If it weren't for the food and water and the horses, I could stay here forever …

We make love one last time before we go. As Jake is taking off the condom he looks up at me, concerned.

'Shit,' he says. 'It's got a tear in it.'

I sit up and inspect it. He's right.

'Shit,' I echo. I was the one who put it on. I must have done it wrong.

'When's your period due?' he asks.

'Umm …' I'm thinking, but my brain's stopped working. 'Everything's out of whack. My cycle's all over the place.' As I count back, I momentarily leave my body and see us sitting on the bed, connected, totally at ease now in our nakedness.

'I'm not certain,' I say hopefully. 'But I think it'll be okay.' I'm trying to convince myself too. A niggling shadow tries to settle over me but I push it away. There's nothing I can do about and I don't want this time to be clouded with worry. Anyway, I honestly can't remember.

As we make our way back to Tom and Sarah's farm, retracing our steps, a creeping melancholy steals over me. Maybe it's always this way when magic happens—there's a price to pay. But I don't want it to end. Every hoof fall is bringing us closer to our normal lives and I don't want to think about mine, even with the possibility of Jake in it now.

Thankfully the others aren't around when we get back. We stable the horses and Jake writes a note, then we head to Dione's on the scooter. I invite Jake to stay over. When he says yes, my lightness comes back and the melancholy withdraws. Is this what love is? Am I going to turn into a needy, neurotic person who only feels complete with her partner beside her?

'I'm starving,' says Jake, looking in the fridge, clearly feeling at home. I can see that he's disappointed.

'Hang on,' I say. 'I'll go look for eggs.'

'I'll come with you,' he says, and I smile. Maybe he's going to be needy and neurotic too.

The chickens took-took at us as we approach, telling me off for being away, hopeful for some food scraps. There have been slim pickings for weeks.

I pick a few salad leaves out of Dione's veggie patch and drop the green goodies for them as I open their gate.

When I go around to the laying box there are only two eggs.

'It's weird,' I say. 'We should be getting double the amount.'
Jake looks at the eggs and shrugs.

'Come on,' I say, looking back at his stunned face, surveying
the secret veggie garden. 'Let's go eat.'

I make an omelette and Jake uses up some salad leaves from
the garden, along with the last of the cherry tomatoes. The meal
is simple and delicious and his dressing is incredible. He is over
the moon about Dione's veggies—I can see she's gone up in
his estimation.

We take our cups of tea out to the sofa on the deck. The crick-
ets are still going. We talk for a while, then just sit, leaning into
one another, listening to the sounds of the night.

21

What?!

I know it sounds corny but 'falling madly in love' pretty much nails it.

I love being with him, listening to him, laughing and sharing my stories with him. Everything sparkles when he's here. And he's been here for weeks! We so happily wrap ourselves up in each other that we rarely leave Dione's house, our island—the place where all the pieces of ourselves come together, bit by bit, every curve and corner fitting perfectly. One time, I even surprise myself with a crazy thought—maybe it's good *not* having anyone else in my life, no-one to answer to or distract me from being with him.

Apart from Melissa, that is. But she lives so far away and brings only good distractions anyway, like wanting more designs! She came for a visit last week and brought the fabric swatches with her. They looked amazing! She'd heard that we'd been up to the shack, so she didn't seem surprised when Jake answered the door with me. She was so laid back, it felt like we'd been together all along. After she left, I tried ringing Lucy but it went straight to her message bank. I have so much to tell her. Maybe I'll call her again and leave a message saying I've fallen madly in love and she has to ring me back to find out more.

I've had a couple of freak-outs, too—just privately in the middle of the night—about falling too fast, too deep. But I shook the fear off purposefully, imagining a dog just out of the water, shaking itself. And woke Jake instead … with kisses.

I don't know how long this is going to last. I don't even want to think about it, I just want to *be*. With Jake. Life is sweet, delicious even—especially since the SIF seem to have dropped off the radar.

The only downer is money. I have three hundred and seven dollars left, not counting Dad's allowance, which I'm not going to touch. He's left a couple of messages since I got out, but I erased them as soon as I heard his voice. He chose not to help me when I was in there, so I'm choosing not to know him now.

I'm worried about not being able to meet the water delivery bill next month, and the food bills. I'm going to have to use Dione's spare cash supply. I'm pretty sure she wouldn't mind. She was always paid in cash.

Jake has started his weekend shifts for the lifesavers, and begins uni next week. I go with him to the beach to get my ocean hit, but I don't sit with him. I let him focus on the job while I get used to being on a different beach—this one is a long way from the ones I know. It's strange, as I sit looking at the water and making holes in the sand with my feet I can feel my body yearning for him, like my insides are being pulled towards him. I love it when he finishes and we zip-lock together again, complete in our connection.

We drive into town every week for water and food, and to check the mail, then head home to cook or walk or make love or listen to music.

◈

'What's that?' Jake asks, eyeing the official-looking letter in my hand. We're on the bench outside the mail boxes and my world has stopped. The MBD Centre wants me to report in. I've missed my last two donations.

My mouth goes desert dry. I haven't thought about my period for weeks. It's like something inside me switched off when the SIF were interrogating me—I thought it was my cycle that had stopped, but clearly it was my brain. How could I be so dumb?

All of a sudden I can see with horrible clarity all the missed signals from my body. Tender breasts and a funny, metallic taste in my mouth. A couple of mornings I've even felt a bit nauseous, but only fleetingly. How has this been happening right under my nose? Right *inside* me. I've been so wrapped up in Jake, nothing else has … I should have …

'You're frowning. What's up?'

I don't know what to say. I'm so scared of shattering the magic that's been growing around us.

'Ora?'

'I think I'm pregnant,' I blurt.

He looks at me. I stare straight ahead. For a long time, not knowing where to put any part of myself.

I feel him hear the words, resist them, question them. And struggle to accept them. He still hasn't said anything. I turn and look him square in the face.

'This is from the MBD Centre … they want me to go in for tests. It must have been up at the shack … We've been so careful.' I'm kind of stunned by the irony—all the times since, when we've stopped to make sure this wouldn't happen.

'Holy shit, Ora,' he says. 'Maybe you've got it wrong?'

I shrug. I don't know. I'm completely lost.

Finally he says, 'Let's go get a test.'

We head for the pharmacy. I wait outside in a haze of disbelief. This is not happening. Jake comes out empty-handed, and crest-fallen—he couldn't get far enough around the counter to grab one.

Ever since the Safety for the Future Program, people have to show ID and sign for a test, which is then followed up by a mandatory re-test at the doctors.

'There were too many people. And cameras,' he says, looking distractedly down the street.

I can't be pregnant. Please, please don't let me be pregnant.

'Dione may have a spare test in her gear,' I whisper.

We don't talk on the way home. I can't look at Jake. This is all his fault.

No. It's all *my* fault. I was the one who put the condom on. But he should have checked—I didn't know what I was doing. But it's not the first time a condom has torn.

It's the manufacturer's fault.

Maybe I'm not even pregnant. I am so scared.

I run up to the cottage. When I open the front door, Dione's scent hits me and I let out a sob. It's like she was here just a minute ago. I haven't set foot in this place since the garden birth.

As I step over the threshold, flashbacks from the woman's birth come thick and fast, and I reel under their weight. I feel sick.

There's hardly anything here. Dione must have got rid of everything before the SIF arrived. I'm shocked at how different it looks. She's made the basement look exactly like a spa—all evidence of the birthing centre is gone, like it never existed.

I sit on the floor with my back against the tub and cry until my insides hurt. This cannot be happening. I don't know how you can go from not feeling pregnant to feeling pregnant in the flicker of a summons.

Jake appears at the top of the steps. He comes down carefully, looking a hundred years older.

'I can't find a test,' I say. 'Dione's cleared everything out.'

Jake's looking around, taking in the 'spa', maybe imagining the births that have happened in the tub. He slides down beside me and puts his hand over mine.

'I've been working it out. We've been here for over seven weeks and you haven't had a period,' Jake says, sounding all practical. 'Can you remember when your last one was?'

'I've been trying!' I sound whiny.

I take a breath in and start again. 'I haven't had one since … a couple of weeks after I came out of the SIF. I remember being disappointed that Melissa wasn't at the MBD Centre. That was the last time.'

'Okay.' He sounds more hopeful. 'So that's at least, what … nearly three months ago?'

I nod. His hope is infectious.

'And if we *had* conceived, it could only have been when we were up at the shack, yes?'

I nod again.

'So it's much more likely that you've been stressed by all the SIF stuff and your period has stopped, which means maybe, you're probably not even fertile at the moment.'

'Yeah! Maybe. I remember hearing something about how women who've been traumatised can stop having their periods. And I hardly had any blood to give them last time.'

'Exactly,' Jake says triumphantly. He puts his arm around my shoulder and squeezes me close. 'So it's much more likely to be that.'

I nod again, relief flooding through me. The thought of not being pregnant is perfect. But then another thought strikes me.

'What about the MBD Centre? What if they test and I *am* pregnant? I'll have to go into one of the centres, Jake. I can't. I can't be locked up again.' My breath begins to catch.

'Shh,' he holds me tighter. 'Ora, it's okay. I read the rules on the back of the letter. You don't have to have a test yet. You're *allowed* to miss two donations per year. It's just that you haven't been twice in a row, so they've noticed. I don't think you'll be tested as long as you turn up next time with blood.'

'Are you sure? Mum was tested for not going twice in a row!'

'How many years ago was that? Five? Six maybe?'

I nod.

'They were just trying to prove a point. The scheme was new. Things are different now. If they question you, you can tell them you've been through some trauma—they'll know you were held by the SIF—and your period is all over the place. I think it will be okay. We just need to find you some blood.'

22

Evidence

'What?'

Melissa is looking at us like we're bonkers. We're sitting around Dione's table over cups of tea.

'I don't think I am, but just in case, if I was, I just … I'm not ready … well, for any of it, but I couldn't handle the SIF being involved right now. But I really don't think I am anyway, so I know it seems kind of odd …'

She doesn't say anything. Jake fills the silence.

'She just doesn't want to go anywhere near a doctor or anyone who's connected to the SIF, that's all.'

'So …' I sound so lame. 'I remember how you said you saved some blood for … for the earth each time. And I was … wondering if you'd …'

'Give it to you instead?'

I nod and look at my hands, clasped tightly in my lap. I feel like an irresponsible teenager sitting with a disapproving parent.

'It broke, okay?' God, I sound desperate.

'What?'

'The condom. It broke. It wasn't like we … weren't careful …'

Melissa holds up her hand. 'Whoa! Too much information. This is crazy. I can't believe it.' We sit in awkward silence. 'I'm only just getting over the shock of Sarah,' she says, shaking her head sorrowfully. 'And now there might be another baby on the horizon.'

'Sarah?' Jake looks concerned. 'What's up with Sarah?'

'You know she's back, right?' Neither of us knew. 'Jake, she's a real mess. I don't know what they did to her in there but she won't touch the baby. She won't pick her up. And poor Little Tom can't work out why his mum's turned into a zombie. I think she's got some kind of trauma thing going on. I shouldn't have left them today but I had to get away. It's doing my head in.'

Melissa keeps looking at me strangely. Maybe she's disappointed. Can't she see that this wasn't my fault? And we don't even know for sure.

She finally agrees to meet me at the MBD Centre. She'll let me know when. Any day now, she reckons.

᪥

Our bliss bubble has popped, leaving a rumbling, thunder cloud in its place. I feel completely trapped by the possibility that my life might be changed forever. Devouring movies is the only thing that helps, getting involved in other people's dramas and watching the screen instead of Jake's eyes.

We have our first fight and Jake storms off—or tries to—looking ridiculous on his moped. I'm glad he goes. It was just a joke. We've been competing to see who can make the best omelette, and when I make a comment about this one being his sloppiest yet— I'm just trying to connect—he loses it. He scowls at me and says he's sick of eggs. I say something terrible, like why doesn't he go back to his old life, and he storms out.

It's the first night we've been apart in over eight weeks and

I hate it. After my anger subsides I'm left with the familiar gaping hole, except now it's bigger and more treacherous than ever. I hardly sleep, listening and hoping that every sound is him returning.

He finally comes back in the morning and we cling to each other like we've just survived a war.

After that, things are good for a few days.

Even the trip to the MBD Centre goes well. Melissa is a bit frosty, but we get talking about her designs and it distracts us both. The official doesn't say a word when I hand over the pot. She just takes it, scans the barcode with all my details, puts it in the fridge and gives me a shower token. She doesn't even check me off against the computer.

Jake and I celebrate and stay up late, listening to music, like none of this is happening.

The next morning, I vomit. I get up to pee and my head swims and belly does a somersault, trying to flip its contents upwards, except there's nothing there. Jake hears me retching and comes in to see me heaving over the toilet. He doesn't say anything, just puts his hand on my back and stays with me.

The evidence is screaming at us, scrawling black paint all over the walls.

I make my way back to bed and burrow under the covers. The maybe has just turned into a most bloody likely. I can't be. I *cannot* be.

Jake cuddles me through the covers and asks if I want him to stay, but I need to be alone.

I hold my tears in until he's left for uni.

I cry for most of the day. Every time I stop, another thought arrives, sparking a fresh torrent of tears. My life is over before it's begun. I'm too young! I've had so little fun.

I want my mum.

My pillow is sodden and my throat hurts from sobbing.

Maybe I'll miscarry from all the crying.

I don't want to be pregnant.

Where is Dione? Please don't let her be dead. I need her. Do I really have lots of cells multiplying inside me? It isn't possible. How can my body sustain a new life?

I need to vomit again.

Later, after hunger drives me to the kitchen, I'm standing against the bench chewing a dry cracker when I see my sketchpad, abandoned on the sideboard. The tears begin again. What about my art? I'm supposed to be choosing a course, building my portfolio, not moping about in my t-shirt and undies, contemplating the prospect of being a mother.

With a surge of anger, I grab a charcoal stick and strike it over the paper, again and again until it breaks and crumbles into pieces. I get another and make a frenzied mess of chaotic black lines as I howl out my rage and confusion.

I stomp back to bed and toss and turn for hours. What would it be like to have a baby in my arms? My baby. Jake's baby. It's the first time I've let myself hold the thought, like the tiniest bud between my fingertips. Then I flick it away and fall into confusion again, more tears and finally an uncomfortable sleep.

Jake wakes me up by sitting on the bed beside me. I open an eye and see him holding the sketchpad.

'Ora, this is incredible.'

I've no idea what he's talking about. I can barely see, my eyes feel so swollen. It looks like an ugly black mess of hate to me.

'Can you see it?'

I sigh and sit up and try to see what he's seeing.

'There,' he points to the darkest part. 'It's an eye.'

I look a bit longer and then goose-bumps prickle along my arms.

'And here,' he points to a tail. 'And here, these are wings.' The eyes are unmistakeable. The dragon is here in the room with us.

I am speechless. As if I'm not half mad with fear and confusion already!

It suddenly dawns on me that this is the final piece of evidence. I truly am, without a doubt, pregnant. And somehow this dragon has something to do with it.

'I'm pregnant Jake,' I say, looking at the picture.

He looks at me briefly, then back to the dragon.

'I know,' he says quietly.

The longest silence stretches between us. He's waiting for me to say something. I'm relieved he's not asking what 'we' are going to do. It is about him too, but it's my body.

With a new life growing inside it.

A solitary tear rolls down my cheek.

He's keeping a respectful silence. Out of love, I think.

'If I have this baby,' I start slowly, 'I'll be only nineteen.' His eyes widen slightly, and he nods briefly in acknowledgement.

'If I don't have this baby it will be a huge, almighty relief,' I say, needing to laugh. He joins in, but it's hollow. 'And ... it will feel like something between us has been lost forever ...'

Where did that come from?

We can't look at each other. Too abruptly, unexpectedly, there's something real growing out of what we've shared. How would it feel to scratch that out? What would it mean?

'I'm not talking physically. I mean ... energetically ...' I still can't look at him, or explain properly. 'And then there's the physical side. The actual getting rid of it. We'd have to find someone who would help us and risk more SIF stuff.'

'Ora,' he says quietly, 'I don't know if I'm ready to be a father.'

'Of course you're not ready,' I snap. 'Neither of us is *ready*. This wasn't in our plans. This was the last thing either of us wanted.' I pause. More tears are welling as feelings of loss surge up. Loss of our freedom; the easy joy we've shared.

'I just don't get it,' I say. 'What are the chances of something like this happening? How many times do condoms rip? And what are the chances of getting pregnant, even when they do? And what are the chances of getting pregnant the very first weekend you make love in your entire life? Is that it? Is that all the fun I get before I have to become a mother? Is that all the fun *we* get?'

Jake looks at me. There's tenderness in his eyes. Pain.

'Say something.'

'There's too much going on in my head! I don't know what to say.' He pauses. 'I want it and I don't. I'm mad and I'm elated. I want to talk about termination and I don't. I want to be a dad and do a better job of it than mine did. And I don't. Because what if I can't? How would we manage? What about uni? What about *your* life? There are too many questions, Ora. I don't know the answers.' He trails off.

We sit for ages, side by side, not moving, trying to make sense of this wild card that life has thrown at us. He moves slightly and his body brushes my nipple. A spark flies through me and the promise of temporary relief alights in my body. I move to sit astride him and kiss him slowly, first on both eyelids and then all over his face. By the time I reach his lips we're off, eager to lose ourselves in each other and get away from the responsibility piling up on our shoulders.

In amongst our passion, he pauses about to reach for a condom, but I motion for him to carry on and he does. It's the sweetest moment letting him come inside me, looking into his eyes, allowing all of him in me. Seconds later, an overwhelming *yes* rushes through me—that inner voice again. This time I'm listening.

Later, much later, as we lie in the darkness, I realise there have been far too many endings in my life. I know it's the least sensible thing in the world, but I'm not going to initiate another. I'm not going to have something else to lament the loss of.

I am over grief.

And I am starting to want this baby.

23

Gumnut

'm letting the reality sink into my being. My morning sickness continues, driving out any residual doubt.

Jake tapes my mess of charcoal to the kitchen wall and spends a lot of time in front of it, drinking coffee. I don't say anything but I can see him sinking lower under the weight of this new future. It's like his heart grows heavier each day under the dragon's watchful gaze. Every now and then I catch him looking at me. I can't read what he's thinking.

A few mornings later, after vomiting a million times, I go into the kitchen and the dragon is gone. My heart misses a beat, but then I see it on top of the fridge, rolled up neatly with an elastic band.

'Good morning,' Jake arrives through the back door holding eggs. 'Scrambled or fried?' He kisses me as he goes by.

'Neither,' I say, as a wave of nausea dares me to run back to the bathroom. Instead I sink into one of the chairs, concentrating on the table's cool wood under my hands.

Jakes eyes are twinkling and he looks like he's about to start whistling.

'What's up with you?'

'Well, after mourning my youth and freedom and seeing endless years of heaviness and responsibility ahead, I've decided to get on with it and come around to the idea of being a dad.'

Before I know it I'm in his arms, hugging him. We look at each other and start laughing—madly—and do a silly dance. Waves of elation roll through me—it's going to be okay. More than okay— he's happy! As we spin around, the worries and the fears fall away and it's just us, in this moment.

Three!

Much later, the weight returns, but it isn't as heavy. We spend our days jumping between parallel universes—denial, where we just carry on like it will always and only be the two of us. And then acceptance, where we get serious and wonder what life will be like with a baby.

The day we decide to move into Dione's bedroom is one of our responsible days. Her bed is so much bigger than mine. Jake suggests it gently, pointing out that neither of us is sleeping well. I feel a bit weird agreeing, like I'm accepting Dione's gone. Forever.

'It'll be better for you *and* the baby.'

He's feeling all paternal after our visit to Tom and Sarah's.

'Sarah's still in a state though, isn't she?' Jake says, clearly still bruised after she shouted at him.

'I don't think she liked your comment,' I venture, gently.

'All I said was, "You're looking better"!'

'You hit a nerve. She feels so bad about not connecting with the baby in the beginning.'

'But they're connecting now! I thought that was worth noting.'

I shrug.

'She was so negative, Ora. All that stuff about the Program! It was like she was trying to scare us.'

'You don't know what she's been through.'

'Neither do you.'

'I think I know a bit more than you.'

'She wouldn't stop talking about the violent births. And the drugs. It was doing my head in. How could she even know if she was so drugged out?'

'She's been really traumatised, Jake. And from my experience of the SIF, I can believe it.'

'The Programs aren't run by the SIF, Ora.'

'Huh!'

'What does that mean?'

We've started to raise our voices.

'I don't want to talk about this now.' He looks shocked that I'm shutting him down.

'But we need to talk about it, Ora.'

'I'm going for a walk.'

'But it's dark.'

I grab my jacket off the chair.

'We need to make a decision about where—'

'Won't be long.'

Apart from spending time outside, I want to be in bed a lot. Maybe it's my brain trying to get used to the idea of being pregnant or maybe it's my body making me rest, but the place where I'm happiest is snuggled up in bed, sometimes sleeping, sometimes thinking. I've never thought seriously about having a baby before—I'm still getting used to having a boyfriend!

I'm also mourning my alternate future. It's like a chasm that opens up sometimes, and there's no way across to the other side— a beautiful field of dreams where my artist's life was meant to be, lost forever.

The sea is still my balm and I go there as much as I can. I'm also gardening madly, turning hidden veggies into an art. I get a buzz out of creating new recipes from the food I've grown and a hit out of defying the SIF. More and more, I understand where Dione was coming from. Maybe it's got something to do with having been inside *and* survived. I'm not petrified of them anymore. Sure, I'm scared, but the fear isn't enough to stop me. Besides, the SIF visits are almost non-existent now. Apart from going to the MBD Centre with Melissa, I hardly spare them a thought.

Jake has nicknamed the baby Gumnut. We spend ages talking about our childhoods and laughing about what he'll be like as a dad and what sort of mum I'll be. I know we're living in the clouds, but the waves of grief have stopped knocking me over and it feels good. Me, Jake and Gumnut.

The first few times I feel the baby move it's vague, almost like a school of tiny fish zigzagging around inside me. I'm not sure it's real, it's so distant. Soon though, the unmistakeable feel of a gentle prod from inside becomes the starting point of many conversations between me and the baby. Sometimes I speak out loud, but usually it's a silent dialogue, me talking to Gumnut, him listening. I don't know why, but I think it's a he.

24

Thief

One cold, wintery morning when I go out to collect the eggs and find only one, I make a decision—to catch the thief. I know the chooks are still laying, I'm just not getting to the eggs in time. My guess is it's a raven or a rat, but I don't understand why there aren't any shells left lying around. I decide to film the hen house. When I know what it is, I can set a trap.

After a long search, I find the video camera in a box at the back of Dione's wardrobe. Luckily the old-fashioned charger is still with it. There's a tape inside with some footage of me and Holly on one of our visits. It gets me right in the heart when I watch it. And watch it and watch it. At the very end, there's a close-up of her. Looking into my sister's eyes takes me full circle, from feeling momentarily complete back to hollowed-out numbness.

When Jake gets home he finds me on the sofa, teary and morbid but kind of happy too. After he's pressed pause and held me for a while, he starts talking about the chickens. It's a good distraction. He coaxes me into making a short film where he and the chickens are the main characters. It's totally stupid, and exactly what I need.

We decide to tape the camera to one of the branches above the chicken coop. I'm just about to go up the ladder when Jake does his, 'Let me do it, you're pregnant' thing. A couple of times when I've gone to lift something he's gently placed his hand on my arm and taken it from me. Mostly I like it—he's doing it in a loving way.

Sure enough, the next morning there are only two eggs waiting for me. I drag the ladder out and, pen-knife in hand, climb up to the branch. Just as I'm cutting the tape the ladder starts to wobble. I call out as I start to fall. My hand grabs onto the tree and I cling on with all my might until the ladder is still again. What a wake-up call! I have to remember there are two of us now.

Eventually, finally, I'm sitting in front of the laptop with the camera rigged up.

After a few seconds I switch it to fast forward. In the middle of a yawn as I debate getting something more to eat, a movement on the screen catches my eye. I press rewind.

What I see next sends me into a complete spin. Shock and disbelief; certainty, fury, elation. The shadowy figure that emerges on the screen isn't an animal. It's Dione.

My mouth is dry and I start to feel nauseous. There are a hundred questions racing through my mind.

Jake is as shocked as I was, and has to watch the scene a few times to let it sink in.

'All the hours I've spent worrying about her, fretting, longing for news. Any news. And she's been here all along! Stealing eggs, and half the veggies from the garden, no doubt. Why didn't she let me know she was here? I don't understand, it's not like I would've—'

'Ora,' Jake interrupts. 'Can I jus—'

'I know she worries about safety but she goes over the top with the protection thing. Maybe she was thinking the less I knew the better. But all the sa—'

'Ora!' Jake says firmly. I stop talking. He looks worried. 'I just need to think.'

'What about? It's simple. We're going to spring a trap and catch her.'

'And the SIF?' he asks.

'What d'you mean?'

'C'mon, Ora. They're still sniffing around. D'you want to get taken in again?'

'They stopped watching this place weeks ago. I should know. I'm the one here all the time.'

'They want Dione and they won't rest until they've got her. Why d'you think she's kept herself hidden all this time?' He pauses. 'She's not stupid, Ora.'

'What? And I am?'

'That's not what I said.'

'I thought you'd be on my side!'

'It's not about sides!'

'Don't you understand how I'm feeling?' I ask with a shaky voice.

He looks like he's going to fire some comment back but takes a deep breath instead. 'I'm just taking it in. This is big—it changes everything. Things were starting to feel really good. Not having to think about the SIF all the time. Just living ... Now I'm going to have to go on hyper-drive again.'

We sit for a while in silence, the righteous wind seeping out of my sails. What Jake says is true. Everything is about to change. My thoughts flit from us to Dione. I start to see Dione's point of view more clearly, remembering the danger she's in. The danger we're in.

'I'll have to move out,' Jake says after a big sigh.

'What?'

'I'm sleeping in her bed, Ora.'

'She won't care!' I cannot believe what he's just said.

'We haven't even asked her.'

'She hasn't been here to ask! The first sign of trouble and you're bailing?'

'Of course not!'

I move to the other end of the sofa and glare at him.

'I can't believe you're talking about leaving. We're having a baby, in case you've forgotten!'

'I didn't mean leave YOU!'

Here is another man bailing on me. All the pain of Dad not being around surfaces and I fling it all at him. Jake shouts back, defending himself, saying I'm off with the fairies half the time and how dare I accuse him of bailing when all he's done is stick by me. We rant and rave and I say all sorts of things I don't mean. The pent-up stress of the baby and the news of Dione's return is swirling in the room. I'm just taking a breath to launch another barrage when I feel a third presence in the room. I look to the doorway and there, standing quietly, looking out of place in her own home, is Dione.

'The ladder,' she gestures to the garden. 'I guessed something was up so I peeked through the window ... saw you both watching ...' She trails off and points half-heartedly at the laptop.

Jake stands up wide eyed. He looks like he doesn't know whether to shake hands with Dione or run. I want to laugh. Then Dione and I lock eyes. The element of surprise is all hers. I could hit her. Instead I just sit mutely, concentrating on the dirt under my nails. She moves into one of the armchairs, lowering herself carefully.

Jake sits too.

Nobody says anything. Jake clears his throat a couple of times, as if he's going to speak but thinks better of it.

Eventually I blurt out, 'Shame you only show yourself when you have to!' My voice is all wrong. Yowly.

No-one says anything.

'Have you forgotten your manners, Dione?'

She looks at me, sorrow and fatigue pulling at her features. I can see her searching for the right words but I steam in before she says anything.

'I know you've met Jake before. We've been sleeping in your bed. I hope you don't mind but I thought you were dead. We're having a baby in December, in case you didn't get that bit when you were spying on us through the window.' Tears prick my eyes. I hate her and I hate myself. 'I decided to start a new family seeing as mine are all dead or useless … But Jake has just told me he's moving out …' I'm trying to hold it together but failing miserably.

Jake moves in beside me and goes to put his arm around me but I push him away. He stays close anyway. Dione sits quietly, taking us both in. She looks shocked.

'Oh, Ora,' she says finally.

She gets up and comes to sit on the arm of the sofa so I'm sandwiched between her and Jake, who whispers that he isn't going anywhere, and puts his arm around me. Dione leans in, holding my right hand in both of hers, squeezing it gently. I close my eyes, wanting to believe I'm safe.

We sit for ages.

'What a mess I've made of everything,' Dione says eventually, sounding far away.

I look at my aunt properly—she looks old. Her skin is all pasty and her eyes are dull. I wish she didn't look so feeble.

'Where have you been?' I ask. She can't have seen sunlight for months.

'Up at the B&B.' She smiles cautiously, pausing to see if I'm ready to hear. I raise my eyebrows in a question.

'I never showed you but there's a small space under the garage that the first owner dug out. The entrance is via one of the storage cupboards in the laundry room. I don't know what the crazy guy was thinking but he saved my life. The SIF had no idea.'

'You can't have been living in a hole all this time?' Jake sounds incredulous.

'No.' Dione smiles, looking tired again. 'I spent days down there initially, when the SIF were here all the time. But when their searches dropped off I started coming out more, spending time in the cottage, keeping well back from the windows. I could always hear them coming. You almost caught me a few weeks ago Ora, when you burst in.'

So that's why it felt like Dione had just been there.

'I only come outside at night,' she says, moving back to her chair. 'And I keep close to the cottage unless I have to come down here for food.'

Dione looks at me for a long time and I don't say anything. Then I guess what she's thinking.

'The condom broke,' I say shortly. I want her to know—it's important. She nods.

'December?' she asks about the due date.

'December.' I can see a mixture of disappointment and concern in her eyes.

'Is it okay with you if we carry on living here?' Jake asks tentatively.

'Of course,' Dione replies. 'Everything needs to stay the same—we've got to keep the SIF away.'

'They're not getting their hands on my baby,' I put my hands protectively over Gumnut.

Dione smiles.

'I'm beginning to understand,' I say. 'About why you did what you did. And the mothers, too ... I *still* think you're all crazy!' I smile, holding my belly again. 'But everything's changing ... The thought of someone having power over him—'

'Oh, it's a "him", is it?'

'Gumnut,' Jake chimes in, grinning widely. 'But …' he clears his throat. 'We haven't decided where we're having him yet.'

'Not in the Program,' I say vehemently, surprising myself. I say it again more gently.

Jake looks shocked, then stands up and stretches. 'I think I might get some air.' He nods at Dione as he goes out.

More silence.

'So … are you going to stick around?' I ask, feeling shy but desperately needing her to say yes.

'You betcha,' she says, sounding more like her old self.

Warm relief flushes through me. She starts chuckling.

'What?' I ask.

'Well, it's just that old patterns die hard … every time I decide to quit being a midwife, something happens and I can never say no.'

'What? That's so unfair! That's like putting all your activist stuff on *my* shoulders!'

'I didn't mean it like that.'

'I still have to forgive you for getting me into trouble with the SIF!'

'You're right, Ora.'

'And for disappearing on me!'

'You're right again.' She's looking so old. 'I just wanted you to understand, that's all. I won't say another word.'

25

Dad

By the time Jake returns I'm yawning. Dione leaves, telling us not to go to the cottage under any circumstances—she'll come for a visit soon. Taking a handful of books off her shelves, she steals out into the night.

The atmosphere is cold between Jake and me as we get ready for bed. I crack a joke about him sticking around after all, but it lands flat and he keeps his back to me as he curls up for sleep. But I wrap myself around him and cuddle in anyway.

In the morning when we wake, we're entwined like usual, and we spend a long time just looking. Not talking, but reading each other's eyes. Finally, he says, 'I'm not ready to share you.'

I don't know what to say. I'm tempted to make another joke, one about being a piece of meat who isn't ready to be carved up, but I don't.

'That's an interesting way of putting it.'

'Last night was weird. I'm not used to someone else being around. And what about when the baby comes?'

'You're worried about sharing me with the baby?'

He just looks at me.

'It's not about sharing me, Jake,' I'm trying to be gentle. I don't want to argue again.

'I'm just used to having you to myself.' He sounds grumpy, and now my hackles are rising.

'Well, excuse me for having *one* other person in my life and another due in December!'

'I'm just telling you how it's already changed.' He sounds sad. 'It was sweet. What we had.'

'Yeah, and we'll still have it most of the time. It's not like Dione's going to come out every minute, dancing with bells on.'

He smiles and my heart melts a little.

'I've felt so loved, these past few weeks, living with you. It's been perfect. Apart from missing Dione and the odd SIF car going by …'

'Yeah, you're right.'

'But nothing lasts, Jake. Everything dies.'

'No need to be dramatic.' He holds me tightly.

'It does, though.'

'Can we talk about the birth instead?'

I'm still not ready for this conversation.

'I know you said last night you didn't want to go into the Program but I think we should talk about it.'

My mobile rings and I jump up to get it, grateful for the interruption. I don't recognise the number.

'Ora!' Dad's gravelly voice booms, stilling my blood. 'Are you at the house?'

My heart's pounding in my chest—the last call from him heralded the SIF.

'Yes,' I manage.

'Great! I'm at Adelaide Station. I'll be there as soon as I can. My battery's dyi—' And he's gone.

My legs are jelly. I'm totally blank.

Jake comes up behind me and hugs my belly. He takes the phone and puts it back on the dresser. 'Who was that?'

'Looks like you're going to have to carve me up into a few more pieces.'

'What?'

'That was Dad. He'll be here in a couple of hours.'

'Shit!'

I want to run.

'What d'you want me to do?' he asks.

'How should I know?' Panic strangles my voice. A few weeks ago, I decided I was never going to see my dad again. Now he's on his way here, like he's come for a holiday.

My eyes scan the room, searching out an answer on the walls. 'His battery died. I can't even call him back to tell him not to come.' I move towards the door.

'Where are you going?'

'To ask Dione what to do.'

'Don't go up there!' There's an edge to his voice.

I pause.

'She can't help us. We've got to sort this out ourselves.'

I sit down at the kitchen table.

And that's where we are when the doorbell rings. We've both dressed, and forced some food down—Jake makes me eat, saying it'll help me think straighter.

Jake gets up, gesturing for me to stay at the table.

'He's my dad, my responsibility.' I stand up.

'Let me open the door and introduce myself.'

I shake my head.

'It's a guy thing,' he sounds determined.

'But—'

'You have to let me.'

My throat goes dry and I sit again, watching Jake's back as he goes. I wish I could see Dad's face, expecting me but getting Jake. But at the same time, I don't want to see him at all.

I wish this wasn't happening.

Jake starts to speak but stops to clear his throat. Then he says clearly, 'I'm Jake, Mr James. Ora's partner.'

They must be shaking hands. I hear Dad use his work voice. 'Douglas James.'

What? He never calls himself Douglas! I wish I could see his face.

I stand up, push in my chair and wait, barely remembering to breathe. They walk into the kitchen, Jake first, then Dad. Jake comes around the table and stands beside me, putting his arm around my waist—another guy thing that isn't lost on me.

Dad and I look at each other. I'm glad the table is between us. He looks smaller.

I nod a hello. 'Dad,' is all I can manage.

His eyes fill with tears. I am so not ready for him to cry. I grip the back of the chair.

I can see he's struggling. He forces his lips into a smile but fails miserably as they curl back into sorrow. The tears slide down his cheeks and he furiously brushes them away.

I start to move towards him but stop myself. I vowed never to see him again.

Suddenly Snake whispers from nowhere, making me start. 'Ora, your mother would want you to give him a chance.'

Oh, piss off!

'Look at him, Ora. He's a wreck. He's had no-one. NO-ONE. No Dione. No Jake. No-one.'

Why did he have to show up now?

His shoulders are heaving and quiet sobs are forcing their way out. I don't want to hear my crazy snake's voice but my feet are moving towards him.

I look at Jake. Why doesn't he say something?

'Does anyone want a cup of tea?' he asks, picking up the kettle.

I take another step but I don't want to. But he's my dad. Another reluctant step. I want to stay this side of the table. My own tears are streaming now. I'm at the end of the table and as I move around it, he takes two strides to reach me and we hug fiercely.

'I hate you, Dad,' I whisper through uneven sobs. 'I *hate* you,' I say louder, and punch him on the back. 'Why didn't you come and get me?'

'I know, love,' he says into my hair. 'I hate me too.'

He smells of home.

He lets out a deep sound. Relief, maybe. And grief. I can hardly breathe.

'I'm pregnant, Dad,' I say quickly, into his neck. His body goes still. He releases me a little and then unravels himself fully, searching my face for answers.

His eyes fly to Jake, who's very busy with his back to us, making the tea. I can see Dad gearing up to shout at him.

'Dad!'

He looks back at me, confusion all over his face.

'Be nice.' The air between us goes cold. 'You have no right to say *anything*, but if you do, make sure it's positive, or you can go back to where you came from. Do you know how long the SIF kept me in that cage for? You're luck—'

'Here's your tea, Ora.' Jake passes me a cup and stands between us, looking at me intently. I snatch the cup, spilling half the tea.

'Douglas,' Jake says, passing Dad his mug.

Dad seems bewildered. He looks down at the tea and then back to Jake.

'Doug. My name's Doug.'

I empty out a big breath of air and sit down at the table. Dad takes the seat next to me and Jakes sits opposite.

No-one speaks. What is there to say? Dad abandoned me three times: First when I was living with him, second when I was living with Dione, and third—the worst—when the SIF locked me up. I don't trust myself to speak.

Eventually he starts mumbling.

'After that call from the SIF, Ora, I could tell you were up to no good.'

I begin to protest but Jake presses his toes into my foot under the table, pleading with his eyes for me to listen.

'I jumped in the car and drove halfway across the country to get here,' he continues. 'But the road and the night got me thinking and by the time dawn arrived I'd turned back. I needed to be sure of the facts … When I got home, I rang an old mate who used to work for the SIF and asked him to find out more. I also tried Dione's phone a hundred times. By the time he came back to me, they'd already got you.' Dad looks into his tea with laser-like intensity—for a moment I think his cup might explode. 'And God knows what's happened to Dione.'

'My friend told me how to play them, Ora. It was so hard—to sit there and pretend I didn't care. They'd ring all hours, morning and night, goading me, telling me what you'd done. I broke my hand after one of the calls.' He holds up his misshapen fingers.

'But I just had to sit there and make them believe I didn't care. I took his advice because I was in a nightmare and needed a lifeline.' He looks at me hard. There's so much pain in his eyes. It's a different kind of pain though, not like his grief for Mum and Holly. This pain is alive and kicking.

'And I didn't know whether you'd done all those things or not. When I heard you were out, I was paralysed. I was so scared you'd turned into some kind of activist monster.'

I stare into my cup. Dione's kitchen clock is ticking very loudly. In the swirl of confusion, no words form.

'I tried ringing a few times but you never answered.' He sniffs.

I can feel myself warming a little, melting the icy shards of despair that formed while I was locked up.

'I tried Dione too.' He looks at me intently, 'Where is she, Ora?'

My instincts start screaming at me. Dione is not safe with him here!

'I don't know, Dad,' I lie. Just like that. The words slip off my tongue as easily as if I'm back in the interrogation room. I press my foot hard on top of Jake's, willing him to back me up. Dad looks at him and he nods a curt little nod.

'Stupid bitch.'

'Dad!'

'She could've got you killed. I hope she's fallen down a hole and died.'

'Shut up!' I yell.

'She got you into all of this.' He points at my belly.

'She didn't get me pregnant, Dad! You don't give a shit about me. You wouldn't even speak to me on the phone. You *left* me in there.' Jake can't stop me now. I'm off, the ragged memories of the SIF tearing me in half.

'*She* was the reason you were in there!'

'It's never been about me, has it Dad? Even when I was at home, you'd stopped seeing me, hearing me. You didn't care about *me*. Too wrapped up in your own pain. I bet it was easy leaving me in there. You probably didn't even notice.'

'Ora,' Jake begins. I ignore him and shout harder.

'Dione *cares* for me—for *me*—she *cares*! You've got your head so far up your arse that you wouldn't know how to pull it out even if you wanted to! When Mum and Holly died, you might as well have died too!'

Dad looks horrified. I sneer.

'The SIF got you to come here, didn't they? Your crying act almost had me ...' I can't believe it. 'They asked you to find Dione, didn't they? Well, I hope your choice was worth it, Dad, because you've lost me now.' My voice drops to a whisper. 'Now you've lost everyone. All your family, Dad, your whole family … gone.' I stop and gulp down a sob, catching my breath.

Jake sits, totally at a loss, and Dad doesn't look much better. I turn and run, slamming the door, and fling myself onto my old bed. I can barely breathe for crying.

I hear the car going down the driveway and hope Jake is taking Dad to the station. But then Jake comes in—Dad has gone into town in the ute. He'll be back later.

'I don't want him here, Jake. He's working for the SIF.'

He snuggles up to me on the single bed and neither of us talks for a long time.

'I know he's hurt you, Ora, but I can't believe he'd do that.'

'He wants to get at Dione. He doesn't see things like you.' I'm getting wound up again.

'He's pissed off with Dione, sure, but he came here for you, Ora.' Jake looks at me earnestly. 'Seems like he's really trying.'

'Hmph,' I reply.

'At least he's not drowned himself in the bottle,' Jake says bitterly.

'Grief or the bottle, what's the difference?' I reply, just as bitter.

'A lot,' Jake says.

'They both suck you dry, Jake.'

'Yeah, but you choose grog. You don't choose grief, it chooses you.'

'You still get to choose how you respond,' I argue. 'And Dad chose to get so swallowed up by it that he forgot about me.'

'He's making a different choice now, isn't he?'

'Too late, Jake. Too bloody late.'

He's looking at me with despairing eyes. 'I just see a man who wants his daughter back.'

'Will you take him to the station?'

'Really?'

I nod, feeling fresh tears brewing. I have to send Dad away. Protect Dione.

I stay in bed. After an hour or so Jake brings me a sandwich before going to do some study. When Dad returns, I hear him and Jake murmuring, then footsteps and a knock at my door. I pull the covers over my head and curl into a ball.

The door opens gently.

'Ora?' Dad says. I hold my breath. 'Ora.' He comes in and stands beside the bed.

Is that his hand on my shoulder?

'I'm going to go. I don't want to but ... if you really don't want me here ...'

I squeeze my eyes shut, trying to block out his voice.

'I'm sorry, love,' he pauses. 'Guess I stuffed up pretty bad.'

There is a long silence. He takes his hand away, 'You know where I am, Ora.' He sounds empty.

The door clicks shut. Soon after, the engine starts. My tears flow again. The little girl in me wants to run after him, call him back. But I don't.

26

Letter

I feel flat for days. Even Dione's visits don't lift me.

I know they're both worried, but I can't help it. I'm being tossed about like tumbleweed, riddled with guilt one minute—Mum would not be pleased—hateful and blaming the next. Traumatic flashbacks to the SIF. Doubt. Maybe he isn't in league with them ... But what if he is? What if he tells them I'm pregnant?

Jake tries to distract me—everything from picnics to breakfast in bed to surprise movie nights. None of it works.

'D'you realise you're doing exactly the same thing as your dad?' he says one day when he gets home from uni and I'm still in bed.

'What do you mean?' I ask.

'You judged your dad for "choosing" to get lost in his grief.' I don't like his tone. 'And now you're doing the same.'

'What do you mean?' I repeat.

'You're choosing to get lost inside yourself.'

I'm dumbfounded.

'I feel like you don't see me anymore, Ora. All you do, *all* day, is lie here like a vegetable. It's been weeks! You're completely self-absorbed.'

He's working himself up.

'How d'you think Gumnut is going to like having a zombie for a mother? Maybe we should find another family for him, once he's born?'

A whoosh of heat courses through me and my temper catches ablaze. How dare he strike out at me about being a bad mother? The baby isn't even here yet! What does he know about babies? And he certainly doesn't know about mothers—he behaves like he doesn't even have one!

He calls me disengaged and self-pitying, says that I'm too afraid to think about the birth.

We stab and strike at each other with our words. We're so blind with fury that we're just screaming, not listening. The pain and confusion that have been festering inside me come out in a torrent. I stop making sense and become a mass of profanities, shouting and crying.

It's exhausting.

Spent, I sit back on the bed and close my mouth. Jake is silent too. Then I take in a huge gulp of air and blow it out again, puffing up my cheeks. And another gulp, like I'm coming up for air.

I'm totally finished with being a zombie. All this heat has woken me up. I'm alive again.

I look at Jake and grin at him. He comes over to hug me and I squeeze him tight.

'God, I've missed you,' he says.

'I'm sorry, Jake,' I reply, marvelling at his ability to let things drop so quickly. And then, after a long while, 'I'm back, I promise.'

Dione looks relieved when she next comes to visit. She mentions the colour has returned to my cheeks.

As long as I don't think about Dad I'm okay.

Unfortunately I'm not that good at controlling my thoughts.

❧

We start to see more and more of Dione. She says she's totally over her own company. As the days slip into weeks and my belly begins to swell, we even start having dinner together. The SIF are busy on some water theft crackdown and none of us has seen or felt them around for months. Maybe they've finally forgotten about us.

Jake seems to like Dione, but I can tell he prefers it when it's just the two of us. He hasn't spoken again of 'sharing' me, or of the birth, but sometimes he's mega-grumpy for no reason.

One day, towards the end of spring, a letter arrives addressed to me. It has the government's official seal on it.

Here we go. I take a deep breath and slit open the envelope. It's a short letter, instructing me to report in weekly to the nearest SIF office—in the city—as a result of recent investigations into my 'case'.

Why now?

Will they notice Gumnut? How am I going to hide him? Why weekly? Why now? What's changed?

Dad?

Surely not … He couldn't possibly have …

I refuse to follow this thought any further, and for once my mind obeys.

Why can't my life ever settle down? Whenever I drop my guard and start to breathe normally, the SIF appear and everything turns to shit. I am so over being controlled by them.

Jake and Dione talk long into the night about a plan. I resume my blob-like state—staring into the distance. It probably looks like I've totally checked out, but inside I am frantic. I cannot go back to the SIF. They'll see Gumnut and lock me up and then take him away forever. I should have gone into the Program. What have I done?

'I think we should disappear,' Jake is saying.

'You keep saying that, Jake,' Dione says, exasperation creeping into her voice. 'But it's not that easy.'

'Well, at least I'm saying something.' Jake looks pointedly at me.

'Look what happened last time,' Dione says. 'Ora didn't exactly get very far.'

'But you didn't plan!' Jake's voice is getting louder. 'And you had no time. Of course she got caught. If we plan properly we can disguise ourselves, go interstate. Somewhere really busy where we can disappear into the crowd, like ... like the Gold Coast! I've never stayed in a hotel before.'

'You're crazy.' Dione smiles. Is she taking him seriously?

'Or we could go bush,' Jake says, sounding desperate. 'If we're clever enough and leave no tracks, they'll never find us.'

Dione shrugs. She is at least considering this.

'Is it too late to go into the Program?' I ask quietly.

'I'm not sure that Ora wants to have her baby in the middle of nowhere,' she says, completely ignoring me.

'You'll be with us, won't you?' Jake asks. 'You know what you're doing.'

'I want to go into the Program,' I say, louder this time.

'You're kidding,' Dione says, incredulous.

Jake speaks over her. 'How can you say that *now*? It's too late.'

'I can't lose Gumnut,' I say quietly.

'You've been to the MBD Centre too many times. They'll know you've been faking. I tried talking to you about this months ago!'

'I can't meet any SIF officers. I'll crack ...'

Dione and Jake look at me. There's a long silence.

'What date do you have to report in?' Dione asks finally.

'The third of November,' I whisper.

'In four days,' Jake says.

I can almost hear him thinking. He's working out whether four days is long enough to get away, far enough away from here.

'What if they want to examine me?' I say, feeling the panic rise again. 'If they do a check-up of some kind they'll see.'

'They won't do a medical, Ora,' Dione reassures me. 'They've got no reason to.'

'How do you know that? What if Dad's told them?' I say, finally naming my fear. I immediately want to swallow it back after the way they both look at me.

'Ora—' Jake starts.

'No way!' Dione cuts him off. 'There's no way your dad would dob you in.' She speaks slowly and clearly, making sure the words sink in. 'Me, maybe, but he's not going to put you at risk. He wouldn't.'

I just look at her.

'I've known him for years, Ora, and I know he would *never* put you in harm's way. That's just not who he is.'

I nod and decide to keep these particular fears to myself from now on.

'I think you're going to have to go in, Ora,' Jake says very gently, like I'm a jittery horse about to bolt. 'Just once.'

I shake my head fiercely. No way! 'What if they don't let me out again? What if they keep me there? I can't. I can't!' My eyes are nearly popping out of my head.

All I get back is silence and long stares.

'We just don't have enough time to plan, Ora,' Jake says. 'If we're going to take off we need to have a plan.'

'Fuck the planning!' I shout, fear frothing inside me. 'You're not the ones who have to go in there and face them. What do we need a plan for? Let's just get in the car and drive!'

'We'd need a different car,' Dione says quietly.

'Maybe we won't even go by car,' Jake says. 'Train or bus might be safer.' He goes quiet. 'Maybe Tom's got an old car he could lend us, or … a boat.' He starts to look excited. 'We could go by boat!'

'Wha—?' Dione starts to say.

'Tom's got an old boat in the barn. It's one of those sailor trailer ones, a twenty-five footer. She hasn't been out for years but I know her well. I grew up sailing her! Hey, we could sail to New Zealand!'

He looks like he's ready to party.

'I don't know anything about boats,' Dione says. 'Would a boat that size fit all three of us?'

'For sure! And have enough space for supplies. It'd need some work though. Some patching up and a good clean out.'

'How experienced are you at sailing?' Dione's looking interested.

'Very,' Jake replies. 'I sailed nearly every weekend for two years with Tom, Melissa and my sisters. We'd sail to different beaches and camp overnight. It was awesome.'

'It's one thing to sail around the coast and another to cross the Tasman,' Dione says. 'I've heard it can get wild out there.'

'You're right.' He slumps. 'If it was just me I'd do it. Can either of you sail?'

We shake our heads.

'Who am I kidding? The boat's not made to cross a wild ocean,' he says quietly.

'But there's nothing to stop us sailing around the coast,' Dione says. 'We could go to Queensland. I'm a quick learner, and if we follow the coastline and just go ashore for supplies, we'll have the perfect hiding place! As long as the SIF don't get wind of it, and we're not recognised.' Dione is looking deadly serious.

I am starting to like the idea too. If we have to disappear, we'll need to keep moving, and there'll be fewer people to worry about on the ocean. And there's nowhere I feel more at home.

Jake is picking up the phone, to ring Tom no doubt, but Dione stops him.

'Better play it safe. It's the weekend tomorrow. A trip up there would look like a normal visit.'

27

The Plan

Things move fast; much faster than my pregnant body can keep up with. I am consumed with fear.

Dione's decided to come with us to Tom and Sarah's; it makes sense to move her to the boat straightaway, even though it'll put Tom and Sarah in danger and they haven't even said yes yet. But it'll only be for a few days, and the SIF have no idea she was involved in Little Tom's birth.

On the drive up, she stows herself in the boot of the car. When we get there, Jake parks as close to the front veranda as he can, then opens the boot. Sarah and Tom nearly fall over when they see Dione climbing out.

'I knew you'd be right!' Tom booms as he strides over to give her a big hug, followed closely by Sarah, who has the baby in a sling. Melissa has Little Tom on her hip. He's grown so much.

Jake sounds very together when he explains our plan to them. They listen intently, nodding and agreeing. The warmth of their support is infectious and it melts some of my fear. Jake is in full action mode, his mind firing details as he goes over the minutiae of the plan. Listening to him makes me wish I could take him with me to the SIF.

Tom says there's a lot of work to be done on the boat. Dione volunteers to do it, if they don't mind her staying. They agree she'll clear out below deck first, so she can hide out down there for the next few days. Luckily the driveway is long enough to hear cars coming, and if visitors arrive by foot, Tom says his dogs will let them know.

My weekly appointments are scheduled for Tuesdays, so the plan is to be ready by next Friday. That way, when I don't turn up for the second meeting, we'll have a few days' lead on them.

'We just have to be careful when we put the boat in the sea,' Tom says. 'That'll be the most dangerous time for being spotted. There's no reason the SIF should even know I've got a boat, so the longer we keep that from them the better.'

We all signal our agreement.

'I reckon they won't be putting much time into you two, any-way. But they won't like it when you disappear on them. That'll make three of you.'

'What about the baby?' Melissa asks. She's been very quiet.

'What do you mean?' Jake says.

'The baby!' She points at my belly like we're all stupid. 'How does the baby fit into your plans to sail around the world? It's due in a couple of months.'

Everyone looks at me for an answer.

There's a horrible silence.

'It's ... too late to go into the Program,' I manage eventually.

'Thank God!' Sarah huffs.

'You're not going to have it on the boat?' Melissa asks, all self-righteous.

'We haven't got that far,' Jake says quietly.

'There aren't that many options Melissa, if you're outside the system.' Dione adds.

'But what if something goes wrong?'

Another silence. Melissa is speaking my own words from a few months ago.

'What if the baby di—'

'Shhh!' I say. 'I don't need your concern Melissa.'

'What if you—'

'Shut up!' I'm rattled. 'We need to focus on the trip right now, Mel.' She's looking at me like I'm nuts. 'What choice do we have? If I give myself up, they'll take the baby away.'

'But they might not.'

'I'm already on their blacklist. There's no way they'll let me keep him.'

Silence.

'Can we please just focus on the plan?' My voice is getting higher.

Melissa walks out of the room.

I feel so heavy all of a sudden. I want to slide off my chair, onto the floor.

Tom starts talking about the boat again, and soon they're back on track.

I manage to stay in my seat.

'So after today, we won't contact you,' Jake says. 'But I'll come up one night next week with all our stuff.'

'I'll buy your food for you, enough for the first couple of weeks,' Sarah says as she sets out knives and forks on the table. 'And we can put it straight in the boat.'

'Thanks, Sarah.' Jake smiles. 'Ora and I can get the bus into the city on the Friday, and then a train and a bus to the jetty later.'

'What about the chickens?' Dione asks.

'What?' Jake says.

'What'll we do with the chooks?'

'We'll just have to leave their door open and hope for the best,' Jake says. 'They might start roosting in the trees if they've got any sense.'

'Is there room on the boat?' she asks. She loves those chickens.

'Aren't you sick of eggs?' Jake looks perplexed.

I start giggling, but no-one else sees the funny side.

'I do have a large cage you could stick on the deck,' Tom says, eyes twinkling.

'Yeah, and how suspicious would that look to other boats?' Jake doesn't like his plans being tweaked. 'I'll put them in a cardboard box and bring them up here when I drop off our gear,' he says, sounding final. 'You won't mind a few more, will you?' Tom and Sarah shake their heads.

Dione opens her mouth to say something but thinks better of it. I can't stop laughing in a crazy, neurotic way. Everyone carries on like they don't notice, even though they're casting sideways looks at me, which just makes me laugh harder.

'The only bit that doesn't sit right is you meeting us at the beach. There are too many houses overlooking the beach,' Tom says a few minutes later. I've quietened down a bit and am just grinning now. 'I'd like to have you hidden in the boat before we put her in the water. That way it'll look like it's just me going for some night fishing.'

They talk some more and agree on a nature reserve on the way to the beach where Jake and I can wait. They know the roads well.

'Okay,' says Jake. 'If we think of anything else we'll have to save it for the night I bring up our gear.'

We are quiet as we eat the lunch Sarah has served. Melissa doesn't come back.

As we're leaving she appears.

'I'm sorry.' She's crossing her arms tightly across her chest.

'I thought *you* were the rebel,' I say to her, attempting a smile.

'Only about the little stuff. I can't believe you're doing this ...'

'Neither can I.'

We hug goodbye.

'Take care,' she says, looking sad.

❧

For the next three days, Jake is in another world. He spends a lot of time at the library, not wanting to be tracked on his own laptop, searching out good spots to moor along the coast. He also disappears into Dione's garage for hours, going through her camping gear. He keeps talking through plans and details and lists.

My stomach is constantly burning and my neck is so tight I can't look over my right shoulder. I am seizing up. I really need to share what's happening inside my head but Jake's too busy. I stomp around the garden and complain to the chooks instead. And to Gumnut.

I can't think about the birth. It's too far away.

The tent is still up the mountain. We can't bring ourselves to go up there but Dione has a good supply of gear at home. Mini-camping stoves, torches, sleeping bags. And a whole range of utensils.

I have far too much time on my hands. Worry and fear have wormed their way into my brain and are eating away at my cells, making room for more worms. Packing clothes and a couple of books takes me less than a morning. Sarah gave me a bag of stuff for Gumnut, but I can't look at it yet. Every time I attempt to project into the future, I only get as far as the SIF appointment.

I try on about thirty different outfits, desperately trying to work out which one shows the least amount of 'bump'. I spend hours looking in the mirror, side-on, front-on, side-on again.

The weather is still quite cold. I hope it'll be cool enough for me to wear my big sloppy sweater. It's bottle green and baggy enough to hide everything. With my long flowing skirt it looks okay—smart even.

I lie awake at night remembering the rat and the slug. My

blood chills as I replay their interrogations again and again. I can't stop. I hate them with every cell in my body. I take to praying—to who, I don't know—'Please don't let it be them, please don't let it be them.'

I do a drum journey several times a day. Lion and Snake appear without fail. Lion's quiet presence reassures me and Snake's words are both strengthening and annoying. Every time I meet them it's in a barren, rust-coloured land. It's totally flat and the only movement is the wind sweeping across the bare plains.

I need more ideas. How will I keep my cool in there? I ask Snake. *If it was just me it'd be okay, but what if they find out about Gumnut?*

'The more you worry, Ora, the worse it will be.'

I know that! But how … how do I stop worrying?

'Have you called on Dragon?'

Huh? I haven't thought of Dragon for ages.

'What do dragons guard, Ora?'

Treasure.

'What kind of treasure?'

All kinds. Snake can be so annoying. She's waiting for me to say more. *Jewels and gold and stuff.*

'Exactly. You need to ask Dragon for protection.'

As her words sink in I start to breathe more deeply. Of course! A quiet surge of strength and knowing washes through me.

I emerge from the drum journey with a plan. I'll need my candle. I also take the rose quartz crystal I bought in the city ages ago.

Jake is busy—no surprises there. I tell him I'm going for a walk to clear my head, which is kind of true. He barely acknowledges me anyway. Maybe I'll explain afterwards.

I walk up behind the cottage. The earth still feels damp from the morning dew. I don't walk for long, just far enough into the bush to feel alone. I stop at a large rock and place my candle and crystal on top of it.

I light the candle, trying to remember the ceremony I went to with Dione before Christmas, to celebrate the solstice. I face each of the four directions, welcoming them one at a time, and the elements too. I've never done anything like this, and it feels weird. But special.

Then I turn back to the rock, close my eyes and say out loud, 'Dear Dragon, I am calling to ask for your help. Tomorrow, when I go to the SIF, I need Gumnut to be safe. No-one can notice him. I just need to go in there, answer the questions without freaking out, and then leave. Please give me strength, dear Dragon, and come with me.'

I stop and listen. Nothing happens.

A bird flaps its wings in one of the trees, making me jump. I look around, half expecting to see Dragon. Then I close my eyes again.

'And if I get scared or lose it or start to give myself away, please will you help me? Gumnut is like gold to me and I know you protect gold. Please, will you protect him?'

I open my eyes to more silence. I don't have anything else to say. My heart is sinking. Where is she? I wait and I wait but nothing happens. Eventually, I turn slowly to each direction with a heavy heart, then blow out the candle. I sit and listen to the tiny birds fluttering and chirping in the bushes. When the wax has set and I've run out of hope I pack up my things and walk stiffly home. My back gets sore quickly these days; the muscles are softening, and I'm not used to sitting on the hard ground with a pregnant belly.

I decide to tell Jake how crap I'm feeling. I just don't think I can go through with this. But when I reach the veggie patch, I am startled out of my head. Suddenly there are wings flapping right above me. She is here, announcing her powerful presence; the heat pulsating from her body. I know if I look I won't see her, but she is here!

For the first time since being summoned by the SIF, I dare to hope.

28

SIF HQ.

Despite Dragon's visit, I barely sleep on Monday night. Jake's breathing is slow and deep and I envy him his oblivion. I shake his shoulder gently but he doesn't wake. There's nothing he can say to make me feel better anyway. He's buckling under the weight of planning and endless lists of marinas and currents and tides. He's printed out a whole book's worth, saying he isn't going to risk taking the laptop, and that we won't get good reception anyway.

The trip seems like a lifetime away.

I get out of bed quietly and walk into the night-filled garden. It's chilly out here, after the heat of the spring sunshine. I wrap the doona from my old bed more tightly around me and lean against the wattle tree out the front. The stars are as abundant as ever, making me feel tiny—alone and connected all at once.

The flyscreen door creaks and Jake stands on the veranda stretching and peering into the dark with sleepy eyes. I smile. His night vision is terrible.

'I'm over here,' I whisper into the darkness.

He comes over and sits down beside me.

'You okay?' He sounds too loud.

I nod. If I shake my head I'll howl.

He takes my hand and holds it up to his cheek. 'We'll be on the ocean soon, Ora.'

I nod again, not trusting myself to speak.

'You know you'll be fine today?' He looks at me. 'I know you will. I know you'll be safe and so will Gumnut.'

I can see he's waiting for me to say something but I can't. He gives up and says, 'I'm going to come into the building with you and wait in reception.' I start to protest, but he continues. 'They know we're together, right? So let's act like it.'

'But it'll look obvious, like you're being over-protective or something,' I say slowly. 'Like we've got something to hide.' I am weary. So tired of trying to out-think the SIF, trying to predict their next move and imagine how things will look to them. It's all so ridiculous, and I'm trapped in the middle of it.

'Don't change the plans now, Jake. I can't cope.'

'But we never made a plan.'

I sigh. 'In my head, I've always gone in alone, and that's what I need to do.'

There's a brief silence.

'Shit, Ora. I'm sorry.' His eyes shine as they search my own. 'I've been so focused on the trip, I haven't spent any time with you.'

'It's okay, Jake,' I whisper.

'No it's not!' He is angry. 'It's fucked. This is all fucked!'

I squeeze his hand. I don't have the energy for words.

❧

He drops me off in the city, a few blocks from SIF HQ. By the time I reach the building I'm hot. The day isn't a scorcher, but it's too warm for my outfit. The towering blocks reach into the sky. The whole city street is lined with them, on both sides. I look up past all the grey-black bricks and thousands of tinted windows and see the strip of blue sky mirroring the road. I flash back to how cold I was in that hellhole and shiver, suddenly glad of my jumper.

I summon Dragon. Lion and Snake too. *All of you. Please come, now.* Fleetingly, Mum and Holly flash into my mind, but thankfully Dragon's wings distract me, reminding me to connect to the earth. I imagine great roots growing out of the soles of my feet and drawing energy from the earth, filling me with power. I don't hear a voice from her, like I do with Snake, but I know which ideas are hers.

I haven't touched my belly since the car. It's become second nature for my hands to track Gumnut, but I am terrified of giving the game away with an unconscious caress. At the last minute, before leaving, I remembered a huge chunky ring from Mum's suitcase—it's a large wooden disc, and it's hideous. But it's doing the job; every time I go to reach for my baby, I feel the ring and stop.

On my wrist sits my power band. That's what Jake called it in the early hours under the wattle tree, when he gave it to me. It's his leather bracelet, which is also too big for me. As he tied it on he said, 'I imbue this band with all the power of the universe,' and I knew he meant it, even though he was using his jokey voice.

I open the heavy door of the building and stand back, imagining my entourage flying, slithering and padding into the foyer. Deep breath. Up to the desk, steady, steady. My clothes can't ripple against me. Steady.

A receptionist looks up from her keyboard. Her eyes are hard and her skin tight. No warm words of welcome. She studies me coldly, waiting.

'I have an appointment at ten,' I say.

She looks at me like I'm an idiot. 'Name?'

'Ora James.'

She's looking with more interest now. The ring reminds me to keep my hand from my belly.

'Take a seat.' She gestures with her head and picks up the phone.

Steady, steady. Just a few steps to the seats. Everyone is looking, staring, seeing Gumnut.

'Remember your gold, Ora.' Snake sounds distant but I hear her clearly.

There is nowhere for Dragon to fit! The space isn't high enough for her to fly. Where is she?

'Ora!' Slug's voice, all cheery to my left. 'How nice to see you.'

I am leaning forwards with my elbows on my knees, hiding Gumnut, practising being disengaged. I have to use every ounce of my will to look at her. The hatred is mutual but she's wearing a smile over hers.

'Come this way.' She sweeps ahead of me and for that I am grateful. I try to do a Jake-like glide out of my seat and nearly trip on my skirt. A droplet of sweat trickles down my spine.

It's a long walk. I trail behind, noticing her uniform is gone, replaced by a too-tight navy skirt and crisp white shirt, which she has tucked in, making her bum look bumpy. A bumpy slug. Eventually she stops at a door and turns to look at me. As her eyes scan me from top to toe with frosty focus, Dragon lands, right between us. I stand up straighter and lift my chin defiantly, making her look at my face, which now mirrors her disdain.

'You look out of shape,' I say, shocking us both. Antagonising her is just plain dumb.

Her upper lip turns into a sneer, revealing tartar laden teeth. She is about to utter something in response but thinks better of it. She pushes the door with a shove and steps aside, waving me into the room impatiently.

Steady, steady.

Same old, same old. One table, three chairs; two on one side, one on the other. I know which is mine. Steady.

The door closes and I'm alone, under surveillance again. I put my forearms on the table, lean forward and play with the ring. My body language *has* to read like I don't give a shit. Bored, nonchalant.

Can they see how frantic I am?

As usual, they make me wait. I breathe. I talk to Snake. Lion sits by the door, guarding it for me. And I feel Dragon. Just before the door opens she lets loose a great jet of fire, then smoke fills the room, cleansing it, filling it with power. Our power.

I lift my chin as Slug comes in followed by a new man carrying a file. He's small, with short dark hair, long sideburns, a sharp nose, grey eyes.

'This must be Ora! I'm Shane Wilkins, Managing Director of the Department of Public Relations and Media.' He holds out his hand.

I look at it like it's a poisoned mitt. No way am I going to touch any SIF worker voluntarily. I nod in acknowledgement and he frowns just slightly, withdrawing his hand.

'Now … Ora, we've asked you to start coming in for …' He checks the file, but I reckon he knows it already, 'a weekly appointment.'

Indignant rage is roaring inside me, battling my fear for top billing. Neither will translate well into words. I purse my lips together tightly. He goes on.

'An unfortunate …' He pauses, looking for the right word, '… development has transpired.'

This time he pauses for effect, looking at me directly.

'The man who brought your case …' He pauses again. This guy is so slow. Bumbling. How is he the head of anything? '…to our attention in the first place … has been in touch with … the free media. For money, no doubt,' he says scornfully to Slug. 'It seems, Ora … you're going to be news …'

I stop twiddling the ring on my finger. 'Remember to breathe, Ora,' Snake whispers.

'So as this is a … delicate situation … As Head of Media, I've been asked to … guide you through this.' He isn't used to being a bully, that's for sure.

Slug is.

'And you *will* cooperate, as will your boyfriend, do you understand?' she says, shoving her face close to mine.

I nod, taking a deep breath. *This* is why I'm here. They don't know about Gumnut! Dad hasn't dobbed us in! They haven't even asked about Dione. I start to relax as relief spreads through my body in a warm rush.

Slug's fist bashes the table. I jump, and so does Mediaworm.

'This is not a smiling matter, you little shit.' She's starting to show her colours. Mediaworm's eyes bulge before he remembers who he is—a big knob. 'I *know* you have something to do with this, and even though I didn't get you before, it's not going away.' Her spittle lands on my cheek. 'As soon as we find that couple, we've got you.'

'It is important that you follow our instructions fully,' Mediaworm continues in his scratchy voice, trying to take control. 'This is a very … delicate situation.'

I nod. I need to get some enthusiasm happening; the sooner I give them confidence that I'll 'cooperate' the sooner I'll be out of here.

It takes another two hours. Once Mediaworm finds his flow he goes on and on and on. My forearms hurt like hell from leaning on the table, but it's the best position to hide Gumnut. I don't stop playing with my ring.

I see Slug look at it a couple of times. She clearly thinks it's hideous. But to her, all of me is hideous.

I hear some of what he says: report them as soon as they show themselves; don't talk to the press full stop; repeat 'No comment' over and over; under no circumstances let them into the house; if they do persuade me to talk to them, deny I was ever held by the SIF. He pushes a card across the table.

'That's my mobile,' he says, pointing. The whites of his fingernails have been cut into right-angled corners. 'And that's the office.'

I nod again. I haven't said one word to him. Slug, who's been leaning back in her chair for most of the lecture, is fidgeting. I am longing to move. To talk to Jake. My mobile has vibrated twice in my bag.

'So if you haven't any questions … you just need to sign this.' He pushes a three-page document across the table.

'It's a lot of legal … blurb. Basically you need to promise us that you won't talk.'

I read it. Twice. It's hard to understand. I don't think I sign my life away.

'So,' he says. 'We'll see you next Tuesday. We'll use each session to … debrief and give you … advice on how to … proceed.'

I want to roll my eyes. His voice and his stilted speech have got under my skin like parasites. I am sweating and my arms are bruised lumps of lead.

I nod again. *Yes, yes. Hurry up.*

'I estimate … they will visit you tomorrow … or the next day. We have a legal injunction out on them … but they are finding a way around it as we speak.'

I sigh and a yawn comes out. I close my mouth too late. He's seen it. Slug grins. He stands up abruptly, nods a curt goodbye and leaves.

She gestures at me to get up. We stand at the same time and she goes through the door ahead of me.

'Just remember,' she says, stopping in the doorway, 'stick to the rules, otherwise we'll get you—it would be my personal pleasure. Stay out of the way. That's the best place for you.' And with that she is gone.

I have to find my way back to the exit, willing myself not to run. As I escape into the bright daylight, there is Jake, pacing up and down, and a wave of love floods through me. When he sees me, he sprints over and scoops me up in a big hug.

'It's okay, Jake. I'm okay,' I say in a muffled voice against his chest. He looks at me for reassurance, then we remember where we are. 'Come on,' I say. 'I'll tell you in the car.'

I am bubbling over with relief—I'm free! And away from the SIF! Gumnut is mine still, they're not going to take him.

Jake says he's happy, but he isn't pleased about the free media.

'They're not called hounds for nothing. Now we've got two lots of bullies on our backs. We're going to have to be extra careful.'

He is quiet on the drive home, brows knitted, as he thinks of more plans and ways to stay safe. Slug was right about one thing. We'd all be a lot safer if I was hidden away.

29

Change of Plan

It's Jake's turn not to sleep. He's a lot noisier about it than I was, sighing loudly and tossing from side to side. I've never seen him so jittery. By the time morning creeps in he looks manic, like he could be brewing a fever.

My night wasn't much better, packed full of replays of Mediaworm and Slug. What if a camera caught me at a bad angle and revealed my pregnant belly? Or worse, what if Slug clicks that something was up and calls me back in again?

Maybe that's why we change the plan.

By the time we're out of bed, both Jake and I have lost our cool. When he suggests we go up to Tom and Melissa's together with all our gear, I jump at the idea. We go into rush mode, like we know someone's coming to get us.

Jake is really spooked by the press situation. When he was seventeen a friend of his died in a car crash and the media made a huge deal out of it, turning the tragedy into a flashy news story about drink driving and misguided youth. He says they're only interested in making a story, not the truth.

'They could muck things up for us,' he says quietly. 'The last thing the government wants is a big birth saga. Not now that things are running smoothly for them.'

I hear what he's saying but am so consumed with my own worries that I don't have room for any more.

It's only when our car tears up Tom and Sarah's driveway that we breathe out and smile again—a safe haven. But Tom is not pleased to see us. He's full of scowls as he walks towards the car. He was up a ladder, tending to one of his beloved plum trees.

'What's with the change of plan?' he says hotly, leaning in. Maybe he's worried.

'The media dogs are onto the story,' Jake says in a rush. 'We wanted to get away before they start on us.'

Tom shakes his head slowly. 'What am I meant to do with Dione's car? That could lead me right into their hands. Besides, the boat's not ready.'

'But the press are onto us. That's why Ora had to report to the SIF.'

'We're not leaving early, Jake. Don't change a good plan unless you have to. That's when mistakes happen.'

They stare at each other for a long time.

'You can handle it.' Tom sounds adamant.

'We'll go back then,' Jake looks crestfallen. 'We'll unpack the gear and get back.'

Tom nods and breaks into a smile. 'But you're here now, so let's have a cuppa. There's even some cake.' He chuckles, 'The little 'un will be pleased to see you, even if I'm not!'

We're quiet as we stand in the kitchen, drinking our tea. It has shocked me the way Jake gave in so quickly, like a puppy wanting to please his master. It's the first time I've seen weakness in him, and I don't like it. I want him to be strong all the time.

'Best we drive the car into the barn and unpack from there, Jake,' Tom says as he puts his cup on the bench. 'Ora, you stay here. I know you'll want to see Dione, but the quicker we get back to plan A, the better. Once we've emptied the car you two should head home.'

I want Tom to come with us too. Even though his bossiness is annoying, it's also reassuring. He is older and wiser than Jake—eight years older—and he'll know what to do if the SIF catch up with us. Or the media.

I suddenly feel bad for comparing. If ever there was a time Jake needs me to believe in him, it's now. I think about how much he's giving up. He could be hanging out at the beach and having fun at uni rather than organising a grand vanishing act and preparing to become a father.

Sarah and I sit on the veranda steps waiting, neither of us in the mood for small talk. I want to see Dione, but I remind myself I'll be with her the day after tomorrow.

We drive back up the hill to Dione's with heavy hearts. I'm about to tell Jake how amazing he is when I'm distracted by a dark car speeding by in the opposite direction. The windows are tinted, so I can't see who's in the car, but instinctively I know it's the media. My hand goes to my belly.

'Great,' Jake says, two minutes later. 'We're being followed.'

I look back and sure enough, the car has turned around.

'We can do this, Jake,' I say, squeezing his leg. He blows out of his mouth, sounding like a horse, and I want to giggle. But laughter won't help.

Surprisingly, I feel okay—surely I can handle a couple of press guys? My biggest challenge will be holding my tongue. I have so much pent-up rage bursting to cut loose, and more than a few ideas about how messed up our system is.

We speed up the driveway, jerk to a halt and race inside. Jake grabs a black pen and writes in thick letters on a piece of paper,

'No comment.' He puts it on the doormat and slams the door just as they're crowning the driveway. I race around closing blinds and bolting doors. We stand in the kitchen, wordless, the tension swimming laps around us.

Two pairs of feet sound on the veranda boards. They pause, probably reading the note. One of them rings the bell anyway. Jake takes my hand and we look at each other, barely breathing.

The bell rings again. We continue to find solace in each other's eyes. They have a brief, mumbled conversation and then start walking around the veranda. I can tell they're trying to look through the windows.

Jake pulls out his phone. 'I'm calling the SIF,' he says in a croaky voice. And again, shouting, 'I'm calling the SIF, NOW!'

They must hear. They talk to each other in low voices. Two men. They ring the doorbell again. We stay planted to the spot and only breathe properly when we hear doors slamming and the car receding.

'They'll be back tomorrow,' Jake says.

'I know, but we'll be gone the day after,' I reply cheerily.

Jake punches the wall. 'Tom should have let us stay.'

I pull the blinds up and a movement catches my eye outside the window.

'Shit!' I say. 'We forgot the chooks.'

'What?'

'We forgot to take the chooks to Tom and Sarah's.'

'Huh,' he says, so not bothered.

I look at him coldly.

'Well, we can't do anything about them now!' he snaps. 'We're *not* going again.'

'We can't just leave them to die! Dione loves those birds. And so do I.'

'You eat those birds.'

I look at him, surprised by the swipe. I've started eating meat again after years of being a vegetarian. Dione suggested it as a way of relieving my tiredness. She guessed my iron levels were low because of the pregnancy, so once a week we buy a chicken from the guy down the road.

'Hey, I know,' Jake says. 'How about I give them a quick and kindly death instead of a fox's massacre and we take them with us in the cool bag?' He thinks it's a joke, but it's just more nastiness, and I crumple. The stress of the past few days combined with the thought of the chickens dying undoes me. I sit at the table, put my head on my arms and let out a wail.

Jake storms up the corridor, shouting and growling. He sounds like an animal. The stress is getting to him too.

He comes back a little later and sits beside me. 'I'm sorry,' he says. 'That was a bad joke. There's just too much to think about, Ora.' He pauses. 'Finding a foster home for the chickens isn't a priority right now.'

I am so tired. I can't move. I can't believe I'm crying *again*. He leans in and hugs me.

'I feel like all I do is cry.' Some of my tears have made it to the floor. I sit back and sniff.

'I love that you cry,' he says, handing me a tea towel.

I blow my nose and smile. 'Are you some kind of masochist or something?'

'No!' He laughs. 'I just think it's good that you let it out. Think how messed up you'd be if you didn't.'

'Thanks a lot!'

'I didn't mean it like that. It's just ... what you've been through in your life is *not* normal.' I start to reply but he steams on. 'Most people would be on some kind of drugs by now, or have turned psycho. But you just keep on keeping on. You're really strong. That's just one reason why I love you, by the way. But if you didn't cry, where would you put all the pain?'

I don't know what to say. It's confronting to hear him

acknowledge my pain. It makes it real, and I don't know if that's a good thing.

'I …' I say. 'Maybe I *should* try drugs?' It's a lame joke.

'Well, that's up to you,' he says, not even smiling. 'But crying is completely fine with me.'

'How did you get to be so good at therapy?' I give him a little shove.

'I was the only male in a house full of females, remember?'

I smile. 'Well, being around women that much must have rubbed off on you.'

'Ha!' he gives me a little shove back and we hug again.

'Ora, if anything happens to me, I—'

'Don't talk like that, Jake.'

'I need you to know how much I love you, Ora James.'

We hold each other tightly. 'None of this feels real,' he says. 'It's all so fragile.'

'And if anything happens to me,' I whisper, 'will you be everything to Gumnut?' He squeezes me. Tears roll down my cheeks again. 'Will you let him know that I love him fiercely? Like a lioness?'

I look into his eyes and feel like I'm seeing into his heart. It makes me want to look away. But I don't. I hold his gaze and feel the final veil fall from my heart, allowing him to see all of me.

'When Mum and Holly were killed, I promised myself never to … I didn't think I'd ever let myself … fully love. Completely, but I …' I take a breath, 'My heart feels whole again,' I say, and then we kiss for a very long time.

∽

Much later, after we've slept away some of the afternoon, Jake gets up and goes outside. Gumnut is doing a workout so I don't manage to get back to sleep, but I lie there with my eyes closed, enjoying the feel of his movements.

I hear some hammering, and eventually wander out to have a look. When Jake sees me walking over he screams at me to get back inside. I realise I'm just in a T-shirt and undies. The media could be lurking anywhere and my pregnant belly is completely on show. How could I be so stupid?

I feel stifled again, caged in. It's definitely time to leave. I walk from room to room and wonder whether Gumnut will ever know this house. I have a sudden flashback of me and Holly bouncing on the sofas.

'Hey, Ora,' Jake shouts through the back door. 'Come and have a look. But put some clothes on.'

I pull on my skirt and jumper and go outside.

'I did it for *you*, not them,' he says with a grin, looking at the chicken coop. 'There's enough feed to last a couple of months.'

I clap my hands and do a silly jig. He's amazing! He's rigged up a feeding shoot from the drum of grain to the chickens' feeder, so that once they've eaten a certain amount, more grain will be released. The water system is the same.

'You're a genius!' I say.

'Well, hopefully it'll work until Tom or Sarah get here to pick them up.'

'You won't be eaten by Mr Fox after all,' I say in a silly voice to the chooks as they scratch contentedly in the dirt. I give him a big hug. 'I LOVE you, Jake Seaboy, father of my child!'

'Shhhh!' he says, looking around warily. 'Come on, let's get inside.'

30

Leaving

The next day, we hide inside, spending most of it in bed. We won't have much privacy on the boat, so we might as well enjoy ourselves now. We have another visit from the media in the afternoon, but they don't stay for long.

The following morning, we pack up the house wordlessly, clean out the fridge and turn off the electricity. If anyone looks closely they'll soon realise we've shut it up. We just hope we'll be long gone by then.

I say goodbye to the chickens and the veggies and walk around to the front of the house, avoiding the front door. I feel like if I walk out that door, I'll never return. Instead, I watch Jake close it firmly and walk down the veranda steps. He takes my hand and, without a backwards glance, we walk down the driveway.

I am in my raincoat. It doesn't look like it's going to rain, but it's as good as my green jumper for covering me up. I haven't walked to the bus stop in ages—since my pregnancy started to show and I stopped going to the beach. A bubble of excitement builds inside me.

Dragon swoops, surprising me out of my reverie. I look up and there is the dark car coming towards us. It slows as it goes by, the occupants blatantly checking us out. My hand in my pocket goes straight to my belly. Sure enough, the car turns around and sidles up next to us.

'Just keep walking,' Jake says, squeezing my hand. 'Don't say anything.'

I smile in spite of the tension. It feels so good to have Jake beside me.

The car window comes down and a man in a charcoal shirt leans out of the passenger window. He's wearing dark glasses and has big hair. I don't look closely, but I bet his teeth are pearly white.

'Hello Ora and …?' He sounds friendly. He waits for Jake to give his name but there's no way that's going to happen. 'My name's Keith Waterhouse,' the guy continues, 'and this is Bob Jenkins. We know the SIF have told you not to talk to us, but unlike them, we're on your side.'

Dragon lands on the roof of their car, which is keeping pace with our steps.

'Like you, we don't agree with the birthing system and we want to change things. It's stories like yours, Ora, that will make people think—and then act. We need the brave ones to speak out. To let people know there *are* other options.'

The energy of the man is magnetic. I want to look at him, even if he is doing the hard sell. His words make sense. Our feet scrunch on the unmade road and so do the tyres of the car. They're keeping tempo with us exactly. I'm glad Jake is between them and me.

'We have another story like your aunt's, Ora.' My name sounds different, like he's rolling the 'r'. 'A midwife who's been practising undercover in another state. The SIF have got her now, but she talked to us before they took her in. It took them months to catch her. They'll get your aunt too, but you just might save her if you speak *now*.'

We carry on walking, looking into the distance.

'Do you know where Dione is, Ora?'

The man is almost halfway out of the car window by now. His torso is reaching towards us; he is so close. If Jake wanted to, he could hit him. I think he wants to.

'We've got a lot of money for you, Ora, if you talk. My boss really wants this story, and when she wants something she pays a high price. Just a chat, Ora? It won't take long. We could come back later?'

'Tonight,' I say, turning to look straight at him.

Jake almost crushes my hand. Dragon flaps her wings. She's flying just above the car now.

'No!' I say. 'Not tonight, tomorrow. I'll talk to you tomorrow.'

'Great! That's great. Hey, we could give you a lift, if you like.' He sounds too friendly. 'Where are you going?'

'She said tomorrow. Now leave us alone,' Jake snarls at the man.

The man nods and sits back inside the car.

'Tomorrow then,' he says, beaming at me. As the car drives off he closes the window.

I don't want to look at Jake.

'What did you say that for?' He is fuming.

'Well, you didn't say anything, did you?'

'You have to *ignore* them. I told you that. Now, if they snoop around they'll see that we've left. I can't believe you just did that!'

'I had to get them to leave, Jake. I am so ready to spill my guts, I can feel it.'

Jake scowls into the distance. He's furious.

'It's all building up inside me. The stress and the anger, being locked up, all the injustice.' I stop walking and look at him, rage simmering in my belly. 'Why should I have to run like a criminal just so I can have my baby *normally*?'

He keeps quiet. Maybe he can see that I'll bite his head off if he says anything more. *I* am the one carrying this baby, carrying the trauma of the SIF, carrying the weight of Dione's story.

We don't say another word until we're in the city.

Any other time, a day in the city could have been fun, but killing time is not fun. What money we have, we want to save, so we wander about aimlessly, feeling lost.

Eventually, we find refuge in a bookshop specialising in architecture and landscape design. There are comfortable armchairs that invite you to sit and read. The books are huge and glossy and I get lost in the images, full of amazing buildings that blend seamlessly with the landscapes. My fingers itch for my pencils and sketchpad.

Jake comes over and guides me quick-sharp out of the shop.

'The sooner we hide you the better,' he says, taking my hand. 'Did you see the way you were sitting?'

'I made sure my belly was hidden. Nobody saw!'

'I did!'

'But you *know*.' I sigh and look back at the shop longingly, wondering if this is how it's going to be forever; never still for long, constantly on the lookout for trouble.

We decide to head off to the meeting point early, fed up with the bustle and fumes of the city, feeling purposeless among the busy people rushing past.

The train lulls me with its low-key hum; my eyes grow heavy and I follow my thoughts inside to Gumnut. Whenever I focus on him, he moves, as though in direct response to my attention. I smile and snuggle into Jake, savouring the moment. We should've just caught trains all day.

As we wait for the bus to take us to the reserve, Jake starts whistling. I know it's his way of dealing with the stress, but it's tuneless and annoying and the sound really gets to me. It's like some crazy jingle that goes on and on. I want to tell him to shut up.

The fumes on the bus make me queasy. I open the window and put my head against the glass, feeling the cold sink into my skin. It's so good to see the ocean again. Today it's the deepest blue, beckoning and soothing.

The muscles around Gumnut start to twitch, like they have a life of their own. It's the oddest sensation. I put my hands in my coat pockets and then over my belly and feel the skin contract, oddly fascinated by how stretched it is and how clearly I can feel Gumnut's elbow—or maybe it's a foot? My whole front is twitching, all tight and hard around his little form!

'Jake! I think Gumnut's coming.'

His head whips around and his eyes goggle, making him look like a cartoon character. I want to laugh but then my belly goes into spasm again. I put his hand over Gumnut so he can feel the movement of my muscles. His eyes widen slightly in wonder.

'Does it hurt?' he asks. I shake my head.

'They're Braxton Hicks.' A woman pokes her head between us from the seat behind. We turn to look at her, horrified that she's broken our cover. 'I saw when you stood up to open the window. Don't worry,' she says quietly, seeing the panic on our faces. 'I won't tell. I used to be a midwife … once upon a time.'

Neither of us says anything. We're too filled with terror.

'The baby's not coming yet. You'll know when it is. Your muscles are just practising.' She sits back and says a bit louder, 'I wondered why you were wearing such a big coat on a day like this.'

''Scuse us,' Jake says, standing up and taking my hand. 'This is our stop.' I open my mouth to say something, close it again and follow him down the aisle. I wave to the woman as the bus goes past.

'Be careful,' she mouths back at me.

'Shit!' Jake says. 'Shit! This is great. We're probably all over the

CCTV in that bookshop, and now we've been clocked by the local sticky beak. Great, Ora. Fucking great!'

'It's not my fault!' We are shouting. I see an old man across the road stop and stare.

I balloon my coat out with my hands in the pockets and start walking in the wake of the bus.

We walk the rest of the way, even though I'm tired and sore and still worried that the baby's coming.

31

The *Artemis*

An hour and a half later, hot and bothered, we finally arrive at the meeting point. The nature reserve isn't far from the beach, and as Tom predicted, no-one's here. It's just a piece of land with some trees and lots of birds.

I am so thirsty, but we've run out of water. We spread my coat out on the ground and sprawl in the afternoon sun. It feels good to be off my feet. I haven't walked so much in ages, and my legs aren't used to the extra weight. I've gone soft.

As darkness falls we hear a car approaching. It's Tom in his four-wheel drive, towing the huge boat on the trailer behind him. How are we ever going to get it into the sea without being seen? I have to force my shoulders down as they tense up towards my ears. I don't know if we're going to make it.

Tom's big smile helps reassure me. He doesn't chat, just gives us both a brief hug and says, 'Right, let's do it.'

Sarah leans across the driver's seat to the open door. 'We'll miss you,' she says, and I feel like flinging myself into her arms.

'I'll miss you too,' I say, restraining myself. 'And you,' I add, blowing a kiss to Little Tom in the back seat, who waves.

Tom has got a ladder out of the car and propped it against the back of the boat.

'Come on, you two,' he says. 'Onwards and upwards!'

We follow him to the end of the trailer.

'Now, just stay in the cabin until I bang my fist on the deck. No poking your heads out, d'you hear?'

Jake and I nod definitely.

'Right.' Tom holds out his hand to help me onto the ladder. 'Thank you,' I say, gratitude thickening my voice. I lean down to give him a big hug, then trundle up the ladder. The rust on the rungs feels prickly under my hands. After I hitch myself clumsily into the boat, Jake passes up my things and follows me. Tom claps him on the back as he goes.

'See you in a bit,' he says, and turns briskly away.

❧

The boat—Artemis—is blue and white. At the back, where we're standing, is a sunken, rectangular cockpit flanked by bench seats covered in faded blue cushions. The tiller reaches a little way into the cockpit and is smooth and well-worn. The outboard motor beside the rudder looks powerful, and I can smell fuel.

The vertical pole of the mainsail reaches into the sky and the sail itself is wrapped around the boom, which goes from the front of the boat to the back, stretching across the cockpit. There isn't much space. At all. I want to get off already. How dumb was I? Just because I love the ocean doesn't mean I love sailing boats. I feel like chucking my guts up, and we haven't even hit water yet! Oh Gumnut.

'Keep moving,' Jake says, nodding in the direction of the cabin. A few steps forward and I'm at the entrance of 'below'. Two timber rails line three steep steps leading into the cabin. A tiny kitchen is on the left and wooden lockers and a door are on the right. Beyond the kitchen there's a table with seats, flanked by a bench seat with another long blue cushion.

It's even more cramped down here. At the end of the cabin, I see through a small doorway a double bed that tapers into a 'V', hugging the line of the boat's bow. Evenly spaced circular windows are at eye level allowing what little light remains to come in. I can just stand, but Jake has to stoop.

Dione jumps up from the bench seat and gives me a hug. We nearly fall over as the car pulls away, towing us towards the sea. We plonk down. Jake sits at the table sideways, his long legs taking up all the space. A wave of claustrophobia overwhelms me. I want to rush back up to the fresh air, but force myself to stay seated.

Dione leans forward to greet Jake and smiles at us broadly.

'Oh, it's good to see you both!' She looks very much at home down here, but she's used to small spaces. I'm too caught up in my discomfort to reply. Right now, all my energy is going into keeping me from opening the hatch and throwing myself onto the moving tarmac.

The car turns left and we all lean accordingly to keep our balance. Jake looks around and says with a nod, 'You've done a great job, Dione.'

There is so much wood down here, from lockers to table to bench seats. It's a deep honey colour, shining under the strong-smelling polish.

'Most of the work was on the outside,' she says. I can see she's pleased with herself. 'Patching up scratches, and a chip in the hull. But I got it all done. Cleaning up down here was the fun part.'

I look around, struggling to believe that this will be my home for the next however long. Jake looks so happy. Is it just me who feels like a factory hen? Gumnut kicks, reminding me of the bus journey.

'I thought the baby was coming,' I say, looking at Dione, exhaustion pressing in on me. She squeezes my hand.

'A woman on the bus told us she was having early contractions. Braxton Kicks or something?' Jake adds, looking concerned.

'Braxton Hicks,' Dione says, frowning. 'What woman?'

'An ex-midwife,' I say. 'She seemed okay.'

Dione nods. 'They're practice contractions, nothing to worry about, but you do look tired. Have you had enough to drink today?'

I shake my head, feeling thirsty again. Dione heads for the little kitchen, swaying as she goes. The boat is quite steady on the trailer—it feels like we're on a bus. I watch as she takes out a plastic tumbler from one of the lockers above and pumps the water at a small sink.

'We've twenty litres of drinking water under here.' She points under the bench. 'And another forty stored at the back of the boat.'

'Does the watermaker still work?' Jake asks.

'Yep.' Dione says. 'It's old but it works.'

'Watermaker?'

'It's a hand pump that desalinates the seawater. It takes ages, but it'll be a life saver,' Dione says. 'Who knows where we'll be able to pick up water for sale?'

Jake nods. 'I've done my homework. I know all the safe places to stop. Boat ramps and jetties are the quietest. We can go in on the dinghy and catch a bus to the nearest shops, if we have to. If we're sick of desalinated water, we can buy water there.'

'And blow the budget,' Dione says.

Jake shrugs.

'Where's the toilet?' I ask, realising I haven't seen one. Jake nods at the door near the cabin steps, opposite the kitchen.

'That's the toilet?'

'Just for number twos,' Dione says chirpily, opening the door. 'The bucket beside it is for number ones; the wee can be tipped overboard straight away.'

'How glamorous,' I say.

'Sand is a wonderful thing for getting rid of smells.' Dione points to the pail and tray on the other side of the portaloo. 'You just sprinkle it on afterwards, whack the lid back on and you're sorted.'

Well, whoopie do. I'm about to say something but the whole boat tilts suddenly. I guess we're driving down the boat ramp.

We make a very smooth transition from land to sea and I get to try out Dione's sand theory straight away, because as soon as we start rocking on the water I have to vomit. Thankfully I make it to the portaloo. Dione is beside me instantly, holding back my hair. I'm sure I've gone green.

Tom starts the outboard and we begin to chug along, which only adds to the frequency of my retching.

'Will Gumnut be alright?' I wail, feeling like he must be dying with me.

'He'll be fine,' Dione soothes.

Jake, who's been pacing, goes to open the hatch but Dione stops him.

'Jake! Not yet!' He sits down again with a *humph*. I spend a long time leaning over the little toilet. When I finally crawl back to the seat I notice how dark the cabin has become—we're not going to turn on any lights until we're further out to sea.

I lie the full length of the bench seat and groan. Dione and Jake, who are sitting at the table, take it turns to lean forward and stroke my leg (Jake) and shoulder (Dione). We have to wait whole lifetimes before the signal finally comes from above. Jake is up and out before I've made it to my feet. I am stiff, tired and nauseous.

The cockpit feels slightly roomier somehow, now that we're surrounded by sea. The dark-blue sail is still wrapped neatly around the boom and something resembling a small surge of excitement distracts me from the sickness as I imagine it billowing in the wind.

The engine is off now and we drift gently along, standing and staring out to sea. The sea is calm and inky black against the night sky, which is filled with low-lying clouds lit up by a quarter moon. Words feel too small for all this space.

Finally, Tom breaks the silence. 'I saw Sarah pull up on the beach a little way back, so I'll jump in here and the tide will take me in to her.'

He takes off his T-shirt and chucks it to Jake, telling him to keep it.

Tom steps nimbly onto the ladder at the back of the boat. 'So look after yourselves, orright?' He looks pointedly at my pregnant belly, and then at Dione and Jake. Then he starts down the rungs.

'Brrr!' he says, dipping a toe into the sea. 'The drink's a bit cold tonight.' And with that he is gone, swimming strongly towards the shore. I want him to turn around and come back to us. I take Jake's hand as we watch him getting further away. It's so far! When we planned this it sounded so easy, but the shore is miles away. What if he doesn't make it?

We carry on drifting slowly, listening to the lap of water against the boat. Dione and Jake aren't saying anything. They're just looking intensely after Tom's disappearing strokes.

'Is he going to be alright?' I sound so anxious. 'This doesn't feel right. It's too far.'

'He's a good swimmer,' Jake says, but that's all. I want to hear him say he'll be fine.

'When we see Sarah's headlights come on we'll know he's made it,' Dione says. We are being pulled by the tide towards the beach. 'That'll be our signal to get moving.'

'What will we do if they don't turn on?' I have to ask. I need them to reassure me. But they just keep staring into the void. 'Say something!'

'Tom reckoned it would take him half an hour,' Jake says, checking his watch. 'It's been ten minutes.'

'Ten minutes! I can't wait another twenty,' I whine.

'Relax, Ora,' Dione says, rubbing my back.

'This is a stupid idea. This whole boat thing's a stupid idea!' I want to jump in after Tom. Another wave of nausea hits me and I lean over the side, retching, even though there's nothing left in my stomach, not even bile.

'Okay Ora, this is a good opportunity to practise for the birth. I want you to breathe with me.'

'Get stuffed, Dione!' I say, and move to go back down below. But the thought of that tiny space makes me want to puke. So I sit heavily, banging my back against the side of the boat.

'Ora,' Dione sounds more commanding. 'I want you to breathe in through your nose for four, hold for four, then breathe out through your mouth for six. Come on. Do it with me. We'll make the breaths longer as we go.'

I shake my head.

'You're being stupid now.' Dione sounds all matronly.

I have to do something to get out of this state. I want off this boat so badly.

'Fine,' I agree begrudgingly.

Soon enough she's got me breathing out for eight.

'Twenty minutes,' Jake says.

My panic attack has passed. I carry on breathing with Dione and finally, finally! There are the lights. We stand and watch as the car disappears up the boat ramp, two red eyes receding.

I groan in relief.

Jake is smiling broadly and gives me a squeeze. Dione salutes the shore—a silent thank you. A wave of self-consciousness washes over me. I hope Dione was distracting herself, as well as me, with her counting and timing.

'Right!' Jake says, sounding firm. 'Time to leave Adelaide. Melbourne, Sydney, the Gold Coast—here we come!' He starts up the outboard and points us out to sea.

Dione goes below, saying it's well past dinner time. I stay on the bench by the cockpit, watching Jake at the helm, feeling the cool sea air push at my face and trying not to retch at the fumes from the engine.

32

On Board

The water feels choppy but according to Jake it's calm. I dread what it'll be like in a storm. The little boat keeps bobbing about, making my stomach dance in my mouth. The others tuck into a quiche that Sarah has made. I can't even look at it. I stay up on deck while they eat. Jake has motored us to what he hopes is a quiet spot. The water slaps the boat as billows of waves try to take us with them, stretching and testing the anchor.

When I am so cold that I don't feel sick anymore I go below, too tired to unpack. It seems like months since we dropped our bags of clothes and books at Tom and Sarah's. I just want to get into bed.

It's far too cramped in this tiny, pointed room. I crawl onto the bed—standing's impossible—and take off my clothes lying down. I snuggle into the comfy mattress; the blue sheets still smell of washing powder. It's going to be weird sleeping in the same space as Dione. I'll have to sleep with the door open, so I hope she doesn't snore.

My whole body is so sore. I listen to Jake and Dione moving about the boat and smile—we did it! When Jake comes to bed, he has to crawl over me—I need to be by the door so I can get to the bucket quickly. I pray that I'm done with vomiting for today.

Jake snuggles in with a huge sigh.

'You are a star!' I whisper. 'Your plan worked and it was a *brilliant* idea and … I love you!' I want to make up for my comment earlier, when I was panicking about Tom.

Jake squeezes me and asks me how I'm feeling.

'Better,' I say. 'Just sore. Where's Dione?'

'She's taken her swag up on deck.' He sounds so tired. His planning has been painstaking. Navigation charts, tidal tables, safe places to anchor and go ashore. It took a whole suitcase to fit all the maps and notes he's collected.

It'll be a fine line between staying near enough to the coast to be safe, but far enough away to avoid being spotted. We can't anchor in any shipping channels—it's illegal, and besides, big tankers would mow us down in a minute. We'll have to choose remote stretches of shore with quiet bays to stop at each night. Or maybe some uninhabited islands. I know Jake will be an amazing skipper. I just hope I find my sea legs.

I force myself to imagine our little boat is being held by the 'calm' and caring ocean. I need to get over the buffeting of the waves and stop worrying about gales and squalls and tidal waves.

In the morning I'm as grumpy as a hungry bear, and Jake and Dione aren't much better. The relief of getting away from the SIF and the media has evaporated into our new reality: there is *no* space. This cramped dance is to be our lives now for however long, constantly bumping into corners, or each other. I feel oversized and hemmed in and am longing to jump off.

The highlight of the first day is hoisting the sail. It takes all of us to coordinate the movement, holding different ropes and watching Jake scale the mast to unhitch the trapped material. Finally we're off, propelled by the power of the wind, and I feel like we're flying across the water. Even Dione whoops for joy.

And then we go back to trying to find space on board. We're not used to living in each other's pockets. The dream of the open ocean is a paradox; all the space is in the sea while here on the boat, it's like being in a lift.

Several days go by before we find our rhythm, but gradually, our frowns begin to settle into smiles.

My favourite spot is at the front of the boat, on deck. I spread out like a jellyfish, covering nearly the whole bow with my new dress. Melissa made it for me and packed it in our things, as a surprise. It's dark grey linen and has her stylish motif all along the edges. I love its long, simple A-line shape. I think I'm going to live in it. It's the perfect colour for absorbing the sun's rays.

From my spot, I watch sleepily as Jake teaches Dione the art of sailing, while I suck on slices of ginger root. The fiery zing has saved my life, and Gumnut's. I am so thankful for Sarah's intuition—she packed the biggest root of ginger I've ever seen and it's helped me keep some of my food down. I don't know if my stomach will ever get used to the constant motion.

Time slows and so does my thinking. After days—or is it weeks?—I stop worrying about the SIF. The ocean lulls my senses when it's calm and sharpens them in choppy waters. I breathe more deeply. The wind closes me off from the world and the sun opens me up. I spend a lot of time looking at the horizon or into the sea below. So do the others. When we see other boats, we wave, but are careful to keep our distance.

We eat heaps of fish and try not to think about the mercury consumption. I've held the Best Catcher's prize for three days in a row now, and Dione still holds the title of Best Chef—it's a wonder what comes out of our little galley.

Jake and Dione like to pass the time in heated political debate; about the government, the SIF's power, education, health, the earth, you name it. Sometimes I listen. A lot of the time I don't. They both have strong opinions and constantly try to outdo each other. I wonder if these conversations remind Dione of Mum.

Mostly I sit and sketch. Or read. Or daydream. I long to be alone, and grow to love the bed that's become my nest and cave. Dione says it's a sign. I'm getting ready for the baby.

Jake and I sometimes talk late into the night—our only alone time. He's told me how distant I've become, and that he misses me. At first, I didn't know what to say. But since he's mentioned it I can feel myself slipping into another zone. It's subtle, but he's right. It's like I'm making space for Gumnut, and I have to cut him off to do that. I've tried to explain, but I don't think he gets it.

During one of Jake's trips ashore for supplies, Dione and I fish from the front of the anchored boat. We are expert now at casting our rods, and there's an easy silence between us. It gives me time to study the light blue of the sky touching the deep aquamarine of the ocean. An occasional cloud turns the sea air chilly but the sun wins out, warming us again.

'How are you feeling about the birth?' Dione asks conversationally.

'Like it's a long way off.' I hope that will be the end of the discussion, but she's waiting for more. 'I'm still a month away, Dione. And that's from forty weeks. In your book it says forty-*two* weeks is a common gestation time.'

'Sometimes they come sooner.'

I don't reply.

'Where do you see yourself having the baby?' I recognise her midwife's tone immediately.

'I'd ... like to have him in the water,' I say in a rush. Saying it makes it real. She's tried to talk about it a few times before, but I'm still not ready.

Dione smiles slightly. 'I thought you might, being such a fish yourself. You know you'll need a birthing tub for that, though? It's way too cold in the sea.'

I nod. 'I keep thinking about the way Gumnut is going to come into the world and what a big thing it is for the baby. The way their heads are squashed, and their lungs too.'

'It's good for them!'

I look at her sideways.

'That's what kickstarts their little bodies,' she says.

'And,' I go on, ignoring her, 'what a shock it must be coming into the world from a dark, watery womb.'

'At least your baby will decide when he's coming out. Imagine what a shock they get when they're unzipped and plucked out like a wisdom tooth.' Dione presses her lips together, probably holding back her diatribe.

'All I know is that I want it to be quiet and dark and as soft as possible.'

Dione sighs, and I can see she's choosing her words carefully. 'You know it'll probably take hours, and you'll probably beg for pain killers?'

'Of course I do, I've had my head stuck in your bible for the past week. Haven't you noticed?' Even though her midwife book has far too much information, I've still read it cover to cover. It's either that or the shampoo bottle—I've read everything else. I hope Jake finds some books when he's ashore.

'I've seen you with it,' Dione replies. 'I just need to know what you want to do about the pain.'

'I don't know!'

'You need to let me in a bit,' she says gently.

'I don't *know*. None of it feels real. I read that book over and over and it all seems so heady and *un*real but then I feel him kick or catch myself talking to him and it's like he's been with me forever. But I just can't see past the here and now.'

She nods, waiting for me to say more.

'I'm scared. What if something goes wrong? What if he dies? What if I die? Once you said that birth and death are two sides of the same coin. I keep hearing that and it scares me.'

'You'll be alright,' she says quietly.

'You don't know that!'

'You're right, I don't *know*. That's the whole crux of birth. Even in the Program they don't know for sure how it's going to go.' She blows out of her mouth like she's trying to calm everything down with her breath. 'My gut feeling is ... that it will be okay. But having said that ...' She sounds a bit harder now, and I guess she's getting to the point of the conversation. '...you don't want to plan to be in the middle of the ocean when the baby comes. It would be better to be on land. '

'Like we have a choice.' I hear myself sounding bitter.

'We do have a choice, Ora.'

'Oh, okay then ... I choose my house that burnt down. If you could just magically restore it and then organise a private jet to fly me there when labour starts, that would be great.'

'There is always a choice, Ora.'

'Bullshit! There was no choice when Mum and Holly died, or when the SIF caught me and locked me up like a dog. And there is no choice about where to have this baby. You don't know what you're talking about.' I slide off the bow and climb clumsily across to the cockpit, holding onto the rail.

'When I was hiding in my hole in the cottage, do you know what kept me sane?' Dione is raising her voice, making sure her words reach me across the length of the boat.

The wind and the waves have picked up. My thoughts flicker to Jake trying to row back in the dinghy. Dione puts her fishing rod in the holding slot and comes after me.

'Every day,' she sits down opposite me on the cockpit bench, '*Every single day*, I had to remind myself that I had a choice. Would I break out and run down the hill like a madwoman throwing my life away? Or would I breathe my way through it and use my imagination to set me free?'

'Well, whoopie-do for you,' I say.

'I bet you did the same in your cell,' she says. 'You made choices, even if you didn't know it.'

'Enough of the lecture already,' I say, standing up.

'No, this is important.' She takes my hand and I feel a flood of warmth, but I resist it. 'We need to have this conversation, Ora. We need to have a plan.'

I snatch my hand away and stomp down the steps to my mattress retreat, shutting the little door with a feeble bang. I look up at the low ceiling and remember being in that cell. And then I remember Snake and Lion. They were the ones who got me through. But I didn't 'choose' to think about them. They just appeared when I was desperate and alone.

Maybe they were just part of my imagination? But they felt more real than that. They were my guides. But ... I'm confused.

I reach up to the little shelf above the bed and get my music player—silently thanking Jake for charging it yesterday in the sun. I put the earplugs in and settle into the embrace of the mattress, covering my eyes with the pillow and already feeling the comfort of where I'm going ...

Lion is with me immediately, underneath our tree. I put my arms around his neck and feel an enormous surge of love. We turn and head into the tree. I expect to go down the stairs but he leads me up, spiralling into the clouds.

It's white and empty, but soft and welcoming. And quiet. There is Snake, dancing on her coils, looking friendly and wild at the same time.

'Ora! How lovely to see you.'

I've missed you, I smile.

'You've come about the baby.' She looks at me with her knowing eyes.

The birth, actually … I … I'm scared.

'Every woman is, Ora. It's part of the journey. Any rite of passage involves fear. Fear of the unknown and fear from hearing stories of those who have gone before you and suffered. Be gentle with yourself and remember to trust.'

But I don't know how I'm going to be. I feel all choked up. *And I don't how to trust.*

Someone comes up behind me and puts their arms around my belly. I recognise her instantly.

Mum! I try to turn but she holds me snugly in her arms. I relax back into her, tears of joy pricking my eyes.

'You'll be fine, Ora. You'll go well,' she whispers into my ear.

I want you to be there.

'I know you do, love.' She rocks me like she used to do when I was upset. 'I will be in my own way. Know that I'll be close.'

I give a quick nod, trying to be brave.

'You're going to be a mother, Ora,' she says, stroking my belly. 'This baby is very lucky, my love, to have you.'

I turn but she's gone. I kneel with my hands on the earth and cry bitter tears, swimming in my loss.

The drumbeat begins to slow and Lion appears to take me back. I switch off the sounds, knowing it's pointless to try again, and surrender to the tears, allowing Mum's absence to wash through me.

My thoughts drift to Dione, and then to my baby. I hope he can't feel my grief.

33

Dad Again

The light is fading when Jake finally returns with a dinghy full of goodies. I hear his voice and go up to meet him. He looks worn out. Dione is on deck grabbing the bags as he passes them up to her. They see my red eyes, but neither of them comments.

This has been Jake's third trip 'into the fray', as he calls it. Each trip takes a toll—the stress of staying undercover when he doesn't know where he is and the weight of the fuel and all the bags and supplies. Dione goes with him every other trip—they shouldn't be seen too much together.

Whenever we can, we get off the boat. I get a break every time we stop at a deserted beach, and there are plenty of those along the way. We throw down anchor and swim or row ashore, celebrating the feel of the solid earth beneath our feet. I walk and walk and bask on the land and always feel torn as evening creeps in. We've talked about camping overnight, but haven't managed it yet.

After passing up the last bag, Jake hauls himself into the boat and fishes out a crumpled piece of paper. 'The good news is I got your ginger root. The bad news is this,' he says, passing the paper to me. 'I printed it at the library.' We sit on the benches, bags of shopping covering the sunken floor at our feet, and I open the folded paper.

I gasp. There is a picture of me looking out at the world, and a small one of Jake that I've never seen before. The headline screams, 'Where is Ora James?' I start to scrunch it up.

'Hang on!' Dione says, reaching across and snatching it out of my hands. 'I want to read it.' She studies the article.

'That's the picture we sent your dad last Christmas. He must have given it to them.'

'What?' I say. My brain isn't working. Was it the SIF or the press who have run this story?

'Read it out.' I'm ready to hear it now.

> 'Ora James of Long Gully Road, Adelaide was last seen with boyfriend Jake Watson on 6 November. The pair was seen in central Adelaide at Scapes Bookshop and later at Seaford Station. James lived with her aunt, Dione Oakton, who has been missing since February this year. It is believed Oakton had been illegally practising as an independent midwife prior to her disappearance. All three are wanted for questioning by the SIF, who have declined to comment further.
>
> 'Emergency Physician Douglas James has appealed to the general public for any news of his daughter's whereabouts. He told journalists that Ora had developed a recent health condition and may be in need of urgent medical attention.'

'What?' I am stunned. Dione holds up her hand. There's more.

> 'Dione Oakton assisted women to birth

*outside of the Safety for the Future
Program. According to reliable sources,
she operated an underground birthing centre at the back of her property and may
have also attended homebirths. If caught
and charged, Ms Oakton will face a life
sentence in prison.*

*'Douglas James commented, "I can't
believe that woman dragged my daughter
into this. Ora would only have gone along
with it because she didn't think she had a
choice." Mr James then broke down, pleading with members of the public to come
forward with information about his only
surviving daughter. Tragically, Mr James'
wife and older daughter were killed in a
house fire over five years ago. Please contact journalist Keith Waterhouse with any
relevant information.'*

'And then it gives contact details,' Dione says quietly, folding the paper neatly. She has read steadily all the way through,
her voice even, but she looks pale. Who wouldn't, after reading
in black and white that they have a life sentence hanging over
their head?

'Let's just go to New Zealand!' Jake says. He has such a hunted
look in his eyes. 'Tonight! It'll only take us a week. We've got
enough food.' He stands up and shoves the bags out of the way.
'Ora can have the baby there! In a proper hospital!' He jumps
down into the cabin. 'I'm checking the weather reports.' The VHF
radio is his lifeline.

Dione and I look at each other. I have a lump in my throat.
There is no way I'm going to lose her to jail.

'I'm sorry,' I say. 'About Dad.'

'It's okay. He's got a lot to blame me for.'

'But he didn't have to—'

'He trusted me to look after you,' she cuts me off. 'And look what a fine job I've done.' She points at my belly. '*And* on the run from the SIF!'

'But he—'

'And now you're missing. He's got every right to want to see me put away.' She sounds hollow.

I get up and give her a hug but my belly gets in the way.

'I'm sorry about before,' I say.

'It's okay,' she says, sounding even further away.

'Maybe Jake's right,' I say. 'Maybe New Zealand is our only option.'

'No!' She pulls away and looks at me intently. 'No way are we crossing the Tasman in this little boat. That would be insane. I'm not going to be responsible for you drowning as well.'

Jake comes back up looking bleak. The weather report is bad—a storm is heading our way. We won't be sailing any-where tonight.

We take the bags down to the cabin. Jake secures the deck and then comes in, closing the hatch. We all huddle together around the table, burying our sorrows in the tasteless government food we've grown used to and trying to ignore the ever-growing waves.

'We're doing okay as we are,' Dione says. 'We just need to keep going.' She sounds so certain. I wonder how she's really feel-ing. She's so hard to read.

'I feel too vulnerable here,' Jake says. 'If they find out where we are—and they may already have guessed, seeing as they've tracked us to Seaford Station—we won't be able to get away.'

'But it'll be the same wherever we hide,' Dione says.

'Medical condition!' I scoff. All my old hurts and suspicions about Dad are rearing up again. 'How ridiculous!'

'Health condition,' Jake corrects. 'Your dad said health condi-tion, not medical condition.'

'What's the bloody difference? I don't know why he had to say any of it.' I want them to agree with me; to join forces and rant about Dad. But neither of them is biting. 'That report is all his fault, you know. Giving them my photo! What was he thinking?'

'That he wants his pregnant daughter to be safe?' Jake says.

'Oh, Mr Know-it-All!'

'You just don't get him, that's all,' Jake says quietly, not backing down.

'Oh, so now you're the expert on my dad?'

'Hang on,' Dione commands, swallowing the last of her chocolate quickly. 'Fighting isn't going to help. We need to stay focused, stick together and keep out of the way. They won't find us if we do that.'

'Those newspaper guys are better detectives than the whole SIF put together,' says Jake. 'If they want to find us they will. Do you think Doug rang them out of the blue? Do you think he even knew Ora had gone? No way!

'The bloodsuckers would've paid him a visit and scared the hell out of him. Asked him questions about Ora, implying she was in danger again. Then they would have left. Can you imagine his distress? You're missing! Of course he ended up talking to them. If he was really the bastard you think he is, he'd have told them you were pregnant!'

Maybe he has a point.

'He doesn't know Dione is with us,' Jake continues. 'For all he knows I might be forcing you to have the baby up a tree!'

'Okay!' I say. 'Point taken.'

We're all silent again.

'Maybe you should ring him, next time you go ashore?' I suddenly want to make it better for him.

'Could they trace the call from a phone box?' Dione asks.

We purposely left our mobiles at home. Tom convinced us that if we had them we'd use them.

'I dunno,' Jake says. 'If I had my mobile I could google it,' he cracks. I don't smile and neither does Dione.

'What about a postcard?' I suggest, but they both shake their heads, saying the postmark would give us away.

'He'll just have to suffer in silence,' Jake says, but his voice is gentle.

It's true, but it bothers me. Thinking about Dad puts me on such a rollercoaster. I don't know what I feel anymore.

'I'd better not come ashore again,' Dione says, sounding flat. Jake agrees.

I realise I'm eating, even though my belly is bursting and the waves are making me feel sick.

'Do you think we should make the supplies last a bit longer?' I say, looking at the others, who are munching away too. 'So we don't have to risk going ashore so often?' Dione and Jake nod reluctantly and start putting the food away.

'The good thing is, we haven't used much fuel,' Jake says, sounding a bit brighter. 'That's the hardest thing to restock.'

When the storm hits, it's the biggest one yet. I don't manage to get to the bucket before I vomit.

34

Row, row, row your boat

We start talking about going ashore and holing up in a big hotel, if I could just make it into the room without being seen. The hunt is truly on and it's making us feel tense and exposed. The ocean no longer feels like the safest place to hide. Jake spotted a helicopter in the distance. It probably wasn't for us, but we're spooked.

We're not too far from the Gold Coast, which is ironic as this was Jake's first suggestion of where to hide. Dione thinks we have the cash to cover a room. I try not to think how risky it'll be; Jake paying cash at a hotel while Dione and I hide out the back.

We have fake IDs. Tom made them for us.

This is crazy.

But we are desperate.

I start noticing every detail around me. I have to distract myself; a creeping terror is encircling me. I make up names for the different types of waves and become so attuned to the stars and the tides that I start to wonder if I'm related to the tribes who navigate the seas by them.

I don't know what to say to Jake and Dione anymore. I try to think of things but I only come up with small talk that dies in my head before the words get out. They seem as lost as me. I am glad for the nights when Jake and I snuggle together, still connected.

Every time I think of the next trip ashore I feel my ribs knit together in my chest. Soon there's a knot there all the time, and two and a half weeks later it's ready to explode. Jake has had to go in for the fifth and last time—we don't have enough fuel to get us to the Gold Coast, or food. The wind has deserted us for days, forcing Jake to use the outboard to move us further along the coast.

I don't want him to go—why can't we just risk it?—but he won't listen. We need more food and he wants to get more gas for the cooker, too. We're a week away from going back to land for-ever. The plan is to find a house to rent, and some kind of work.

Jake sails us towards the coast and puts down anchor when we can just see the shore. All the time I'm pleading with him not to go. We end up having a spat before he leaves, me desperate for him to stay, him determined to go. Two hours later, when Dione and I are in our usual fishing spot on the deck, I am relieved to see him returning.

'Looks like Jake's back already,' I say to Dione.

She looks through the binoculars for ages, then looks at me. 'That's not Jake.'

'Are you sure?' She *must* be wrong.

She looks again. 'It's a wooden rowboat and the guy looks bigger.'

'Shit!' I say, feeling the panic rise, remembering the chopper from yesterday. The three of us had been below deck, which was a com-plete stroke of luck—Dione had been doing a check-up on me and Gumnut, and Jake had wanted to be there. We held our breath as it flew over a couple of times, shaking and rattling our insides with its thunderous thrum, filling us with terror. But when it took off and nothing happened we convinced ourselves that luck was on our side.

We had to. We had nowhere else to go.

'I'm going to have to hide below,' Dione says, ducking along to the cockpit already.

'Shit!' I look at my bare belly. I'm wearing my bikini to get a half-hour of morning sun. I follow Dione.

By the time I reach the cabin Dione is already hidden in my bed with the door shut. I fling on my grey dress and look down. All I see is bump—who am I kidding? My baby is due in a few days' time. I wish Gumnut was already out, he'd be so much easier to hide.

I scramble back up to my fishing position, grabbing my sunnies and hat. It seems to take the man ages to get close enough for me to see him clearly; the steady paddle of oars is driving me insane.

As he draws closer, I recognise the flashy smile. It's the guy from the car who tried to charm me into talking, the same one who wrote the report. I take a deep breath and think of Dragon; if ever there was a time Gumnut needed protecting, it's now. Our cover is blown and Mr Big Hair is about to find out I'm pregnant.

'Ora!' He says my name like we've been friends forever. 'Good to see you!'

We both know his excitement is more about his success rather than actually seeing me. I pull my knees up in front of my chest and cover my legs with my dress.

'You remember me, don't you?' he asks, coming in beside the *Artemis* and tying his boat to the ladder. 'I'm from the free media, remember?' His hands, by now, are on either side of the ladder and he is about to step onto it. I am frozen, unable to speak or act, images of snarling dogs and SIF officers flashing through my system.

'Keith,' he says, flashing those impossible teeth again. 'Keith Waterhouse.'

'Stay right there!' My senses return. 'Don't come on the boat!' I command, struck by his stealth, like a panther moving in on its kill.

I watch him pause, undecided, and take my chance.

'Dolphins!' I point. He turns to look behind him. In one

movement I stand up, hold the rail and do a kind of forward roll into the sea. Pure adrenaline shoots me overboard. I have to push out hard with my arms so I don't bang my head. My back takes the impact. The cold water stuns me as I land with a plop.

My sunnies and hat are lost and the dress pulls me down but I kick up to the surface, adjusting to the cold, and start swimming slow strokes towards him, using my breath to calm me. I am much safer submerged in my ocean.

Thankfully, the rowboat is low in the water and I'm able to put my arms over the edge so I'm kind of leaning in as my legs paddle out behind me, hiding Gumnut but keeping my rear end afloat.

'I could have sworn it was dolphins,' I smile.

Keith Waterhouse is looking at me like I'm bonkers.

'Sorry!' I say, smiling harder and looking up at the sky, impersonating a ditzy girl. 'I just …' I search for the right words, '…panicked! I'm not used to company.' I attempt a coy smile and when he smiles back, warmth runs through me. Maybe I can charm him.

'I thought you were going to swim for shore.' He chuckles and stands up, coming towards me. 'Here,' he holds out his hand. 'Let me help you.'

I look at his hand and then at his face and shake my head.

'No offence Keith, but I feel safer here.' Another shy smile. 'It's just … I don't know you and …' I trail off, hoping he doesn't persist.

Thankfully, he sits back down—too close for comfort, but it'll do. He nods his head and smiles. 'You're a hard girl to find, Ora James.'

It feels like he's admiring me. I blush furiously.

'How *did* you find me?' I concentrate on my legs, beating a gentle rhythm in the water, rather than my burning cheeks.

He throws his head back and laughs. 'Now that'd be telling.' Another flashy smile, aimed right at me. This guy is so cocky. I bash harder at the sea with my feet.

'If you don't tell me, I won't talk to you.' I know it's childish, but I can't think what else to say.

He watches me and his lips twitch. How dare he find me amusing! He waits, staring at me for too long, drawing out the moment. I glare back.

'Little Tom,' he says finally.

'Little Tom?' I say in disbelief. 'He can barely talk.'

'It was pure chance and some skilful powers of deduction.' He raises an eyebrow, looking smug. 'I paid Tom and Sarah a visit. We drank tea on the veranda. They weren't talking and I'd almost given up, but then one of the horses got kicked and they both took off to check on it.'

I imagine Little Tom being left on the veranda, looking up with fascination at this smiling man beside him.

'I always carry a few tricks in my pocket,' Keith says, puffing out his chest. 'You never know when you might need them.' Again, that self-satisfied smile. 'So I pulled out my little matchbox car and the boy's face lit up. He reached for it and I said he could have it if he told me where Ora and Jake were. He looked at me with his clear blue eyes and said, quite precisely, "Boat!"' Keith chuckles.

I squint in the bright sunlight, disbelieving, and yet ...

'After that, it was easy. Well, it took a while sifting through the boating license records from years ago but I eventually hit the jackpot and saw that Tom was indeed the owner of a boat, which confirmed the little guy's tale. Then it was just a question of sighting you. It took a while but, like I said, I have my sources.'

'So what d'you want from me?' I ask, hoping to get this man away from here as soon possible.

'I need a good story, Ora.' He sits back and folds his arms, looking dramatic. 'And this one has the potential to change history. For the better. Anyone with half a brain can see things have gone wrong. For women, and especially for babies. And if they lose, we all lose. And I'll admit …' He pauses for effect. 'I could do with a break. I've had a bad run recently.'

It feels like he's telling the truth but I still don't trust him. Keith continues chatting away about the free media being cut-throat and the constant threat of the SIF when they cover edgy stories. Thankfully, he hasn't asked me into the boat again, and has no idea I'm pregnant. After a minute he stops talking about himself and zooms in on me.

'Why did you run, Ora? I hope *we* didn't scare you off? You're the innocent in all of this. You didn't want to be involved, did you?' He looks at me and waits.

I can't help myself. The words find their way out. I can feel myself sliding down the slippery slope into Keith's world of questions and 'stories'. And I know Jake will be furious, but what choice do I have? I can't stay in the sea all day—I'm starting to feel the cold. And that could be bad for Gumnut. I'll only tell him about the SIF.

'And then once they captured you, you were held for … how long?'

'Six days,' I say.

He shakes his head in disgust. 'What were they thinking? You're still a girl!' I flinch inwardly but maybe I do look young right now, with the sun drying my hair into a frizz.

He stops shaking his head and looks directly at me, asking gently, 'Did they torture you?'

Slug and Worm flash into my mind. I almost answer, but stop myself. Jeez, this man is good. Something about him reminds me of Jake, the way he listens so intently—it's like he knows what I've been through, how insane it all is. I want to tell him everything. Even about the births.

'Are you sure you don't want to come and sit up here?' he asks, noticing our positions again.

Jake must have it wrong. How could someone so caring be as calculating?

'Your lips are looking blue.'

I shake my head.

'Your father's pretty cut up. He's really worried about you, Ora.' He holds out his hand again. 'I just need you to tell me more about the SIF and your interrogation. And Dione.'

I've stopped kicking my legs and let them be pulled down by my dress. I don't know what to do or say. I want to speak, but I can't. Is this man good or bad? Here to help or not? Is he like the SIF? Worse? Or better? Maybe he can help us. What about Gumnut? Jake is going to be so mad with me. I need to think. Everything needs to stop, to slow. I am checking out.

He is saying something about the SIF again, taking me back there. I don't want to go back. My arms are so tired. I stop thinking and loosen my grip.

The water comes into my body. I let my dress pull me down. It's heavy. Blissfully heavy. Floating down. So quiet underneath the water. No SIF down here. Maybe I can swim under the boat to the ladder?

A muffled whoosh rocks me and then a hand closes around my wrist, yanking me up.

I try to pull away, but the grip is too hard. He's strong. I barely struggle—there's no point. We both come up coughing—I've swallowed a lot of water. He grabs the side of the rowboat, still hurting my wrist.

'What the bloody hell are you doing?' His teeth flash in the water and sunlight. Not so smiley now.

I remember who I am.

'Let go!' I shout and try again to pull out of his grip. I'm not going anywhere. But I fight on.

'Let me go, you dickhead!' I shout and squirm. A string of

profanities flows from my mouth; everything I wanted to say to Slug and Rat. I am kicking my legs furiously, pulling away from him.

We struggle on. I make up for my weaker body by shouting in his face, at the top of my lungs. I hate him.

I see Dione before he does. She leaps from the *Artemis* onto the rowboat, moving fast. He senses her and turns. Surprise loosens his grip and I pull away. She brings the oar down on top of his head. A loud smack rings out across the water and now it is he who slips under.

Instinct moves me and I grab his chin, bringing him up again. He is heavy. It's just a couple of strokes to the rowboat. I'm breathing hard. Dione leans over and struggles but manages to get her hands under his shoulders. We move as one. As she heaves, I swim under him and push him up by his buttocks. He is almost halfway in. I grab the side of the boat and when she heaves again, I wedge my shoulder under his side and kick my legs, levering him up. Once his backside is in, she lies him down and swings his legs in quickly.

'Are you all right?' Her face is close to mine as she leans over.

'I'm fine.' I am breathing heavily and holding the side of the boat, but I feel okay.

She looks at me a moment longer before dashing up the ladder and onto the *Artemis*. He starts groaning and moving his head. She's back in no time with a rope. Swiftly, she ties his hands and feet. She finishes by tying the end of the rope to the post of the bench.

'Get back on our boat, Ora,' she orders.

I've been lost in her movements. Everything happened so quickly. It's starting to catch up with me.

Obediently, I walk my hands along the rowboat to the *Artemis*. My legs are wobbly as I climb the ladder. I half fall onto the bench at the far end of the cockpit, out of sight of the rowboat. I am going to vomit. There is the empty bucket we use for our catch of the day. I grab it and some seawater comes up. My insides feel like they're coming out.

A terrible pain shoots through me. Dione comes up the ladder as I'm holding my belly.

Wordlessly she puts one hand below my belly button.

'You're having a contraction,' she says, looking concerned.

'This hurts more than a Braxton Hicks,' I say, grimacing.

'That's because it isn't one.' She goes quickly into the cabin and reappears with her midwife's bag. A chill goes down my spine.

'Is the baby coming?' I ask.

She has put her blood pressure band around my arm and is pumping it up. Holding a finger to her lips, she reads the dial.

'It's a bit high,' she says, casting her eyes to the rowboat. Next she picks up her tool that looks like a mini-wooden trumpet and places one end on my belly. She leans over and puts her ear to the other end. She has to move it a couple of times before she finds Gumnut's heartbeat. I wait, hardly breathing.

'All good,' she says with a wide smile.

The pain has gone and I smile back at her weakly.

'Is the baby coming?' I ask again. I need to know.

'I don't know,' she pauses, looking at me hard. 'Possibly. But it might just be shock. And the seawater. We'll keep an eye on you.' She squeezes my shoulder.

'Thanks for saving me,' I say. As if on cue, Keith starts moaning loudly.

'Shit,' says Dione. 'I didn't think of a gag.' He moans again, louder this time, and she starts to laugh. We are soon giggling and cackling like a couple of hyenas.

'Shh,' I say. 'We'll frighten him.' And with that we're off again.

'He'll think we're witches.' She cackles dramatically. We are made crazy by our adrenaline and our victory.

More cramps stop me. They hit like a leaden force, pushing at my womb. Into it, out of it, pulling it. I fall silent and breathe through the pain.

35

Keith Waterhouse

After our laughing fit Dione and I retreat to the cabin. I change out of my wet dress while Dione sits quietly. My body has returned to normal and there is no more pain, but I feel different; something has shifted, like I've changed gear or something. Maybe it's the adrenaline subsiding.

Dione makes us mugs of tea.

'We'll have to hold him hostage now,' she says, sounding serious. 'We could lose everything if we let him go.'

She's right. We sip at our hot tea, thinking through this added complication.

'I'd better go check out his head,' she says after a while, grabbing the first-aid kit and Jake's spare hat. 'Can't have him getting burnt on us.'

'Dione,' I say urgently. 'If Gumnut comes soon, will he be all right?' She looks at me questioningly. 'Given that it's a bit early?'

Dione smiles widely and I am reassured. 'He'll be fine, Ora.' She turns back to the open sky and says, 'I'll be back in a minute.'

I breathe a sigh of relief. And then—I can't help myself—I creep up on deck and move as close as I can to the rowboat without being seen.

'You bitch!' He's shouting. 'You could have killed me!'

He rants on for ages.

Dione is better at keeping quiet than I am. I want to shout back at him. How dare he ruin things for us? I peep over the edge to have a quick look. She is sitting at the end of the rowboat, waiting for him to finish venting.

Finally he stops. After a long silence he says, 'I should have guessed you were with them.'

'I need to check your head,' she says, sounding cold.

'Boy, this is a story!' he says loudly. 'Man, it's so good!' He's the one laughing madly now.

When he quietens, there's a long silence. I have another quick look and see Dione applying something to the bruising. I almost miss what he says next.

'I'm on your side! Don't you see? The SIF won't be far behind me.'

'In my experience, journalists are only ever on their own side,' Dione says. 'If you keep quiet I won't gag you, but if you make too much noise you'll have an old boat rag in your mouth before you can say help.'

She comes swiftly up the ladder, surprising us both as we lock eyes. She pauses just for a second and then walks straight past me and back down to the cabin.

About an hour later I have another contraction.

⁓

Jake returns in the late afternoon. I'm waiting for him on the bow of the *Artemis*. He waves excitedly and is full of smiles. He doesn't see the rowboat until he is very close. His smile morphs into fury. He rows up to where I'm waiting at the bow.

I lean over the rail and whisper in a rush, 'It's the journalist.' He looks at me, not understanding. 'From before. Dione hit him over the head with an oar and he's tied up in his boat.'

Jake nods, keeps quiet, and paddles to the end of the *Artemis*. Dione goes to the ladder and as usual, they unpack the dinghy. Neither of them says a word—they are being watched by Keith, no doubt. I go to help, keeping out of his sight, and see immediately what was making Jake smile. A box with an inflatable child's paddling pool is amongst the shopping. Jake climbs aboard and sees me looking at it.

'You shall go to the ball, Cinderella!' He comes over and kisses me, not letting Keith Waterhouse's presence spoil his surprise. 'I found it in someone's hard rubbish. Must have been in a garage for years! As long as we find a hotel with a balcony, we can heat up some of the water for the tub with the solar shower bags and boil the rest in pots on the camping stove.'

My heart swells with gratitude. He has found a way. I throw my arms around him and kiss him back.

'That's if we can smuggle everything into the hotel room without being seen,' Dione says, reminding us of our imminent plans.

Jake looks up from reading the measurements on the box and eyes the back of the *Artemis*. Without saying anything we head down to the cabin. Dione and I explain what happened earlier.

'This isn't good.' He's biting his nails. He never bites his nails.

'We have to keep him with us,' Dione says. 'There's no other way. I've been thinking it over all afternoon.'

She has as much to lose as we do. Maybe more. No one speaks for a while.

'He says he's on our side,' I say.

They look at me like I'm stupid. My womb inflames again. Every hour this has been happening—like clockwork. I am surprised at how similar it is to period pain.

'You all right?' Dione asks in her midwife's voice.

'No, she's quite mad,' says Jake. 'And has no idea about journalists.'

Dione and I exchange a grin.

'We'll have to keep him captive on the boat until we're in the hotel. We can put an anonymous call in about him when we're safely hidden.

'I want to talk to him,' I say to Jake. I have a plan of my own.

'Again?' Jake sounds suspicious.

'What else can we do?' I'm angry with them for looking down on me but I tell myself to keep calm; we have to stick together.

Nobody says anything. We have reached a stalemate.

'Jake,' Dione says eventually. 'Can I have a look at the maps? I'd like to see where we're at.'

Her request distracts him—he loves those maps. Maybe she's thinking about sailing into shore tonight. When he gets up to find them I get up too; to talk to the man who holds our future in his hands.

'I might be a while,' I say to them both, hoping they understand that I don't want to be disturbed.

36

My Plan

The sun is setting by the time I step onto Keith Waterhouse's rowboat. There is no wind, and the sea is calm in the orange glow. He is lying with his eyes closed and looks very uncomfortable, in spite of the blue cushion Dione put under his head earlier. I feel bad that we've tied him up like this. It smacks of the SIF—it makes me sick to think I have become like them.

It's odd seeing Keith in Jake's hat. He opens his eyes as I sit on the rowboat's bench, next to where his feet are tied.

'Hello, Keith,' I say gingerly with a half-smile.

'Ora,' he says, with no trace of the sophistication from before.

'I'm sorry about this.' I don't know where to look. The sea clunks gently on the side of the boat, water on wood. I hold up my bottle. 'Would you like a sip?'

He nods, so I kneel in beside him—there's not enough space to do anything else—and put the bottle to his lips. He takes great gulps and then nods, signalling when he's had enough. I want to untie him but I talk instead.

'You know you said before you like a good story?' I decide to get straight to the point—I'll lose my nerve otherwise.

He nods, looking wary.

'And that we could change things, by sharing our story?' He nods again.

'Well, I've got something that tops the fact that you've found Dione,' I say, sounding eager now.

His eyes open slightly wider in the fading light.

'I'm pregnant. The baby's due any day now.' I watch as his eyes nearly pop out of his skull.

He lifts his head and looks at my centre. I kneel up and flatten my T-shirt against myself. He lets out a slow whistle, eyes still big. I sit back on the bench. How did my life get to be this crazy?

'So,' I say, 'as you can see we've got a bit of a problem over what to do with you.'

He nods again.

'If we were evil, we'd feed you to the sharks,' I say. It's a bad joke and he doesn't smile. I carry on quickly. 'But I have a plan B instead, if you agree.'

'Do I have a choice?' He smiles wanly.

'If Dione and I tell you our stories—how it all happened for me and why she did what she did—and we let you go, will you give us your word that you won't print anything until a month from now? That way I'll have had Gumnut and we'll be able to disappear.'

'Gumnut?' he asks.

'The baby.' I smile, feeling shy.

'And you'll let me go, just like that?' he asks.

'I've been held against my will before. I won't put anyone else through that, even if it does put our lives in danger.'

He looks at me for what feels like a long time.

'Besides, it's not like we have a spare room. And it can get pretty bitter out here at night.'

He smiles and stares at our floating home, then looks back at me with what seems like respect. 'You've got yourself a deal, Ora James.'

'Ora!' Jake barks from the *Artemis*, making me jump. I turn back and see myself through Jake's eyes, leaning towards Keith, and squirm inside. I give our hostage a small nod. My legs have gone to sleep so I'm none too steady on the rocking boat as I swivel around and head back up the ladder.

Jake's eyes are boring holes into me. I walk past him and step carefully down to the cabin. Dione is waiting for me at the table. The vertical frown mark between her eyes deepens when she sees Jake's face behind me. I slide onto the bench seat opposite her.

'What the fuck are you playing at?' Jake says between gritted teeth. He is trying to pace in the low, tiny space. I have never seen him like this. His eyes are blazing.

'How could you?'

'Hang on a minute,' Dione says, sounding protective.

'She was practically sitting in his lap!'

Dione looks at me and pulls the weirdest face; a frown, a smile and a question all squished into one expression. My giggles from this afternoon are still echoing inside me and I can feel a laugh rolling its way out, but then I look at Jake. Behind his fury I see a deep current of fear and pain in his eyes and my heart stops.

I love this man.

'I'm sorry,' I say to him. 'It must have looked all wrong.'

He sits down on the bench opposite, leans over and holds his head in his hands. He blows a long breath out of his mouth. One of his legs is moving up and down and I can see he's working doubly hard to manage his anger. I don't think he trusts himself to speak.

'I was trying to be friendly, Jake.'

'So I saw,' he snarls.

'I hate that he's tied up.'

'We can't let him go,' Dione says quickly, shaking her head.

'We're no better than the SIF,' I say. 'He's been tied up for hours.'

No-one says anything.

'I was giving him some water,' I say, sounding miserably defensive. I remind myself I haven't done anything wrong. Jake is acting like I've madly pashed him. A kernel of self-righteous anger ignites inside.

He takes a loud breath in and breathes out again.

'I'm sorry too,' he says. 'I overreacted.' He looks up at me with pained eyes. It dawns on me we've never hung out with other guys before, other than Tom.

'He is a bit of a charmer.' Dione smiles.

'He's a sleaze,' Jake says.

I have another contraction. Dione looks at me. She knows. It doesn't last long.

'Whatever he is,' I say, 'we can't keep him here forever.'

I tell them my plan and the three of us argue for an hour.

I have another contraction. The pain is still bearable.

'You should get some sleep,' Dione says.

'I need you to agree first,' I say. 'Both of you. I think this guy is okay. Yes, he may be a sleaze,' I look at Jake. 'But I don't think he's going to put us in danger and we really don't have a choice, unless we throw him overboard tied to the anchor.'

'That's a good idea,' Jake quips.

I am starting to feel so tired.

Finally they agree. I will talk to him first, and tell him my side of the story. Then Dione will share hers and he'll row back to shore with the promise that he won't publish the story for a month. I persuade them that the sooner we talk, the sooner he'll be out of our hair.

'Then I'll go to bed,' I say to Dione. 'And once you've talked to him he can row his way out of our lives.'

Jake looks happy about this part of the plan, but is still uncertain about releasing him.

'I hope you're right about him,' he says, looking at me intensely. He doesn't need to tell me that our freedom depends on it.

Jake goes to untie Keith and Dione makes us some food. The cockpit is the only place where we can all sit, and I wouldn't want Keith in our cabin anyway.

We eat in uncomfortable silence. Keith has tried a couple of jokes but Jake and Dione completely blank him.

It feels like I talk for hours about getting caught and being at the SIF centre. I'm finding it hard to focus. I haven't had another contraction, but I think my baby is coming. It takes every drop of my willpower to continue talking.

I will tell Jake when we're in bed, but for now I hold my secret close. It anchors me as I spill my insides into Keith Waterhouse's phone. He's surprisingly gentle as he picks his way through my story.

I break down when I have to talk about my time at the SIF. Jake holds me and whispers in my ear, reminding me I'm safe now.

Eventually we stop. Keith's battery is running low and he's worried he won't be able to record Dione's story too.

'Shit!' he says forcefully. I realise how much passion he has invested in this story.

'We have a solar charger. You'll have to recharge it in the morning,' I say tiredly. 'I need to go to bed.' I get up and go down to the cabin. All I can think about is lying down. This has been a huge, long day and reliving my story has churned up too much; it feels like a dust storm has blown through every part of me.

I lie on the bed and wait for Jake.

37

Gumnut

'Are you sure?' he asks, incredulous, all his grumpiness over Keith dissipating.

Jake is lying beside me in our little cave, propped up on his elbow, his face above mine. He puts his hand on Gumnut and right on cue I have a contraction.

'Wow!' he says as the skin across my belly tightens. The pain is like a full-on period cramp now, cutting into me. I move onto my side to try and get some relief. Jake can feel when it stops.

'But I don't get how you could just sit up there chatting, knowing that Gumnut is coming!' He looks happy and a bit cross. 'Why didn't you *tell* me?'

'There wasn't the chance,' I say, yawning. 'Everything happened so fast today. I really, really need to sleep, Jake.'

'But how can you be so chilled. Gumnut is coming!'

'Jake,' I say sleepily.

'But does this mean you'll have the baby on the boat?'

'I don't know, it might take hours. I think Dione was checking places out. *Please* can we get some sleep?' It's all I can think about. Who knows how long my early labour will go for but I'm beginning to doubt I'll be leaving the boat pregnant.

'Sure, sure,' he says excitedly. 'D'you want me to get you a glass of water? Any food? You'll wake me up, won't you? It better be sunny tomorrow. I'm glad I filled up the shower bags yesterday. I'll pump up the pool in the morning. Maybe I should do it now?'

'Jaaaake!' I say, almost on the verge of tears.

'Sure, okay. Right.' He leans up and turns off our little overhead light. 'I'm just going to talk to Dione.'

∾

The pain wakes me sporadically throughout the night. When I get up to pee, Dione is on the bench-bed in the cabin. I'm surprised to see her, and realise she must have given up her spot on deck to Keith. I try to pee as quietly as I can, knowing he is lying on the other side of the hatch.

On my way back to bed she asks how I'm going. I whisper that the contractions are coming regularly and everything feels a lot heavier, like Gumnut has moved further down. She asks me to describe the pain and then tells me to get as much sleep as I can, and to drink some water.

'We're not going to make it to land, are we?' I need to offload the worry that's been pulling at my mind.

'I looked on the map and ... for the first time in my life, I don't know what to do. If Keith hadn't been here, maybe, but ... Would you want to go into shore now, even if there was time?'

I shake my head. There's nowhere to go. Not if I want to keep Gumnut.

Dione's face is creased with concern. I've never seen her looking this uncertain. 'I was hoping the contractions would die down,' she says.

A great chasm of fear opens for a brief moment, but I can't go there now. I just need to lie down again. I give her a hug and go back to bed.

Lying down again, I look out the tiny round window and put my hands on my belly.

'I can't wait to meet you,' I say quietly to Gumnut. 'I need you to know that you're going to be born on this boat, so make sure you're okay, okay?' A tear pops out of my eye. What if something goes wrong? What if I can't do it? What if he gets stuck? I can't lose him now, not after everything we've been through.

I close my eyes and get the clearest image of Dragon looking straight at me. I fall into her eyes. Huge, deeply dark, soft, love-filled eyes. My own eyes brim with tears as a startling insight dawns on me—Dragon belongs to Gumnut. She is here for him.

I tingle all over and remember my dance when Dragon first appeared and how Jake was there as well. I have to wake him, this is all too much. I touch Jake's shoulder and he rolls over towards me. His face is beautiful. I kiss his lips and his eyes open widely.

'Are you all right?' he asks urgently, half sitting up.

I smile. 'I'm fine, Jake. Nothing's really happening.' I decide not to tell him about my fears, unsure if he'll get freaked out and lose it. 'I just needed to be with you.'

We are whispering and snuggling.

'You remember my dragon?' I ask him.

'The picture?'

'Yes, and also when we got together?'

He nods and smiles, remembering.

'Well, I thought the dragon was for me. But I've just realised who it's really for.'

'Gumnut?'

'Yes!' I hug him. 'Every time Dragon has appeared, apart from the first time, it's been for Gumnut.'

Jake is as excited as I am, even though he says I'm a loon.

'Maybe that first time was when Gumnut was getting ready

to be conceived!' he says, his eyes glistening in the darkness. 'And then that picture you drew—'

'You're as much of a loon as me!' A contraction seizes me, this one demanding more attention than the last, and I have to use some breath to work through it. Jake shuts up and puts his hand on my leg gently, watching me.

He is with me, quietly supporting me.

When the pain subsides I say, 'I think he's having his second coming now.'

We giggle and cuddle some more, watching our little piece of sky turn from night to day. Jake is doing a good job of distracting me from my fears.

I can do this, I think.

∽

I change my mind soon enough. The contractions start to come closer together, and they steadily get more intense.

I have to get up, which means the whole boat has to get up.

Thankfully the sun rises bright and warm. I notice the waves catching movements of sunlight. The sky is a breathtaking blue. All is clear.

Jake is busying himself with the solar shower bags. He lays them all out on the bow of the boat. I hope the water heats in time.

Up on deck, I manage a 'Good morning' to Keith, but say no more. He has no idea my labour has started and is so busy looking at his phone—willing it to charge—that he doesn't see what's in front of him. His fidgeting annoys me so I retreat below, but there isn't enough room. I need to walk. Jake and Dione come down at different times but I want to be alone. Dione does a quick blood pressure check and listens to Gumnut's heartbeat and then goes back up on deck.

I can hear Jake blowing up the inflatable pool. It's taking ages. Every twenty minutes now a surge takes me. I walk up and down the cabin—four little steps or three big ones, and then I have to turn again.

I think about asking Jake to get us to a beach. I put on my bikini but before I can get up the steps I have to stop and hang onto the table, breathing myself through a surge.

I don't know how long I spend like this. Hours. Backwards and forwards, up and down.

I forget about the beach.

It hurts. I feel sick. I am going to be sick. I reach for the wee bucket. Dione must have washed it out with seawater. I don't care anyway. It feels like my guts are coming up.

The pain in my womb is much worse than any of my fiercest period cramps. I don't think I'm going to be able to do this. I wonder about gas. I like the idea of being knocked out. Why didn't I talk to Dione about pain relief?

Another surge. Rocking. Breathing. Vomiting.

Dione opens the hatch and calls down gently, 'Can I come down?'

I don't look up from the bucket but manage a nod. She sits beside me on the bench seat and rubs my back. Her hand feels good. She ties my hair back.

'Keith has gone,' she says but I don't care.

'It really hurts!' I say to Dione with closed eyes, moving my head from side to side.

'I know. Your body's doing its thing. It's meant to hurt.'

'But I'm not meant to feel pain! This is why we have drugs,' I say indignantly, my voice going up an octave.

'When will the water be ready?' I ask.

'I'm so sorry Ora, there was a problem with the pool. It had a hole in it.'

'No!' I groan, shaking my head from side to side. My natural painkiller option has been taken from me.

'Let's stand you up,' Dione says, taking both my hands.

There isn't room for us both to walk up and down. I feel a strange popping sensation and water gushes down my legs, covering my feet. I am momentarily in awe and disbelief. The sac that has carried my baby all this time has broken open, and I am standing in its puddle.

Over the next half hour I spend all my time getting on and off the portaloo. I kick off my bikini bottoms. They're annoying me. I have this overriding urge to empty my bladder and bowel—especially at the height of a contraction. I stay up this end of the boat.

Dione is with me. She keeps her distance but as soon as I need her she is beside me. She seems to know what I need. A sip of water. A cool face washer. A firm back massage.

Another contraction. I need to hold onto something. The table. If I don't grip the table, I'll be swept away by the pain. I cannot hold this pain inside me. I scream, and my knees buckle.

I want to move. I want to lie down. I don't know what I want. I don't want the next contraction to come.

Dione guides me to my bed. I kneel on the mattress, facing the point of the bow. Dione puts the pillows in front of me and I burrow my head into them. I rock and breathe through the surges as they explode inside me. It's better in here, in my little cave. I lie on my side to rest.

Jake's voice. He leans in and tells me I'm doing great. Right at that moment another wave roars through my body and I do not reply. I am kneeling again, head in the pillows, sounding out the pain.

An enormous contraction rips me apart and I want to run. I can hear my voice, high and strange. *Let me go. No! No! I want the water.* I'm screaming.

Suddenly, I hear Snake's voice. 'Turn and look at the pain,' she instructs.

I can't!

'Turn around, Ora. Step inside the pain. Look at it. It's a wave. Go towards it.'

'Dione!' My voice is so high, I don't recognise myself. 'Make it stop. Give me something. I can't do it.'

Jake is on my other side. He rubs my back but I shake his hand off. I don't want to be touched.

Snake commands me again to look at the pain. I want to run. Dione is telling me to use a deep voice. She wants me to grunt, not shriek. I bury my head deeper into the pillows as she leans over me.

'I can't!' I cry, collapsing onto my side and sobbing.

'Turn and look at the pain,' Snake calls.

The next contraction is coming. I fling my head from side to side. *No! No!* But my body is moving of its own accord, getting up on all fours again, readying for the next barrage.

I stop.

I stop running and turn. The fear slips away. It is the ocean crashing over me, through me. I am inside the pain that is inside me. One word keeps going around in my head: 'Open'. I am kneeling forward, my head in the pillows. My cervix is stretching: wider, wider. Opening. I feel the height of the wave subside and I slide down its back in relief.

I lie on my side and drift in a haze.

Up again, kneeling forward, forearms and knees. Another wave of pain, thundering through me. Between each wave I drift. I am so deeply inside. My eyes are closed. No-one can come in here. It's blissful between the waves.

Another wave, more kneeling. Inside the pain. I lie down, I sleep. Another wave, another sleep. Time stops.

Every now and then I feel Dione press her monitor on my belly, listening to Gumnut's heartbeat. I want her to leave me alone. Jake is here, but not here.

I am shaking violently. I open my eyes. I am cold. I am freezing. My breath is short and I am filled with fear.

'No!' I say. 'I can't. I can't do this. Get me out!' Panic ripples through me over and over. The pain is too strong for me now. Too big. It is moving down into my bottom and legs.

I grasp Dione's hands.

'Dione, make it stop! I can't!' I am screaming. Wild. Clutching. Jake is beside me.

'Jake, make it stop!'

They are talking to me. Talking at me. Telling me I *am* doing it. That I'm nearly there. I feel like I'm disappearing down a plughole. They're not hearing me!

'Is this normal?' Jake asks. He sounds panicked.

This is not fucking normal!

Snake calls to me from deep inside. Her voice is quiet. I have to stop thrashing about so I can hear her. She says something about a point of reckoning. I'm at the threshold. I shut my eyes and I listen. I have opened, she says. I am open. My breath returns. I am okay. I can do this.

I look at Jake and smile. He is with me. Love blazes out of his eyes. Stillness, trust, knowing. I smile again. My heart is full. We stay like this forever.

'I need to poo,' I say, scrambling backwards, out of bed and waddling to the loo.

I don't quite make it, but Dione makes it okay. The warm water feels nice.

She puts towels on the bench. We sit, Dione one side, Jake the other.

The pain returns. It's different now.

I move forwards into a squat. Jake and Dione are beside me on the floor, my arms around their shoulders. I am doing this.

Dione breathes with me.

I feel my baby's head moving down inside me. He feels as big as a melon! I am cracking open. The urge to push is amazing—I could not stop this if I wanted to. I don't want to. My body is driving, my mind sitting, watching, behind a veil.

From somewhere deep, deep inside comes sound. I know it's me, but it isn't me. It is every mother who has gone before me. My throat is opening and so is the rest of me as my baby's head moves down. He is crowning. A crown for him and a ring of fire for me as I stretch around his head. The stinging and heat is phenomenal. I use my breath as he slowly splits me apart.

Pure relief! His head is out.

Dione tells me to reach down. I feel a spongy head and look up in wonder. I motion Jake to reach forward too. He nearly wobbles over. Tears spring into his eyes as he feels our baby's head.

I need to bear down again. I can feel tiny shoulders urging themselves through, and in one swoop he is gliding out of me, into my waiting hands.

I sit back against the bench and lift my baby close. My breaths come in short, excited gasps, full of wonder. He is soft, slippery. Dione places a little blanket over him carefully. Jake kisses me. We are both crying.

Gumnut is looking around with all-seeing eyes. I can't imagine what he's seeing. Then he squeaks, and my heart swells. A little cry. Dione gives him a quick check over and confirms he's a boy. Of course he's a boy! I cuddle him into me and he starts looking for my nipple. He is so tiny and determined, and his little mouth is seeking me out.

I can't stop looking at him. Finally he finds what he wants and latches on. A sharp pain makes me yelp. It takes him a few more goes to attach himself. I feel like I'm all fingers and thumbs—I have no idea what I'm doing.

Dione looks over to the hatch and her face darkens. Jake and I follow her gaze and see Keith. He has opened the hatch and his head and shoulders are inside the cabin with the rest of his body stretched out on the cockpit floor. He is pointing his phone at us.

Filming us.

Dione starts to shout as Jake moves towards him. Gumnut's

whole body jumps. I grip him tighter and say, 'No!' Everyone stops. My baby will not hear words of anger in his first minutes of life. All the power and strength from my birthing body whirls around the room and fills my words. I speak quietly, with complete authority.

'Put the phone on the step and get out.' Keith obediently places his phone on the cabin step and closes the hatch. Were those tears in his eyes?

I look down at Gumnut, who is oblivious and searching for my nipple again. Jake and I return to our baby bubble. Dione gets up and steps over us, moving the phone out of sight. She then puts on some water to boil.

After a while, I need to push again. Still holding my baby, Jake and Dione help me stand. The placenta glides out, a huge chunk of slippery meat. Dione catches it in a bowl and inspects it. All is as it should be. I look into her teary eyes.

There is so much love in this cabin.

∽

With warm, clean water, Dione wipes the blood off my legs and inspects the towels, checking my blood loss. I carefully sit back on the bench and she examines me between my legs.

'You've got a tiny graze,' she says, and I'm surprised that's all there is. I feel so sore, but I'm jubilant. And madly in love with this little being.

Jake cuts the cord.

'My body is amazing,' I say to no one in particular. I feel like I can do anything. 'And you are amazing,' I say to Gumnut. 'We didn't need the water after all.'

Dione smiles, 'You did great.'

'This is all I hoped for.' I look at Gumnut, completely in love.

'Can I hold him?' Jake asks. He is sitting beside me, looking intently at our baby wrapped in a soft blanket.

I have to make myself pass him over.

As I carefully wash and put on my pyjamas, Jake asks dreamily, 'What are we going to call you, little fella?'

'Gumnut!' I say.

I see Dione smiling to herself. She is busy in the kitchen, giving us space as well as keeping an eye on me.

'That's his nickname,' says Jake, clearly besotted. 'He's got to have a proper name.'

'I'm calling him Gumnut.'

'What about Josh?' he asks brightly.

We've had lots of fun laughing and disagreeing about names, but Josh was one of the names we both liked.

'We can call him Josh ... Josh Holly!' I say with inspiration. Jake knows better than to disagree. 'But I'm going to stick to Gumnut for now.'

'Right, you two,' says Dione, bringing over tea and toast. 'Time to eat. Then it's off to bed with the three of you.'

It's dark outside already.

I smile. The *three* of us.

38

Plan A

I don't sleep for long. I keep waking and looking in wonder at my baby, who is lying between us. His journey from womb to world has been a tiring one, and he's sleeping soundly. But I have a constant need to check that he's breathing. I can't believe he's here. His button nose fascinates me—it's tiny! And his miniscule fingernails. When he does open his eyes, they are the deepest blue, ancient and newborn all at once.

Whenever he wakes it takes me a while to get him attached properly for a feed—I'm shocked by how much it hurts when we get it wrong. Toe-curling pain shoots through me as my poor nipple is clamped and pulled by his tiny mouth. It's such a relief when we get it right—for both of us.

My stomach is a spongy mass of skin—what was once stretched taut around my baby now lies in sagging rolls. But none of that matters, not when I look at Gumnut.

By the time first light comes I'm ready to get up. I need to see the horizon. I start to move gingerly out of bed but Jake stirs, so I snuggle back down and we get lost in time together, gazing at this new being between us, drinking him in.

Jake tells me I'm a birthing goddess and I laugh, remembering the rush of power I felt after Gumnut arrived. Josh. Josh Holly.

ॐ

It takes me a while to get up on deck with Gumnut. Walking feels tender but sitting down is worse. Jake is right behind me as I go up the cabin steps. Dione and Keith are sitting, not talking. A sting of repulsion hits me when I see him. He is crumpled and haggard in his suit trousers and shirt, looking like he's had a cold night.

'Good morning,' Dione says gently. 'How did you sleep?'

'Not much,' I reply with a happy smile, hugging Gumnut closer.

I nod briefly at Keith, feeling self-conscious.

'Ora ... and Jake—I am so sorry.'

Nothing like getting straight to the point.

'I owe you a huge apology. I just couldn't help myself. I tried rowing away but I heard you and knew you were giving birth.' He pauses, eyes boring into me. 'I ... can't keep my nose out of other people's business. It was wrong.'

I'm not going to say it's okay.

'You were making these incredible sounds. I'd never heard anything like it. Like some kind of big cat or wild animal, and I just couldn't *not* look.' He's talking fast. 'I tried, I really did. But by *God*! It was amazing. To witness. I mean.'

He's still staring at me intently.

'It felt almost holy! But it was so normal, too.'

His gaze now flits between me, Jake and Dione. There is silence, apart from the waves knocking against the boat, rocking us gently.

Jake is standing beside me with his hands crossed over his chest, totally on edge.

Now Keith pleads. 'I am sorry, Ora.'

The silence becomes unbearable.

'What were you thinking?' I ask. 'Looking is one thing, but filming?'

'I don't know. But recording is what I do. It's terrible, I know. But now … it's done … It … Something like this could reach thousands, Ora.' He looks searchingly into my face. 'It'll show them what birth *can* be like. Things have to change or people will forget—maybe they have already—but it's too important not to try! This could go viral before it gets taken down like all the other birth footage. You've got to let me use it. It's exactly what we need.'

'You're insane!' Jake looks at Keith in disbelief. 'You had no right. *No right!* That was private and you want to make it *public*? We're on the *run*, for God's sake.' His hands are balled into fists.

'Whoa!' Keith waves his arms in defence. 'Let me explain. I've got a plan.' I can see him making himself smaller, like an under-dog with an alpha male. He'll need to talk fast to avoid getting punched in the face.

'I'm on your side. I want to change this … it's out of control. Everyone's forgotten what normal birth is like.' He looks at me admiringly when he says this. 'Babies are *meant* to come out like that. Full stop.'

He's got Jake's grudging attention now. 'Birth isn't meant to happen in factories for the future programs. I *know* it's wrong and I want to stop it. That's the big picture.'

Jake is unclenching his fists. I breathe more easily.

'Little picture, there's you guys. Whether you like it or not, you're birth activists.' He looks at Dione. 'You've always been one. And *you've* just become one,' he says, startling me out of my baby bliss. 'If you don't stand up and fight, who will?'

Dione is smiling at him! This guy is good. He's even got me wondering, in spite of my anger.

'I admit—in the beginning I was just after the story. But last night … Witnessing the birth … I'm totally *in* … completely.' He shrugs, looking surprised at himself.

None of us knows what to say. Maybe he *has* just become enlightened.

'I've been awake all night,' he says finally, straightening up. 'And I've got a plan.' He looks pleased with himself and I can see the familiar Keith Waterhouse returning.

Jake rolls his eyes but says nothing. We don't have anything to lose.

Keith carries on with his rapid-fire talk.

'I want to write this story. And I want to show the birth footage. But first we have to make sure you guys are safe.' He looks up. Dione and I nod to show we're listening.

'Someone owes me a favour. A big one. And the guy in question happens to have a converted warehouse in Melbourne. If you sail down there, I could transport you and hide you in it. It's very liveable. You could stay there indefinitely, until this blows over.'

Jake looks doubtful. 'We don't want anyone to know where we are,' he says.

'No-one needs to.' He pauses to think. 'He's offered it to me before. I could tell him I'm renovating my place. I could supply you with everything you ne—'

'What kind of favour?' Jake interrupts.

'Two years ago I uncovered a fraud—company theft. Great story. The owner of the company couldn't thank me enough. He keeps offering me his place.' Keith looks pleased with himself. 'Treats me like a son … Nice fella. We play squash together.'

'And he'll lend you the place, just like that?' Dione looks dubious.

'Yep. Definitely.'

'What about water?' Dione asks. 'I can't see four of us surviving on your ration, Keith.'

'We'll find a way,' Keith says. 'The hardest thing is going to be getting rid of the boat.' He explains the rest of his plan. It's complicated. It's dodgy. It means we have to trust him.

And it might just work.

They spend ages talking through the possible downfalls. Halfway through, I go and lie down with Gumnut. When will this ever stop?

I come back up feeling fragile. Uncertain. It's all moving too fast again. Yesterday, my baby was still inside me.

Keith has finally convinced Dione and Jake he can help us.

Jake looks at me and Gumnut before going down to the cabin to get Keith's mobile. He holds it out to him. I don't know what to say. This doesn't feel right.

There's silence. The two of them look one another squarely in the face.

A moment passes between them, then they shake on it, the phone in their hands; our fates contained between their palms.

⋙

As Keith leaves in his rowboat, Gumnut starts to cry. His wails unnerve me. I can't comfort him. It's the first time I haven't been able to console him properly. A sense of foreboding creeps into my body; I don't know whether it's to do with Gumnut or with Keith's departure.

I make a mental list of all Keith's promises and wonder if we're completely nuts. What if he gets back to shore, goes to his office and publishes the story? What if he rings the SIF and tells them where we are? What if Gumnut's birth is all over the news tonight?

I have to remind myself that things are looking good so far. Keith rang the guy with the warehouse before he left and has arranged it already. It's all set for nine days' time. We just have to get to Melbourne.

But will he be able to keep from breaking the story until we're safely in the warehouse? I'm not so sure. The thought of going back scares me. It'd make a better story if the SIF caught us first …

When I'm not worrying, I'm feeding Gumnut or changing his nappy or gazing at him for hours. Or trying to sleep. I had no idea how exhausting babies are.

❧

A massive storm hits us three days later. I think we are going to die. I struggle to hold onto the boat and to Gumnut at the same time. Finally, Dione and I manage to attach him to me with a homemade sling she makes out of a torn-up sheet. My hands are now free to grab on for dear life.

Gumnut screams his head off. Jake is up on deck, harnessed to the boat, making sure we stay upright. Dione is down with me, frantically trying to stow everything away. We are battered relentlessly. It feels like we're going to capsize. The worst is when we're airborne, and then the inevitable crash that follows as we smash back into the sea. I begin to pray.

Maybe this is what my foreboding was about. I make so many promises. The roar of the storm is my witness and my torturer, hearing my pleas and howling in my ears that this is the end.

39

Plan B

The next day the sea is completely calm. All we can do is sleep and rest our tender, bruised bodies. Nobody feels like talking. Gumnut is unsettled and I comfort him, wondering how many more storms lie ahead of us.

The next few days slip by uneventfully. It feels strange going back on ourselves, but at least for once we're going *somewhere*, rather than just staying hidden. Suddenly it hits me. Once we're at the warehouse, we'll *always* have to stay hidden. For years! What were we thinking? I can't live like that. None of us can! I rush down the cabin steps, startling Gumnut, who was asleep in my arms.

'Can you stop packing up?' Jake and Dione have been busy sorting through what we're going to take ashore. The boat is anchored and it's almost lunchtime.

'I don't want to go to Melbourne!'

'Wha—' Jake starts to talk, but I interrupt him.

'It doesn't feel right. The closer we get, the more I feel it.

Physically. In my chest and in my gut. I want to trust Keith, but I don't.'

'Ora—'

'Dione, can you just listen? Have either of you thought about the life we're going back to? Even if it all works and we get to the warehouse, change our identities ... we'll still be living like caged mice, with Keith as our keeper. Until he's onto the next story. The SIF will want us more than ever. We have too much to lose.'

'There's still time to stop Keith from running the story,' Jake says.

'He'll use it anyway,' Dione says bleakly. She sighs. 'As much as I want things to change ... I wish he'd never found us.'

'Why didn't I just toss his phone overboard when I had the chance?'

'He's still got our story, Jake,' I say. 'We became his pawns the moment he found us. We should have tossed *him* overboard.'

Dione smiles.

I can feel the heat of certainty rising up through my body. 'I am so *over* being someone else's pawn. Even my blood belongs to the government. My baby will too, if we go back. And now my birth story belongs to Keith. *We'll* belong to Keith if we're not careful. Maybe he will protect us like he promises, but I don't want to live like that.' I look at Jake, then at Dione. She will be the hardest to convince.

'I want to go to New Zealand ... We just survived a massive storm.' I am pleading now. 'Jake, I know you can do this.'

He is quiet, thinking. Weighing up our chances.

'I'd have to go ashore to get more fuel.'

He's putting on his VHF headphones.

Please let the weather report be good.

'Dione?'

'This boat isn't made for the deep, Ora. Do you know how

much bigger the waves are out there?' She's shaking her head. 'It's too dangerous.'

'Having a baby on a boat is dangerous. Being an undercover midwife is dangerous! Growing your own veggies is dangerous!'

'But what if we all drown?'

'I have a gut feeling about this Dione ...'

She smiles at me, catching the echo of her own words from a few weeks ago.

'But what about your dad, Ora? He'd never forgive me if something happens.'

'You'd be dead, so it wouldn't matter! And besides, he still has to forgive you for all the other stuff first.'

'That's not funny. I don't know—'

'I'll write to Dad. I'll explain. Jake can send the letter when he goes to get more fuel. Dad might even join us when we're there. You could practise as a midwife again, without having to hide. Think of all the women you'll help.'

'The weather report is good,' Jake is grinning. 'If we leave today. But that crossing is one of the worst in the world. The winds are unpredictable. They change all the time and can get up to 40 or 50 knots. If a real storm hit, we'd just have to close the hatch and pray. I couldn't sail us through it. It's madness.'

'But it's not *always* stormy ... what about luck?'

'How long will it take?' Dione asks. Is she considering it?

'Up to three weeks max, a lot less if the wind is right. I don't know how far the fuel will take us when the wind's down, but once it runs out we'll still have the sails.'

'Think of the alternative, Dione. Hiding out for years, wondering when the SIF are going to catch us? Or worse, being caught and locked up?'

'When you put it like that ...' she says.

'It's a no-brainer.' Jake is grinning. 'But there's no way we'd survive a big storm.'

'But there might not *be* a big storm.'

'The ocean is much more unpredictable than birth, Ora.'

'I know! And I know there's so much to lose. But I want to take the chance.'

She's shaking her head.

'Please, Dione!'

Silence.

'I must be mad.' She is still shaking her head, but it's in disbelief, not disagreement.

I jump up and hug them both, nearly squishing Gumnut in the process.

'I'll steer us into shore,' Jakes goes up the steps. 'There's an onwater refuelling station not far from here—there's no way I'll be able to carry all the fuel we're going to need. Dione, you'll have to go and get food supplies when we dock.'

'I'd better go write that letter!' I can't believe it.

A new, cold fear unfurls inside me—we *are* insane—but I push it away. Gumnut is fast asleep again, wrapped up in his little bundle of swaddling. I put him down on top of our bed and move in beside him.

It takes me so many goes. When Jake calls down to say we're ten minutes away, I have to scribble my final attempt. I put the letter in an envelope and seal it. Then I put that inside another envelope, along with a note to Dad's neighbour, asking her to pass it on to him. I don't explain why. She must know I'm missing. It's a big risk, but she's an older lady who hated the SIF so if she suspects anything, I don't think she'll tell them—she was always fond of Dad.

We motor into the filling station. I stay below deck with Gumnut. Dione disappears, wearing her big sun hat and sunnies, promising to post the letter. *Please be safe,* I whisper under my breath as she goes. Jake, also wearing his hat and sunnies, fills all the tanks. We have extras under the cockpit benches. He comes down and grabs one of the 50L water containers, saying he's going to fill that with fuel too. We can always make drinking water along the way.

I listen to Jake readying the boat on deck and wait for Dione to return. More tension. More wailing from Gumnut. How does he know when I'm stressed? He feels it more than me. I keep putting him on the boob, which is probably giving him a belly ache, but I need him to keep quiet.

Finally Dione returns, laden with bags. As soon as she's stepped on board, Jake fires up the motor and we're off!

Dione comes down with all the food and starts unpacking. She looks the most worried I've ever seen her. I get up to give her a hug.

'In two to three weeks we'll be free, Dione. I know it feels mad but we're going to make it, I'm sure of it.'

'Oh, I hope so, Ora. I just keep thinking about your dad. And your mum. And Holly.'

I put my hand over her heart. 'They're here. Always.'

'I know that, but I still feel like I'm leaving them. And if something happens ... your dad ...'

'You can't think like that, Dione. Right here, right now, we're heading out on the calm sea and as soon as we get to New Zealand, we'll find a way to let Dad know where we are. *And* contact Lucy! I'm so excited about seeing her again. She doesn't even know about Gumnut.'

'Lucy! When was the last time you spoke to her?'

'Months ago. We kind of lost touch with all the SIF stuff ... but she'll understand when I explain.'

'You sound so certain about it all, Ora,' she says, managing to look happy and sad at the same time.

'So much has happened, Dione. I just want to know what it's like to live normally for once in my life.'

'Well ... in that case, stepping into the here and now.' She goes to get something out of one of the bags. 'And making sure we enjoy the moment while we can ... look what I found in the shops.'

'Champagne!'

'We have to wet the baby's head!'

'Do you think it's wise? The last time we drank champagne was—'

'You can't think like that, Ora. Right here, right now we're heading out on the calm, blue—'

'Okay, okay!' I'm laughing. 'You and Jake will have to drink it. But I'll have a sip.'

I grab some tumblers and we head up on deck.

'Where's Josh?' he asks with one eye on the horizon.

'Sleeping.' I hand him a glass and kiss him.

Dione pops the cork. 'To Gumnut,' she says, pouring out the bubbles.

'To Gumnut,' Jake and I repeat, clinking cups, grinning.

'And to Ora,' Jake kisses me. 'The most amazing woman in the world. My love!'

'To Ora,' Dione says.

'And to freedom!' I say, raising my tumbler to the sky.

'Freedom!' we all shout, waving the cups above our heads.

Right on cue, Gumnut's distinctive cry reaches us.

'Ha!' I say. 'How's that for timing?' They laugh.

I hand Dione my cup and head for the cabin.

A powerful gust of wind ushers me down the steps to my baby. I smile ... It feels like Dragon's wings.

Dear Dad

I am a mother! I still can't believe it. And you are the grandfather of a gorgeous, healthy boy.

I'm still calling him Gumnut. But his other name is Josh Holly, Joshy for short. I'm sitting next to him right now. He's got the most beautiful, ancient eyes. Do you remember once putting an acorn in my hand and telling me I was holding an oak tree? It's like that with Joshy. I can already see who he's going to grow into.

But I don't want him to grow up here.

I used to think I could never leave this country, because of Mum and Holly, but I see now that's not true. The only thing left for me here is you, Dad, and I hope we'll be together again one day. I'm so sorry for all the pain and anguish of these past few years. Losing Mum and Holly and all the SIF stuff has ripped us apart, but we don't have to live the rest of our lives in that story. I think that's one thing I've learnt ... there is always another way.

I was so against Dione's birth stuff when I found out—and just for the record, she never wanted me involved in any of it—but when I got pregnant I began to understand where she was coming from. Suddenly, I had to face all these decisions. I felt so trapped, and I couldn't even think where or how, right up until the birth. I couldn't decide anything ... the only thing I knew for sure was that I wanted Gumnut, and no-one was going to take him away. Not for one minute. So HE was my choice. Just as he is now.

We're sailing to New Zealand, Dad. We all know how dangerous this is. Stupid, even. But it's what we have to do. I've lived through two nightmares already and I will not live through a third. I know in every fibre of my body, if we go back, we'll eventually be caught and they'll take Gumnut. It's ironic, because life is more precious now than ever, but I need to be able to live without looking over my shoulder in fear.

The journalist, Keith Waterhouse, filmed my birth. He plans to broadcast it for thousands to see. I feel like he stole something from me. And Gumnut. This is not my war, Dad, but I keep getting sucked into it. I don't know what will happen. Keith says there's a chance it will help change things. Who knows? I hope it will, but it's another reason to leave.

Jake is an amazing sailor. I trust him, and Dione's pretty good too, now. She doesn't want us to go, but I've persuaded her. I believe that we'll get across the Tasman, if the sea is kind to us. I'm sorry that I stopped trusting you, Dad. It was such a horrible time and I thought you believed in your doctor's oath and the SIF more than me. But I know now, you were just doing what you thought was best ... I guess that's what parents do!

I hope you understand.

I love you

Ora xxx

Acknowledgements

I would like to offer heartfelt gratitude to my writing group the Welcome Swallows. Elizabeth Vercoe and Jenny Heslop helped midwife this book into being, with their encouragement, fine fare and support.

Sincere gratitude to: Rhea Dempsey and Jane Hardwicke Collings for teaching me so much of what I know about birth and holding space for women. Also, to the birthing mamas who I've had the privilege of attending.

There have been many important readers who I am profoundly grateful to: Mum for her time and love. Maria Lerch, Melinda Whyman and Jennie Teskey for their wise words and support. Lorraine Brusch for sharing so openly (and for her generosity and patience in all things web related). Catharine Boothroyd, Sarah Miller and Felicia Pinchen-Hogg for their respected literary insights. Jasmine Varrasso, Kian Mckinnon-Lerch, Ibby Brusch and Calleisha Gregg-Rowan for their thoughtful responses. Anna Foletta and Rachel Watts for their Barefoot love. Jacinta Cross, Grit Opperman, Victoria Cornick, Susan Stark, Susan Pleasant, Kat Worth, Jane Hardwicke Collings, Rhea Dempsey, Eloise Fisher, Alison Priestley and Tanya Strusberg for their time, energy and positive feedback. To intrepid travellers Jonathan Pooley and Dawn Reid for sharing their sailing experience and expertise.

I would also like to thank the 2014 Year 10 English students of Preshil School: Celine, Emma, Zac, Ainslee, Charlie, Katherine, Caleb, Oliver, Tove, Ruby, Ricardo, Zoe, Neeve, Laura, Jack and Charles. Big time thanks to their fantastic English teacher Marisa Lawlor for saying yes and letting me workshop the manuscript with them. Terrifying and edifying all at once!

I would like to acknowledge that the waves of music described in the dance scene in Chapter 17 are based on Gabrielle Roth's 5Rhythms®.

Hearty thanks to Dad and Rena for all their love and time, particularly in the childcare department.

I am extremely grateful to Emily Gale and Vanessa Lanaway for their professional literary advice.

Finally, I would like to thank my family for their support and love, especially Jonathan whose unwavering belief and encouragement has been such a gift.

Charlotte Young grew up in southwest London and went to all sorts of educational establishments, from religious to free-thinking, to right-wing to left. At twenty, she fell in love in a seaside town, lived in France and Sweden for a while and settled in Australia a quarter of a century ago. She lives in Melbourne with her husband and three children. ORA'S GOLD is her first novel.

www.charlotteyoung.com.au